D1548614

It was just a simple visit to the world of the living—her world—with her husband . . .

Who just happens to be Hades, the god of the Dead

MY POWERS COULD burn through me, causing all kinds of pain and anguish before completely destroying me.

Typically, I would use my powers throughout the day in goddess lessons with my mom and then visit Hades. He would show me more tricks and then siphon away the excess powers. I hadn't had much of an opportunity to use my powers today, and I was starting to feel the effects of the buildup.

Hades waited for me to offer him an explanation.

"Today's been so much fun." I walked to the edge of the pier, looking at the churning waves. "So normal. I don't want it to end." I gave a small shrug. "It was almost like a date."

He stiffened, almost imperceptibly, and I let out the breath I'd been holding. He'd admitted to having feelings for me, even being in love, but he still hadn't gotten over the whole age difference thing.

He wrapped an arm around my shoulder, and I looked up at him, my gaze catching on his lips. He'd kissed me three times before. Well, really kissed me not fished my brain for dream images. It was easy to remember because each time was after a near-death experience. Books and movies make it seem like kisses won under emotional duress are somehow extra romantic. The screen goes blank, and you're left with the impression that the characters lived happily ever after, or at least dated like normal people. In reality, being kissed only when something earth-shattering has happened is kind of insulting. I shouldn't have to practically die to get that kind of attention.

Stanly Community College Library
141 College Drive
Albemarle, NC 28001
Phone: (704) 991-0259
www.stanly.edu

The Daughters of Zeus Series

by Kaitlin Bevis

Persephone

Daughter of Earth and Sky

The Iron Queen

Daughter of Earth and Sky

by

Kaitlin Bevis

ImaJinn Books

This is a work of fiction. Names, characters, places and incidents are either the products of the author's imagination or are used fictitiously. Any resemblance to actual persons (living or dead), events or locations is entirely coincidental.

IMAJINN

ImaJinn Books
PO BOX 300921
Memphis, TN 38130
Print ISBN: 978-1-61194-634-5

ImaJinn Books is an Imprint of BelleBooks, Inc.

Copyright © 2012 by Kaitlin Bevis
The Iron Queen (excerpt) copyright © 2013 by Kaitlin Bevis
Melissa (short story) copyright © 2015 by Kaitlin Bevis

Published in the United States of America.

All rights reserved. No part of this book may be reproduced in any form or by any electronic or mechanical means, including information storage and retrieval systems, without permission in writing from the publisher, except by a reviewer, who may quote brief passages in a review.

ImaJinn Books was founded by Linda Kichline.

We at ImaJinn Books enjoy hearing from readers. Visit our websites
ImaJinnBooks.com
BelleBooks.com
BellBridgeBooks.com

#10 9 8 7 6 5 4 3 2

Cover design: Debra Dixon
Interior design: Hank Smith
Photo/Art credits:
Woman (manipulated)-- © Ipb | Dreamstime.com
Texture (manipulated) © Olgakorneeva | Dreamstime.com
Frame © Liudmila Metaeva | Renderosity

:Leds:01:

To My Mom

I wouldn't have been able to get through this year without her.

Chapter I

I'D BEEN HERE before. My bare feet glided over the leaf-strewn path, unharmed by the rocks and twigs crunching beneath me. Massive live oaks draped with Spanish moss created a canopy above me, transforming the forest path into a tunnel of speckled sunlight. The air was heavy with humidity. The moist heat pressed against my skin and stole the breath from my lungs. By the time I reached the path's end, my Eeyore nightshirt clung to my skin.

"Dungeness." I came to a halt when I recognized the sprawling ruins of the ancient ivy-covered brick and stone manor.

Athens Academy took my class on a week-long trip to Georgia's coastal islands freshman year. Cumberland Island was a major highlight because of the sea turtles, wild horses, and these ruins.

"Good job, Persephone," I muttered, kicking at a branch. "You've figured out where you are, but how did you get here?" I knelt to pick up a smooth, white stone, tucking damp tendrils of hair behind my ears so I could see better. The rock looked and felt real. I ran my hand over the smooth stone, turning it over and tracing the shape. The weight of it in my hand reassured me.

I turned, hoping the path held some answers, but it was no longer there. I stood on the grass-covered shoreline looking out to sea. In the distance, a girl stood thigh-high in the ocean, clad in a gown of strategically placed sea foam. Although her back was to me, I could tell she was perfect. The curly ringlets of hair cascading down her flawless cream skin matched the intense orange of the sky as the sun sank in the sea.

I glanced down at my sun-kissed skin. I'd never felt self-conscious because of a tan before but gods. She made pale look really good. A movement caught my attention and I glanced up as she looked over her shoulder, aquamarine eyes meeting mine. Then she spoke. I was shocked to hear Boreas' cold voice roll off her tongue. "Zeus lives."

I stumbled backward. Boreas, the god of winter. My mind flashed back to that horrible day in the clearing last winter. Boreas' cold laughter.

His fingers digging in my hair as he pulled me across the frozen ground. Melissa's eyes widening as she choked on her last breath. The rush of power that gave me the strength to put Death himself, and Boreas, under my control.

A soul for a soul. I'd bargained with Thanatos, the god of death, and killed Boreas without a second thought, saving my best friend.

I wish for you to die, I'd told him.

He'd had no choice but to comply.

Now images shoved their way through my thoughts: Cumberland Island, two sunsets, lightning cracking in the sky. My mind screamed against the onslaught.

Dreaming, you're dreaming. The old me, the one who didn't know that all the myths were real, would have found that realization reassuring. But I knew better now. Gods could dream walk to send messages or attack each other in their sleep. And like it or not, I was one of the few living gods left. My "marriage" to Hades and my high-profile mother had made me a target before. There were measures to protect myself from dream walking gods, I'd just forgotten to use them.

How could I have been so stupid? I gritted my teeth against the pain and forced myself to think the word that would make it all stop.

Dasvidaniya.

I bolted up in bed with a gasp. A weight in my hand made me look down. I unclenched my fist, revealing the white stone from Dungeness.

My blood rushed in my ears as I looked around the room. *It worked.* I took a deep breath and tried to calm down.

I frowned. I'd chosen *Dasvidaniya* because the word had played a pivotal role in some half-remembered cartoon I'd seen years ago. Hypnos, the god of sleep, told me to choose a word or phrase someone else could never guess and to think it every night before bed, and never ever let anyone hear what it was. Like a network password, or a pin, only this password would protect my mind.

And you forgot. Really, Persephone? I groaned and flopped back on the bed. But it had been months since Zeus had sent Boreas to abduct me, and nothing had happened since. I'd grown complacent.

That's no excuse. I glanced at my phone and saw it was almost three in the morning. I had two choices. I could either wake up my mom and tell her about my dream, or risk another attack and do some dream walking of my own to Hades and tell him.

My mom, or my hot husband? Well that was a no-brainer.

I closed my eyes. *Hades.* I directed my thoughts to him. I could sense the energy of all the other sleeping deities, both alive and dead. It was a weird sensation, like catching a glimpse of something out of the corner of my eye only to have it move before I turned my head.

It was easier to find gods I knew. I sensed Hypnos' energy right away, flickering like a strobe light beyond the horizon. He was always the easiest to find because I'd learned to dream walk from him in the Underworld.

I found Hades next, a bundle of dark energy guarded like a fortress. I sent out the mental equivalent of a knock and found myself in the Underworld, standing in his library.

"This better be good," he grumbled. He looked sleepy sitting in his usual oversized leather chair. His arms were crossed and his foot tapped impatiently. The library faded into muted reds and browns, fuzzy and unfocused. Hades on the other hand, was in hyper focus, the sharp angles of his face almost too real in this strange setting.

My heart leapt at the sight of him. His dark curly hair fell into his bright blue eyes. His lips curved in a smile, despite his grouchy tone. My eyes wandered to his firm arms, and I flushed remembering being wrapped in his embrace.

Last winter he'd rescued me from my first encounter with Boreas by taking me to the Underworld. The only catch was that he had to marry me to bring me to the Underworld without being . . . well, dead. Supposedly it didn't mean anything. Marriage between the gods wasn't about love; it was mostly political and job-like. But I didn't think it would be like that for us. Or maybe it would, once he realized what I'd been hiding from him.

Hades' eyes flickered over my face, and he rose from his chair. "What happened? Are you okay?"

I jerked in surprise at the worry in his voice. *He's probably wondering why you invaded his dream if all you're going to do is stare at him, weirdo.* I shook my head to clear it. "Can Boreas still dream walk?"

His face darkened at Boreas' name. "No, he died stripped of his divinity."

"You're sure?" I couldn't keep the tremor out of my voice. I didn't exactly want to have Boreas in my head again, but if it hadn't been him, then that meant it had been someone *else*. And the only other person I could think of was Zeus.

"I'm sure. He's in Tartarus anyway. Even if he somehow retained the ability, the souls in Tartarus are blocked from dream walking." Hades gave me a thoughtful look and ran his fingers through his thick, dark hair. "What's this about?"

I told him about the whole nightmare in a jumbled rush.

Hades blinked. "Slow down." He put his hands on my shoulders. "Start again."

"She was him, I mean, he was her, her voice, it was his. And then he, or she, or whatever, it showed me all of these pictures, and I—"

Hades listened, worry giving way to confusion. "Yeah, okay. That's not working." He leaned down and kissed me.

The connection between us flared to life, and all the images from my dream flowed to him. I still wasn't used to that. Gods married by exchanging power, and that created weird links in their minds. Hades and I had only exchanged a token amount to make the marriage binding, so our connection was limited to when we touched, but if we exchanged more, we could—

Why was I thinking about any of that while Hades was kissing me!

I *really* wanted to relax into his embrace and just enjoy the kiss, but instead I turned my thoughts to an even worse topic. Thanatos.

I'd charmed him to get Melissa's soul back. Charm could work like mind control if you used it right. It shouldn't have worked on another god unless there was a *huge* power differential in my favor. There wasn't. I'd not even come into my powers yet, but I didn't question it when it worked. I'd just been happy to get my friend back.

Have you told . . . anyone that you charmed me? Thanatos had asked.

He'd looked so embarrassed that I'd felt sorry for him. He'd been my friend and one of the few people who I could talk to in the Underworld.

"I hate asking you this, but could you promise not to tell anyone anything about me? It's just that I'd never live it down if anyone ever found out I'd been charmed."

"I promise," I'd assured him like the idiot I was. *"I can't promise Hades won't figure it out, but he won't have any help from me."*

I remembered the relief on his face, how grateful he'd been. How stupidly happy I'd been to do something nice for him after everything he'd done for me. It wasn't until later, when Hades explained I'd only been able to charm Boreas because he'd sworn fealty to Zeus, that I realized how completely and utterly I'd screwed up. Thanatos, Hades' best friend and right-hand man was working with Zeus. And I couldn't tell a soul.

Gods can't lie. My promise was binding. I'd tried everything in the months that had followed. Writing it down, pantomime, *anything*. Nothing worked, and trying made me feel like I was being ripped apart.

Hades' lips were warm on mine. I tried to slip thoughts of Thanatos through the kiss, but my mind rebelled at the idea, and I only managed to convey a troubled feeling. Given the nature of my dream, Hades didn't seem surprised I was worried.

He drew back. For a second, he didn't move. Just looked down at me, his hands resting on my shoulders. Then he jerked his head and cleared his throat, moving back to his chair. "That's . . . something."

"So who did that? What did it mean?" I perched on the arm of his chair. I usually had a better sense of personal space, but Hades was the only thing in this room that looked real and solid. Staying close to him made me feel grounded.

I frowned, comparing the nauseating swirls of unfocused furniture coloring this room with my dream. "Whoever sent that message put a lot of energy into making it feel real."

"It had Poseidon's signature all over it. He considers himself to be quite the *artiste*." Hades waved his hands in the air. A dark, mocking smile played on his lips.

"Poseidon's still alive?" *Could he be working with Zeus?*

Hades nodded. "He won't be working with Zeus, either. They didn't—I mean, don't—get along. From what I could gather from your dream, something is happening in two days at sunset on Cumberland Island. I don't know why the girl was in the dream, but she did mention Zeus."

"This is the first lead we've gotten," I murmured, linking my hand with his. We hadn't learned anything new since Boreas' earth-shattering revelation that Zeus was alive and looking for me.

"I can see what Poseidon wants, why he sent you that image." Hades' eyes met mine. "You don't need to come."

"Yes, I do." A thought occurred to me. "Can you? Leave the Underworld I mean? For that long?"

Hades nodded. "I'll leave Cassandra and the others in charge. I'm due some vacation time. How much time do you need to talk to your mother about leaving?"

I took an inward hiss of breath. I hadn't thought of that yet. "Thirty minutes?"

"See you soon."

Chapter II

I WOKE WITH a start, peeled free of my jersey sheets, and scrambled down from my loft bed. I didn't bother turning on the light, just picked my way across my room by the light of the moon peeking through my lacy curtains and raced down the stairs to the kitchen. My mother sat at the round wooden table, a forgotten cup of tea next to her as she flipped idly through a magazine. Her blond hair was pulled up in a messy bun. A few wisps of hair had escaped and framed her heart-shaped face. People said I looked just like her, but shorter. I didn't see it.

She turned another page in her magazine. Seeing her down here like this was so normal, so mundane, that the sight brought me up short and took me back to the time before I knew gods and goddesses existed outside mythology. Before I knew my mother was actually Demeter and my father was Zeus. Before I'd been stalked by Boreas and forced into hiding in the Underworld. Before Hades . . .

My mother glanced up. "You're up late. Is something wrong?"

I recounted my dream, much calmer now that I knew it wasn't from Zeus. Or maybe I was just calmer because I was talking to my mom in our bright yellow kitchen. *Yellow*, I decided, *is a good color*. It made me think of the sun and warmth and spring. I felt safe in this kitchen. There was something soothing in watching my mom move around the kitchen while she made me a cup of hot chocolate. It was in the high 80s outside, but in Georgia you drink hot drinks for the flavor, not for warmth.

"It was real," I finished, dropping the white rock on the table. "When I woke up, this was in my hand."

"Honey, I don't need to tell you how important it is to guard your mind. Try not to forget again."

My temper flared up so fast it even took me by surprise. But that had been happening a lot lately. "No, you don't need to remind me." I snatched the rock off the table and scooted my chair back. It squeaked in protest along the stone-tiled floor. "Especially since you never told me to guard it in the first place."

I kept trying to get over seventeen years of deception. But somehow knowing it was in my best interest wasn't enough to forgive her for keeping my divinity . . . my life . . . *everything* about me a secret. She'd let me think I was human, but I wasn't, and some part of me had always *felt* different from all the people around me, so I'd just grown up thinking I was a freak. That something was *wrong* with me. As much as I wanted to make things right between my mom and me again, I didn't think that was something I could get over.

Mom rolled her eyes and handed me the mug of hot chocolate. "You haven't been very honest with me either. Zeus lives?"

I squirmed in my seat. "I didn't know how you would feel about the news. You never talk about him." I watched her closely as she poured herself a fresh cup of tea. She seemed to be taking it well. I felt as though a huge weight had been lifted off my shoulders. Keeping that secret for three months had been one of the hardest things I'd ever done.

"Don't worry about me." She set the tea down on the table. "I do wish you had told me earlier. You don't need to get involved with what-ever this is, Persephone. When Zeus sets his mind to something—"

"Why aren't you surprised?" It had taken Hades weeks to stop referring to Zeus in the past tense, and Mom hadn't even paused in pouring her tea. The truth dawned on me with a horrible certainty. "You knew?" She didn't meet my eyes. "Answer me! Did you know Zeus was alive? Yes or no?"

Just because a god can't lie doesn't mean they're always telling the truth. They'd had millennia of practice misleading people.

She lifted her chin. "Don't take that tone with me."

"Are you *really* hiding things from me again?"

Her green eyes cut to me with a withering mom-look. "I'm not the only one who's hidden things."

I laughed in disbelief. "I bet you've been waiting for months to be able to say that. Not telling you about Zeus made me feel sick. I couldn't stand misleading you, but *you* . . . " I waved my hand. "You can't really believe that's even in the same category as letting me believe my father was dead?"

"He is not your fa—" The lie caught in her throat. She closed her eyes and exhaled, putting her fingers to her temples. "What I mean to say is that you can't view Zeus as a father."

I still couldn't wrap my head around the way gods viewed family. Most gods are created, not born, so there are no genetic ties. They don't think of each other as brothers or sisters or daughters or sons. Which in a way was good, because otherwise my marriage to Hades would be really weird. But I hadn't been raised like most gods. I'd grown up thinking I was human, and my mom was still my *mom*. And my dad . . . I'd spent my whole life wondering about him, and now I was just supposed to disregard him because gods don't think of each other that way? I couldn't do it. "Maybe he wants to be more than nothing." The handle of the mug bit into my hand. I hadn't meant to sound hopeful, but Mom didn't miss the plaintive note in my voice.

She stiffened and leaned across the table, eyes wide. "Persephone, if we're lucky, Zeus doesn't even know you exist."

So she didn't tell him about me either. I guess that wasn't surprising. "We're way past him knowing I exist! He sent Boreas after me. He wants me for something. Maybe . . . maybe he just wants to get to know me?"

My mother's face paled. "Zeus doesn't care about anyone but himself. The only thing he wants from anyone is to use them up and to throw them away."

I nodded, my throat aching from holding back tears. I knew she was right. If Zeus had amicable intentions, he wouldn't have sent Boreas. He would have come himself. I'd heard enough about Zeus to know how horrible he was, but I'd never heard anything from Mom. And, judging from the expression on her face, I wasn't about to learn anything new.

My father had been a closed topic my whole life, but it never stopped me from wondering. I'd invented stories, imagining that he was a secret agent, or a rock star, or something. In most of my fantasies he was dead, because what other reason could there possibly be to leave your wife and child? As I grew older, I realized calling my mom his wife might have been the wrong assumption. I'd wondered if she even knew who my father was. But nothing had prepared me for the truth.

I'd secretly hoped my father was someone famous, but never imagined that fame would be for sleeping with everything with a pulse and making humans miserable.

"When?" I asked finally. "When did Zeus escape the Underworld?"

"He never died."

"But Hades *saw* him in the Underworld when Olympus fell and the rest of the gods died." I still wasn't clear on how that had worked, but gods lived off human worship. Without it, they died. By the time Olympus fell, the gods' power had been fading away for want of worship for centuries. The smarter gods, like my mom, had paid attention to all the signs and stocked up on worshipers by cursing them with immortality. Others, like Hades, were just so powerful already that it didn't matter. Undead worship is still worship, so he'd never lost a single follower. The rest weren't so lucky.

While a handful of other gods were still alive, none of them were as powerful as they'd been before. Most of the power my mom had went to keeping her alive. Hades could do quite a bit more, but his power maintained his whole realm. It was a heavy burden. So the gods pretty much lived like regular people now. That was part of why mom had tried to raise me like a human. So many gods failed to adapt to the lifestyle and burnt what little power they had left. She didn't want that for me, so being human was all I knew. But of course *that* had come with its own price.

Mom shook her head. "Hades assumed Zeus died when the rest did, so he extended Zeus a personal invitation to Olympus. Olympus is different from the rest of the Underworld. It was Zeus' realm, so he was able to come and go until his powers dwindled away. He lost his ability to return to Olympus a while ago."

"How long have you known?"

"You're seventeen. Do the math."

I gaped at her, "You said that you waited until the world was safe to have me." She'd made it sound like she'd had some sort of crazy everlasting pregnancy.

"I *did* wait until the world was safe to have you. You weren't un-planned."

"Do you even know how to tell the truth?" I was far too angry to heed the disapproving look my tone provoked.

"Persephone—"

"Don't!" I stood so fast the chair knocked over and fell to the floor with a crash. "There's no point in listening to you if you never actually *say* anything. I'm going to Cumberland Island to figure out what that dream meant. If I'm lucky, Poseidon will give straighter answers than you do."

Something akin to fear flashed across her face, but it was gone before I could figure out what it was. "Persephone, Zeus is a powerful enemy, and he didn't want anyone to know he was alive. That's why I misled you. I don't want you getting involved in this." She spoke calmly, as though she thought laying down the law meant I would obey.

Did she know me so little? Did she think her opinion even counted anymore?

"I *have* to go," I argued. "Who knows what he's up to? It could af-fect all of us!"

Mom must have heard the conviction in my voice because she

stopped arguing and said, "I'll come with you."

"No."

"Persephone, I know we've practiced using your abilities all summer, but you're not ready to try anything on your own yet."

"I know. That's why you're going to give Hades permission to travel to this realm and come with me." Hades didn't technically need permission, a fact that became obvious when he surfaced last year to take me to the Underworld, but trespassing into another god's realm was not something to be taken lightly. Everything would go much smoother with her consent.

"What?" my mother demanded, brow furrowing. "Gods, no! If you're going at all, I am going with you, not that—"

"Be very careful what you say next. That's my husband you're about to insult."

She threw her hands up in the air and stood. "A technicality."

I took a deep breath and tried to still my shaking hands. There was a time to be angry, but this wasn't it. I needed to be logical. "I trust him, in a way that I can't trust you."

"Persephone!" Mom tucked her chair under the table with more force than necessary.

"He's never lied to me, never misled me, and he saved my life on more than one occasion. I need someone at my back who I can trust, and at the moment you don't fit that bill."

"I—"

"Did what you thought was best for me, I know." At her surprised look, I rolled my eyes. "Gods, Mom, I'm not stupid. I didn't think you were lying to be mean. You're my mother; you love me. But you keep trying to protect me when all I really need is to know what's going on. If Zeus really is as dangerous as you say, then I'm going to need someone who will tell the truth, not what they think will be easiest to hear."

She fell silent for a long moment. "Fine," she acquiesced. "You can go tell Hades."

"I told him before I came downstairs. He should be here soon."

She grimaced. "Of course you did."

I tensed, ready for another argument about how I spent too much time with him. A sharp knock at the door saved me from the familiar lecture. I threw the latch to let Hades in.

"Hello." He gave me a rakishly handsome grin.

My knees felt weak, and I'm sure I turned three shades of red, but he had the grace to ignore it.

"Demeter." He nodded his head.

She nodded back and turned her attention to me. Her green eyes flickered over me, and the corners of her mouth turned up in an amused grin. "Persephone, I'm sorry but I can't allow you to leave in that."

Hades glanced at me, and I followed his gaze down to my Eeyore nightshirt. We shared a look. I did have to go get dressed, but I didn't want to leave Hades to be interrogated by my mother. He gave a slight nod, and I sighed and raced upstairs.

Their murmured voices drifted up the stairs behind me. When I reached my room, I threw open my closet and switched on the light. What in the world was I going to wear . . . ?

Forget what I was going to wear! Hades was downstairs with my mom. Alone! Who knew what she was saying to him? I threw on a floral printed dress, ran a brush though my hair, yanked on a pair of sandals, and ran down the stairs.

". . . not angry," Hades was saying. "I know better than anyone how intimidating Zeus can be."

I paused on the last step, standing behind the wall. The soft light cast shadows of my mother and Hades on the pine floor before me.

Her voice was barely a whisper. "Hades, I don't want her involved with any of this."

I stared hard at the yellow wallpaper with lines of miniature pink roses.

"Normally I'd agree with you," Hades replied. "But, I think she needs to do something. She's terrified; I can feel it. You know her better than I do, surely you've noticed."

"Of course she's terrified. She watched her best friend die, and then she killed someone!" Mom's breath caught, and she lowered her voice. "She can't handle any more of this—"

"What? 'God stuff'? This is her life, Demeter, whether you want to admit it or not, and honestly, I don't think she's mature enough to sit things out when she's in over her head. Look at what happened with Boreas."

You mean besides me saving the day? I wondered. Yes, going after Boreas alone had been stupid, but they kept overlooking that everything had ended up more or less okay. Melissa was back from the dead, and Zeus didn't have me yet. I called that a win.

"I didn't say she wouldn't *want* to get involved, Hades." Glasses clinked against the kitchen sink, and there was a sudden rush of water. "I said she shouldn't. She's not mature enough to sit out when she's over her head, but that doesn't mean you give in and let her."

"Yeah, I'm really not going to handle her that way." Hades sounded amused.

"If you can't handle a little immaturity, then maybe you shouldn't rob the cradle."

I could almost hear the muscles in Hades' jaw tighten. "I don't need to *handle* your daughter, Demeter. I need to step out of her way and let her handle herself. In case you haven't noticed, she has a way of getting things done. Now, I could tell her to stay home, and you could watch her like a hawk, but you and I both know that she'd do everything she could to slip past you and end up on Poseidon's beach, alone. And neither one of us wants that."

"I just wish it wasn't Poseidon."

There was something in Mom's voice. Vulnerability? Fear? I frowned. Poseidon was one of the good guys, wasn't he?

"I won't let anything happen to her."

"Your concern for my seventeen-year-old daughter is touching," she said dryly.

I walked off the last step with a stomp. They fell silent when they heard me.

"I'm ready," I said in a cheerful voice, rounding the corner.

"You'll call me when you get there?" Mom asked, sounding exactly like any other worried mother.

"Of course. Oh, and I used your card for the thing."

She blinked. "The thing?"

"UGA."

"Ah, yes. Good luck with that."

I cocked my head and stared at her in surprise. She sounded sincere. "Thank you." I gave her a hug and walked down the wooden steps of our porch with Hades.

I froze mid-step when I saw a pink, unicorn-shaped bag, complete with legs, a tail, and a stuffed head, on the hood of my yellow bug. "What is *that*?"

Hades gave me a confused look. "Your luggage. I hope you'll forgive me for putting a few of your things in my bag. Cassandra said you'd forget to pack, and she was insistent that you'd want your bag, but it doesn't have a lot of room in it . . . " He trailed off, looking between my amused expression and the unicorn. "That's not yours, is it?"

I giggled, imagining him carrying that bag all the way here. Cassandra was a prophet who'd died in the Trojan War. She was Hades' most trusted advisor, but she got bored easily. Picking on Hades was her favorite pastime. "Nope. How long will we be gone?"

Hades opened my trunk and tossed in a nondescript black bag along with the unicorn. "At least two days, maybe more."

"Why drive? I can teleport there."

"You can't teleport with me. This isn't my realm."

"I can share."

Hades gave me a knowing smile. "Try it."

I narrowed my eyes at his smug look and grabbed his hand. "Hold on tight," I cautioned, closing my eyes. I painted a picture of Cumberland Island in my mind, visualizing the live oaks, feeling the humidity, and smelling the air, heavy with salt and flora.

The air whirled around me. Then with a sudden yank that threatened to rip my arm out of my socket, I stumbled back into place. Hades' arm weighed me down like an anchor.

He steadied me. "See? Not. My. Realm."

"I teleported with Melissa."

"She's a native of this realm."

I frowned. "Can I give you the ability to teleport here?"

"You don't have the authority to give away teleportation rights." Hades slammed the trunk. "Only your mom can do that. She rules this realm. So we require . . . transportation." He looked at my car and the left corner of his lip quirked, but then seeing my expression, he rubbed at his chin, covering his mouth with his hand.

"What?" I snatched my keys out of his hand. I love my car. I'd worked in my mother's flower shop for countless hours to buy the daisy-patterned rims, brake-light cut outs, and wildflower vanity plate.

"The Queen of the Underworld drives a bug," Hades snickered. "Sorry, it's just funny. Allow me to drive. I know the way."

"Hell no!" I slid into the driver's seat. Part of me wanted to ask why we didn't just go back in the house and demand my mother give Hades teleportation rights, but the rest of me was excited at the prospect of taking a long drive with Hades. We didn't get much time alone. Plus, as much as I'd love to assume he had the same motivation for *not* asking my mom, there was probably a long and boring explanation why he wouldn't. Gods were weird. "This is my car, and besides, do you even have a license?"

He shot me a withering look.

"Didn't think so," I said triumphantly.

Hades rolled his eyes and slid in after me. I took a final look at my mother's silhouette in the doorway and tightened my grip on the steering wheel.

Hades followed my gaze. "She was trying to protect you."

"I know. That's the worst part. I'm just tired of her deception. I mean, keeping the fact that I was a goddess from me my whole life was one thing, but to *still* keep something from me? That's just . . ." I couldn't put words to the feelings that were bothering me.

"You wanted her to be as honest as you've always perceived her to be."

"Yes."

"It could be worse."

"How?"

"My father ate me."

Chapter III

WE COULDN'T actually drive to Cumberland Island. Instead, we had to drive six hours to St. Mary's Island and then take a ferry.

"You look like you're going to be sick." Hades studied me from the corner of his eye.

I focused on the dimly lit road. The deformed shadows of trees whipped by as we drove down Highway 316. "I don't like the ocean." I shuddered, remembering my class trip to Georgia's islands. I'd been so excited to see the ocean. When I took my first hesitant steps onto the beach and looked into the cerulean waves, I'd felt a horrific certainty that something terrible was lurking beneath them. It was another world down there, and I didn't belong in it.

"That's natural." Hades adjusted his seat, pushing it back so he'd have more leg room. "The sea is Poseidon's realm. You wouldn't want to enter without an invitation."

I held up my hand and squinted against the brights of a car in the other lane. I hated driving at night. Everything was too dark to see or blindingly bright. "Didn't my mom think a complete inability to enter the ocean was important to mention? What if the ferry had sunk or something? Or, I don't know, I just wanted to swim?"

"Poseidon's not unreasonable. Technically you *can* enter; you just have a strong desire not to. Just like me being here. It feels more comfortable with your mother's permission, but I'm capable of entering her realm without it."

I frowned. That didn't work both ways. My mom *couldn't* enter the Underworld with or without Hades' permission. No gods could. Humans either, unless they were demigods, but demigods were just odd. But I guess it made sense. People crossed into Poseidon's realm when they went swimming or Zeus' realm skydiving, but there was no spelunking down to visit dead relatives. The Underworld was just different.

I'd been so excited to go on that trip. I remembered planning, packing, and talking about it for weeks. And my mother had just watched, knowing I would be disappointed. I'd been lonely watching my class-mates play in the waves. What else would I learn about my divinity? How much had I shrugged off as normal? How deep had the deception gone?

Hades broke the silence. "What did you use your mom's credit card for?"

I glanced over at him then back to the road. "Come again?"

"You used your mom's card, for a thing?" He fiddled with the vents, adjusting the air.

I gave him an incredulous look. "Nosy much?"

Headlights illuminated his electric blue eyes as he glowered at me. "Considerate, actually. I could tell you wanted to talk about something else."

"That's a half-truth if I've ever heard one." I laughed. "You're curious. Maybe I used it for something personal."

"Fine. Don't tell me." Hades turned to look out the window.

I sighed. "It was an application for early enrollment at the University of Georgia."

Hades gave me a look full of pity. "You still plan on going to college?"

"Why wouldn't I?"

"You know you're going to be coming into your powers in the next couple of years." Hades reached for the dial on the radio.

"Don't even," I warned him. Hades' eyes sparkled in challenge, and he started thumbing through the songs on my playlist. "Besides, I know how to handle my powers now, thanks to you. Don't worry; I'll still visit the Underworld when I don't need you anymore." I smiled to show I was teasing.

Hades had to channel away all my extra power every night thanks to Orpheus going public with his adventures in the Underworld. The rock star demigod thought that was doing me a favor. Most gods *want* worship, or people simply thinking about them, which constitutes as worship today. But since I hadn't come into my powers, the extra powers that came with "worship," or in this case people speculating whether or not Orpheus had gone nuts, were dangerous.

I wasn't complaining. More time with Hades was always good in my book, and it meant that however much my mom wanted to, she couldn't forbid me from seeing him. He was my lifeline.

"Just be careful." Hades pulled at his seat belt and adjusted it over his shoulder. "I think you'll find once school starts, you're being too ambitious with your schedule between attending court in the Underworld, lessons with your mom, working at the flower shop, and school. College is going to be a lot more demanding."

I frowned and turned on my blinker. Mom said the same thing. I was probably the only teenager on the planet being dissuaded from attending college. I passed a silver car and moved back into the right lane. "How is college any more unnecessary than high school? No one's suggested I drop out of high school."

"Because you need to blend in," Hades explained. "The socialization you learn in school alone is valuable. People get suspicious when they can't find a diploma in your records. It's another mark on the paper trail. You came from somewhere, no reason to suspect you of being anything but human."

I paused, considering. "What about in a hundred years? I'll still be around then, and somehow I doubt my diploma—"

"So you go again. No doubt the customs have changed, so there will be more to learn. Unlike the rest of us, you'll probably look young enough to pull it off without a glamour."

I scowled. I was not repeating high school. Once was bad enough. I also didn't like the reminder that I was probably going to look seventeen for all eternity. I was supposed to grow into my early twenties and *then* stop aging. But dealing with all the power from Orpheus was probably going to make me come into my powers earlier than usual, which was good, and make me stop aging sooner, which was bad.

I know I shouldn't whine about things like immortality, and I know it's shallow, but I'm really short. I was hoping to grow a few more inches so I could do little things, like reach the cups in the top cabinet without having to use a step-stool. "I still don't see why college is a bad idea. It's normal to go to college. Melissa and I are going to move into the apartment above Mom's flower shop. We're going to take all our classes together. It's going to be so much fun." I grinned at Hades. "I might even go Greek. Join a sorority."

He hesitated. *Don't say it*, I urged him silently. *Don't tell me I'm not normal. I know.*

I liked being a goddess and all the perks that came with it. But that didn't mean I was willing to scrap all the plans I'd made for my life before I'd discovered what I was. That was the plus to being immortal. I could live the life I'd envisioned for myself and then do whatever else I was supposed to do as a goddess . . . later.

Of course, some plans would change. I probably wouldn't be buying that house with the white picket fence on the corner of West Lake

Drive and Lumpkin Street. I certainly wasn't going to marry Orpheus and have identical twin girls named Harmony and Melody. I was already married, and I had a castle in the Underworld. But I still wanted to enjoy the steps between.

"So . . . " Hades shifted in his seat to face me. "Your mom said you thought Zeus may just want to . . . get to know you?"

Oh gods! I didn't know what was worse, Mom hating Hades or actually *talking* to him. "I'm not stupid," I snapped. "He sent a serial rapist after me. He couldn't have thought that would end well. It's just . . ." I sighed. "Part of me, a stupid part of me, I'll admit, kind of hopes the whole thing was just a big misunderstanding."

Hades considered that for a moment. "It's not stupid to want that," he spoke with the slow precision of someone choosing each word with careful consideration. "And honestly, if it weren't so dangerous, I'd let you hold on to that . . . fantasy. But you have to understand something about Zeus. There is *nothing* good in him. He's—"

I whipped my head around so fast my neck popped in protest. "How can you say that? He's a part of me!"

Hades held up his hands in surrender. "That isn't what I me—"

"He's just as much a part of me as she is. Everything I am came from them, no matter how much you try to ignore it or how much I wish I could forget it, he's my *father*."

"Okay, pull over."

"What?"

"You're upset and what I'm about to tell you is important, so pull over."

I scowled but pulled off to the side of the road, flipping my hazards on. "What?"

Hades waited until he was sure I had his full attention. "You are not the sum of your parents."

I rolled my eyes. "Yeah, okay. But that doesn't change the fact that—"

"I'm not trying to give you some sort of feel-good speech here." Hades' voice rose in frustration. "I'm serious. You aren't them. They aren't any part of you. They gave you powers and a physical appearance and that's *it*. You are *nothing* like them, and you won't grow up to be like them either."

I ducked my head. "Maybe not the sum of both of them, Hades, but I am something from both of them. If there's nothing good in him then—"

Hades brushed a strand of hair off my face and tilted my chin up till I was looking at him. "That has no bearing on you. Look, do you think I'm evil?"

My mind flashed back to Pirithous, a demigod who'd been working with Boreas, screaming in agony as Hades turned him into stone. "Dark? Yes. Evil? No."

"Well, my parents were. They make Zeus look like a saint. We are not destined to become our parents."

"I killed Boreas, Hades. Without so much as a second thought."

"He deserved it."

And I'm keeping something from you. Something terrible. I opened my mouth and tried to tell him for the thousandth time. My stomach twisted and my pulse raced. I closed my eyes against the dizziness and let it go. The feeling went away instantly.

"Persephone?" Headlights glittered in his eyes.

"If he pulls the long-lost father card, I won't go off to the dark side," I promised him.

Hades let out a deep breath, and his entire body seemed to relax. I blinked. He'd really been worried. He returned his attention to the playlist while I eased the car back on the road. His fingers flipped deftly over the screen. "Orpheus . . . Dusk . . . Orpheus . . . Dusk . . . do you have anything on here that doesn't make people want to jump off a cliff?"

I made an offended noise but was glad to have the conversation return to normal. "I'm driving. When you learn to drive something more modern than a horse and buggy, we can listen to your music."

"I can drive!"

"Did they even have cars the last time you came to the surface?" I teased.

"Yes."

"Not counting the minute and a half you spent rescuing me last year?"

Hades fell silent, and I laughed. "I didn't think so."

Despite my teasing, when I'd been driving three hours, I pulled over and let him drive. He would know how to control anything humans made. All the gods who'd been created did. Gods who'd actually been born, like me, had to learn everything the hard way.

I fell asleep to Hades' running commentary on my playlist. When I opened my eyes, the sun was peeking through the clouds.

"We're here," Hades announced.

I yawned. There was a black leather jacket draped across me that hadn't been there before. It took me a minute to place it before I remembered Hades had been wearing it. He walked around and opened my door. A Greek revival plantation home stood before us, a sign proclaiming it to be the Riverview Hotel.

"I already checked us in," Hades said.

I got out of the car, combed my fingers through my hair, and checked my reflection in the rearview mirror. "I'm sure you're exhausted." I straightened my dress. "So did you just want to crash here and hit Cumberland Island tomorrow?"

"Are you kidding? This is the longest I've been on the surface in . . . " Hades trailed off to think. "Nearly forever. I'm not going to waste a minute sleeping. We should go sightseeing! We've got two days, might as well make the most of them." He gave me a hopeful look.

I yawned again and reached down to adjust the strap on my sandal.

"Unless you're still tired," he amended, sounding crestfallen.

I looked up. His shoulders were slumped as he grabbed his suitcase out of the trunk.

Aww, he wanted to go sightseeing! "Give me five minutes."

Hades led me into the hotel and directed me toward a wooden staircase. I kept a hand on the espresso-colored railing. A striped cat raced past me. It was a really nice hotel, really homey. The top half of the walls were white with curvy, wrought iron lights fastened every few feet, and the bottom half was paneled with the same espresso-colored wood of the staircase. The wood floors were covered with red rugs with paisley patterns printed on them.

"This one." Hades unlocked the door and opened it for me. "And I'm right here." He pointed at the next door before entering his room and closing the door behind him.

I took a quick look around my room before I tossed the unicorn bag onto the massive four-poster bed. A painting of two palm trees on a beach hung above the bed. I stood between the bed and the fireplace and dug through the bag Cassandra packed for me. "Oh, gods."

The short skirt and shiny aquamarine top were thrown to the side. It would have looked great on Cassandra; on me it would look ridiculous. I dug past the sexy sleepwear and found a linen sundress that was more my style.

I ran a brush through my hair, pulling some of it back into a daisy clip, and let the rest of the blond waves cascade down my shoulders. My bright green eyes caught my attention in the mirror. *Oh right.* I closed my eyes and took a deep breath, letting the human glamour settle over me.

I didn't have to change much. I'd passed for human most of my life. When I opened my eyes, they'd dulled to a more natural shade of green. My skin and hair were no longer as bright or glossy. It was probably overkill, but ever since Pirithous had tried to abduct me from my mother's flower shop last year, I'd realized you could never be too careful.

Between Orpheus' publicity stunt and Boreas' freak blizzard that tore through the world last year, the gods were no longer regarded entirely as myths. We still weren't widely worshiped, but the glimmer of belief that we could be real had spread like wildfire, igniting a sense of hope and fear in the human race.

When I stepped into the hall, Hades was leaning against a wall reading a brochure. He'd altered his appearance, too. His unearthly electric blue eyes had dimmed, and his hair was lightened to a normal shade of black. Even his gait had changed from his unnatural, almost predatory walk to a clumsier human stride.

I took in his black T-shirt and blue jeans with an amused smile. "Wow, you look almost normal."

He glanced up from the brochure and gave an uncomfortable looking shrug. "I hate it," he admitted. "I don't know how you can tolerate keeping your glamour up twenty-four seven."

"It gets easier," I assured him. I motioned to the brochure. "Where to?"

WE SPENT A surprisingly normal day together. We walked through Orange Hall Museum, a beautiful antebellum mansion, and explored the rest of the city. According to the dream message, Poseidon wasn't expecting us on Cumberland Island until tomorrow night, and since the island was only accessible by a ferry that ran earlier in the day, there was no getting there today anyway. Plus, I wasn't going to suggest we hurry. I was enjoying my time with Hades.

"I can't believe all the houses have been here since 1820." I motioned toward a brick building down the street. "There's a spot like this in Athens, timeless. If you ignore the cars and stuff, you can imagine back when the streets were dirt, and there were horses and—" I broke off seeing Hades' amused look. "What?"

"I need to take you to Europe. That—" he pointed at the huge white house "—is an infant."

I stuck my tongue out at him and caught sight of a cemetery with a huge statue of an angel. "That more your style?"

Hades didn't answer. I turned to look at him and saw his attention was focused on a man dressed in dark robes across the street. The light bent around him. My throat went dry when I recognized he was a Reaper.

"Is he—" I gasped.

Hades waved to the Reaper, grabbed my arm, and propelled me to the next street. "Just the usual," he assured me. I heard a woman cry out, and Hades picked up the pace.

My pulse was pounding in my throat. People die, it happens. The Reaper was a blessing; it meant that poor soul wouldn't have to sit in its dead rotting body. On an intellectual level, I got it.

But my understanding ended there.

"Look." Hades pushed me toward a small gazebo. Necklaces hung from the roof of the stand, glittering in the sunlight.

I could feel his eyes on me, watching, evaluating whether or not I was about to burst into tears and accuse him of being a heartless god for letting people die.

Well, it wasn't like it hadn't happened before.

"Pretty," I whispered instead, moving closer to the necklaces. I couldn't fall apart every time someone died. I was Queen of the Under-world! It wasn't like the Underworld was some terrible place. The soul would adapt.

I did my best to shove all thoughts of the dead or dying out of my head. I couldn't do anything about it. The necklaces swayed in the breeze. I steadied one and studied it. A small wire basket, about the size of my thumb, kept a small plant in place. It hung on a simple silver chain.

"They're air plants," said the woman behind the register. She moved closer to us. "They don't need soil to grow, just spritz them with water every couple of days and make sure they get plenty of sun." She plucked another necklace off the stand. "Eventually they bloom." She motioned to the splash of red growing from the plant's center.

"Do you get to pick a charm?" Hades asked.

I looked up, unsure of what he was talking about and noticed some of the necklaces had small charms attached to the baskets.

"For an additional five dollars you can—"

"You're going to charge *me?*" Hades' eyebrows shot up.

"It's fine." I reached into my purse to grab some cash and held it out to the woman. Hades intercepted my hand and motioned me to put the money away.

The woman gave Hades a strange look. "Are you someone special?" She frowned like she was trying to place him.

Hades laughed. "You have no idea." He reached into the pocket of his jeans and pulled out a black credit card so dark it seemed to absorb light. It must have felt strange because the woman shuddered when she touched it.

Hades plucked a charm out of a box sitting on the counter top. He showed it to me, and I grinned. It was a pomegranate seed. He'd remembered my favorite fruit.

The woman took the necklace I'd been eyeing and attached the charm to it before giving it back to Hades. "Have a nice day," she said before moving on to another set of tourists so fast you'd have thought hellhounds were chasing her.

"She thinks you're crazy," I told Hades. "Why would you think she wouldn't charge you?"

Hades grinned. "No reason. I just wanted to be memorable."

"Why's that?"

"Can you imagine the look she's going to have on her face when she sees me again? Here." Hades moved behind me, taking the two ends of the necklace. "You were right about what you said in the car earlier." He moved my hair off my neck, and I shivered under the warmth of his fingers. "You're a bit of both of them. Not the evil bits," he added quickly. "You're something different, too." He moved back, and I touched the necklace before adjusting my hair.

"Thank you," I whispered, touched.

"Ah, I just wanted to buy something. No commerce in the Underworld." Hades waved away my thanks and motioned for me to hand him my phone. He pulled up a map of the city and studied it. "Want to go to a movie?" He pointed to a spot on the map. "There's a theater just down the street that way."

"The new *Dusk* movie is out!" I grabbed his hand and pulled him toward the movie theater.

"I meant a good movie."

I let Hades pick the movie, after all, it wasn't like he spent a lot of time on the surface. Afterward, we ate at Seagle's Waterfront Cafe. The view was breathtaking, or would have been had the ocean not sent chills down my back. Hades pulled the chair facing away from the window back for me, and I shot him a grateful look. I loved that I didn't have to explain things like that to him. He probably knew more about me than I did.

Hades dug into his rock shrimp with gusto while I ate my salad. Eating out wasn't always easy for a vegan, but I managed. We talked the entire time, laughing and flirting the day away. Beneath our playful banter, I felt an undercurrent of nerves. I wondered if this was the calm before the storm, and we were both here, clinging to some shred of happiness before it all got ripped away.

The news that Zeus was alive had more of an effect on Hades than I'd anticipated. He'd hidden it well, but I could see he was worried. I didn't know if it was because Zeus was after me, or if it went deeper than that.

I wasn't that worried. Zeus had been alive forever and hadn't done anything noteworthy enough for anyone to find out he was still breathing. Why would he do anything differently now? I was more concerned about Thanatos. He could come and go to the Underworld as he pleased, kill humans with a touch, and had an army of Reapers at his disposal. But Hades didn't know he was a threat.

Later, we walked along the pier hand in hand, enjoying the cool breeze while the sun sank into the sea. A photo booth caught my attention, and I dragged Hades over to it.

"I don't do pictures." Hades pulled back on my hand putting up a token resistance, but I noticed he didn't stop walking in the direction of the photo booth.

"It'll be fun, please!" I pulled on his hand a bit more, and he took another step toward the photo booth.

"Have you ever seen a picture of me?" Hades protested. "Of any of us? It's a thing, we don't—"

I dropped his hand and stared at him in complete shock. "You've *never* had a picture taken?"

"We're immortal. Pictures, paintings, images, they start witch hunts."

I blinked. I'd never considered that. "I guess it makes sense . . . being scared that some dead human will make it to the Underworld and go, 'Hey, that's the guy from the out-of-focus grainy picture I saw once.'"

Hades smirked. "I was thinking more about you."

"I have a driver's license, a passport, a photograph in fifteen years' worth of yearbooks counting preschool, social networking accounts, and a mother who might have actually invented scrapbooking. If having *pictures* taken is some kind of immortal foil, I am thoroughly screwed. But it's fine. You probably wouldn't photograph well anyway," I teased, walking away from the photo booth.

He caught my hand. "Wanna bet?"

Countless dollars and strips of photographs later, Hades and I emerged from the photo booth laughing.

"Burn that one," Hades tore off the last picture of one of the strips.

"Why?" I snatched it back from him. "It's fitting that the Lord of the Underworld look like a corpse."

He snatched it back and tossed it off the pier. "Yeah, looking like a corpse is fine. It's the evidence of the bunny-ears that must be destroyed."

"Fine," I conceded. "As long as you burn this one." I tore off the end of another strip that featured a smear of my face captured mid-motion. A sharp pain went through my head and I grimaced, clutching the picture so tight that it crumpled.

"Everything okay?" Concern clouded his features.

"Just a headache."

"Why didn't you say something?" Hades admonished, pulling me toward the hotel.

I resisted, and he looked at me in surprise. "It can wait," I said, with more confidence than I felt. My powers could burn through me, causing all kinds of pain and anguish before completely destroying me.

Typically, I would use my powers throughout the day in goddess lessons with my mom and then visit Hades. He would show me more tricks and then siphon away the excess powers. I hadn't had much of an opportunity to use my powers today, and I was starting to feel the effects of the buildup.

Hades waited for me to offer him an explanation.

"Today's been so much fun." I walked to the edge of the pier, looking at the churning waves. "So normal. I don't want it to end." I gave a small shrug. "It was almost like a date."

He stiffened, almost imperceptibly, and I let out the breath I'd been holding. He'd admitted to having feelings for me, even being in love, but he still hadn't gotten over the whole age difference thing.

He wrapped an arm around my shoulder, and I looked up at him, my gaze catching on his lips. He'd kissed me three times before. Well, really kissed me not fished my brain for dream images. It was easy to remember because each time was after a near-death experience. Books and movies make it seem like kisses won under emotional duress are somehow extra romantic. The screen goes blank, and you're left with the impression that the characters lived happily ever after, or at least dated like normal people. In reality, being kissed only when something earth-shattering has happened is kind of insulting. I shouldn't have to practically die to get that kind of attention.

"Come on." He gave my shoulder a little squeeze. I followed him back to the hotel, wishing things could be different.

Chapter IV

A BLARING ALARM that sounded like sirens on a submarine jolted me from my dreams. I fumbled for my phone, knocking it off the unfamiliar nightstand. With a frustrated hiss, I scooped the phone off the floor and moved my fingers across the screen to switch off the alarm.

The door to the adjoining suite burst open revealing a wide-eyed Hades. "What was that?"

I untangled myself from the covers and waved my phone with an apologetic smile. "Time to wake up."

He leaned against the door, inhaling sharply. "I thought the building was on fire! You wake up to that every morning?"

My hands moved automatically to fix my hair and straighten my nightgown. I paused at the unfamiliar silky fabric and rolled my eyes, remembering the crazy clothes Cassandra chose for me. "What would happen to us if the building was on fire?"

"And we didn't get out? It would hurt. A lot."

I tilted my head as I took in his black T-shirt and black pants. "Do you ever wear color?"

"Black is a color."

With his dark hair ruffled haphazardly and a crease from his pillow marring his cheeks, Hades looked so disheveled I had to laugh. He usually looked so put together.

Unable to resist, I stood on my tiptoes and brushed the hair out of his face.

"Hey!" His hands lifted to his hair, and he snapped his chin up so I couldn't reach it.

The sudden movement knocked me off balance. I stumbled into him. His strong arms wrapped around me, steadying me.

"You okay?" he murmured. The deep rumble of his words vibrated through me.

"Uh-huh," I managed. My pulse pounded as I realized all that separated us was a nightgown that suddenly felt really flimsy. I looked up at him through my lashes, half hoping he'd make the next move . . . and half terrified.

Hades cleared his throat, hands dropping to his sides. "Um . . . We should get going if we want to catch the boat."

I stepped away from him, cheeks flaming. "Right. Of course." I fled toward the bathroom. When I reached the doorway, I glanced back at him. "Sorry my phone scared you, but thanks for coming to my rescue."

He gave me a slow smile. "Always."

I ducked into the bathroom and changed, glad Cassandra had the foresight to pack hiking gear. Once I braided my hair and donned my human glamour, I sprayed on my sunscreen then wrinkled my nose before spraying insect repellent into a toxic cloud. I coughed, turning around under the mist of DEET.

"What are you doing?" Hades coughed as the door swung open.

"Trust me, you'll need it." I tossed him the bug spray.

He caught it and sprayed it on his broad arms, making a face when the acrid odor hit his nose. "I'm already missing the Underworld," he grumbled.

"That's right, no bugs." I remembered, clipping on my new necklace. "So what happens to them when they die?"

"They go to their own realm in Tartarus."

"You send bugs to hell? Wow, you really don't like them."

Hades tightened the laces on his black hiking boots. "Serial killer hell. The bugs love it. You ready?"

I nodded and followed him back into the room. I threw a few bottles of water from our room's courtesy basket into my backpack purse, and we headed down the hall. I grabbed the picnic lunch we'd ordered from the hotel when we reached the lobby, and Hades moved ahead of me to get the door.

"Hey, you!" A hand grabbed me by the wrist.

"Excuse me?" I twisted around. A woman in a business suit towered over me.

"Where do you think you're going? The rest of the students are waiting outside with the buses." She pushed her glasses up her nose with a pinky and gave me a no-nonsense look. "If you girls keep trying to sneak off, this trip is off next year."

I blinked. "What?"

"You heard me; we already caught your little friends after their adventure last night. Just because you're not in my class doesn't mean you don't have to listen to me, but I'd be more than happy to get Mrs. Powers over here if you'd rather talk to her." The way she said 'Mrs. Powers' sounded like quite a threat.

"I'm not with a group." I tried to pull my hand away, but the woman held fast.

A shadow fell over the woman. She looked behind me, and her jaw went slack. Hades had that effect on people.

"Let her go," he growled.

The woman closed her mouth with a snap and released my hand. "Umm . . . " She stared at Hades for another moment, a blush creeping to her face. "I mean . . . " She cleared her throat and shook her head.

I took pity on her. "I'm not here with a group."

"You're not?"

"No. She's not. And now we're running late," Hades snapped. He ushered me to the door. I followed him even though the woman seemed conflicted about letting me leave with a strange older man.

Once we were out the door, he picked up the pace, and I had to jog to keep up with him. "You know I'm, like, really short, right?"

He slowed. "Why didn't you just charm her?"

I wrinkled my nose. "I don't like charming people. It feels wrong. Besides"—I added when Hades rolled his eyes—"she didn't mean any harm. She thought I was with a school trip or something."

"Charming isn't inherently wrong. In that situation—"

"Oh look, T-shirts!" I cut him off to avoid the lecture. "Look at all the *colors!*" I stopped at a wooden pagoda and grabbed a blue shirt with a picture of dolphins on the front.

Hades snatched the shirt and tossed it back to the T-shirt guy.

"Aw, come on!" I yelled, hurrying after him. "It was pretty!"

"I rule the Underworld! I'm not supposed to look pretty."

"So do I," I teased. "And look, color." I motioned toward my dress.

"Yeah, but you're not just a ruler of the Underworld. You're Goddess of Spring."

"So! What if I'd been some random human? Would you make me go Goth?"

I was still picking on him when we reached the ferry. We paid for tickets and made our way onto the ferry with a group of tourists. My mouth went dry when I looked down at the ocean. I plopped down on an empty wooden bench, staring hard at a black speck on the shiny, white vinyl floor.

Hades sat beside me and put an arm around my shoulder. I closed my eyes and leaned into him as the boat moved away from the shore with a lurch. He felt solid. Safe. Completely unlike the water that surrounded this tiny boat. I swallowed hard and gripped the edge of the bench.

"Here." He took my hand and guided it to my necklace. I jerked in surprise when my fingers brushed against the tiny leaves. They felt *alive*. I've always felt something when I touch plants, a hum of energy. It's not as weird or New Agey as it sounds. Until recently I thought everyone could feel it, but the jolt of energy that came from this plant wasn't subtle.

"It can work as a conduit when you're out of your realm," Hades explained. "You'll always have your powers, no matter where you are, but this lets you pull them from your realm. It's easier, plus it's kind of comforting."

I looked up at him. "Do you have one?"

He nodded and pulled an old iron coin out of his pocket. It was about the size of a dime, but thicker and more misshapen and lumpy. Like it was trying really hard to be round but couldn't quite succeed. A centurion was stamped on one side of the coin, and a bird with huge talons was stamped on the other.

"What is that?"

"An obol. Just a knickknack from one of the shops. A demigod walked out of the Underworld with one of these once, and suddenly all of Greece was using them for currency. They had this crazy idea they could use them to bribe Charon." He touched it to the pomegranate seed on my necklace, and I felt a sudden surge of power.

"Something from each of your realms," he said, pocketing the coin.

A chorus of amazed "oohs" from a group of tourists caught my attention.

"Dolphins," Hades said with a nod to the water.

A pod of dolphins crested the surface, and the tourists laughed with delight. The sight filled me with anxiety I couldn't explain.

Hades took pity on me. "Poseidon's harbingers. He's such a show-off."

"That's kind of cool." I forced myself to laugh to take my mind off the rocking boat and the creepy-ass dolphins. "How come you don't have anything like that?"

"What?" Hades' lips quirked in amusement. "Splitting the ground in two and coming up from the depths of hell wasn't dramatic enough?"

I smirked. "Now who's a show-off?"

When the boat landed on Cumberland Island, I started to depart with the tourists, but Hades held me back.

"You need to charm the captain into coming back for us." He kept his voice low.

"No."

Hades sighed. "Look, we don't have another option. Sunset is well after the last group leaves, and we need a way off this island." He gripped me by the shoulders and looked into my eyes. "If I could do it, I would. All right? I'm sorry, but it has to be you."

"What would you have done if I'd stayed home?" I asked, desperate for another option.

He grinned. "Taken shelter in the Underworld and waited out the apocalypse. When have you ever stayed home when there was a chance for conflict?"

I gave him a playful push but sobered as the Captain approached.

"Is everything all right?" he asked with an easy Southern twang. "If you've changed your mind about visitin', you'll still have to get off I'm afraid. Just a security—"

I'd looked him straight in the eyes, unleashing my charisma. His pupils dilated, and he broke off mid-sentence.

"Easy, Persephone," Hades whispered. "We want him to have his wits about him."

I flushed and eased off the charm. "We're going to be staying longer than the ferry service runs today, and we'll need a ride home when we're done."

"Of course," he breathed, looking awestruck. "I'll wait here for you."

"No, no. That's okay. You take the people back and forth like you normally would. Just give me your cell phone number, and I'll call you—"

"We may need a fast exit," Hades pointed out. "Ask him to leave us his boat."

"No!" I said hastily before the Captain could offer. "If you come back after you take the last group home, will anyone notice?"

"Not if I park at the Carnegie's deck on the little island. They aren't here durin' tourist season."

"Could you get in trouble?" I asked, dreading the answer.

"I'm staff here. I can come and go as I please."

I looked at Hades, and he gave a curt nod. "Thank you," I told the Captain and followed Hades off the boat.

WE SPENT THE remainder of the day poking around Dungeness and learning about sea turtles. When the sun began to sink through the sky, we made our way deeper into the forest. Gradually, the sounds of tourists faded away.

Hades dropped his glamour with a sigh of relief and motioned for me to do the same. "When we see Poseidon, let me do all the talking." Hades slapped at a mosquito. He stepped on a twig, and the sound ricocheted through the forest like a gunshot.

My feet crunched the leaves beside him, and I frowned. "Why?"

"Poseidon is old-fashioned. He—"

"Expects me to be arm candy?" I let out an offended laugh.

Hades gave me a look. "You don't have a lot of experience talking to gods that rank above you. Just this once, defer to experience, okay?"

"I guess he does outrank me." Given my parentage and my marriage, that didn't happen often. "You said Poseidon was okay. Why are you so worried about having a simple conversation with him?"

Hades ran his fingers through his hair and stopped under a giant live oak tree draped with Spanish moss. "That's exactly what I'm talking about. I never said a word regarding Poseidon's character. You inferred that all on your own. I wasn't trying to deceive you. Poseidon may be."

"I'll still be listening," I said, watching the dying light filter through the trees in shadowed patterns.

"Yes, but if you're not speaking, you can't give away more than I want him to know. He also won't be able to lock you into any promises."

I winced, thinking of Thanatos. "I understand."

A rustling of leaves caught my attention, and I glanced behind me. Two beautiful horses emerged from the trees. I caught my breath. They were a deep chestnut brown with black manes and perfectly formed white stars on their foreheads. I felt a strange kinship to the animals. Human intelligence sparkled in their eyes. They bowed their head to Hades and studied me carefully.

"Despoina, Arion," Hades said with a polite nod. "Lead on."

I followed the horses through the forest, wondering how Hades knew their names. We emerged from the forest to a white, sandy beach. I gasped at the sight of the girl from my dream standing thigh-high in the water.

"She can't see us," Hades said under his breath.

I looked again and saw the faint shimmer of a shield surrounding her like a giant bubble that would prevent her from seeing or hearing us.

"Hades!" a jovial voice called.

I turned to see a tall man striding toward us through the shallow surf. He had a flowing blond beard, a deep tan, and was dressed casually in board shorts and nothing else. I raised my eyebrows at his six-pack and gave Hades a speculative look. I'd never seen Hades with his shirt off. Were all gods built like that? I really hoped so.

"Poseidon," Hades said in a civil voice. He shifted, subtly placing himself between Poseidon and me. "It's been a long time."

To anyone who hadn't spent months overanalyzing Hades' every move, he looked perfectly calm. But I could feel the tension radiating off him.

Poseidon stopped an arm's-length away from us and looked at me. I saw his eyes and caught my breath. They swirled with shades of green, blue, and brown-white waves crested in miniature. They were so deep I could feel myself falling into them. I forced myself to meet the crashing and churning waves, not looking away until Poseidon chuckled.

"You're the spitting image of your mother." He grinned at me. "Uncanny. Pleased to meet you in person." He extended his hand.

Hades pushed my hand down before it could meet his. "Don't." His voice was full of warning. I followed his gaze to Poseidon, confused by the sudden malice in Hades' eyes.

Poseidon laughed. "Oh Hades, you've got it bad. There's little need to worry. I don't often have interest in children."

Interesting wording. "Didn't often." "Little need." No wonder Hades looked so tense. This guy was slimy. What would have happened if I'd shaken his hand?

Poseidon must have said something I missed because Hades bristled like an angry cat. I recognized the look in Poseidon's eye. I'd seen it in my classmates as they teased their younger siblings, pushing every button they had. I fiddled with my necklace and turned my attention to the girl in the water. She seemed frozen there, and I wondered what kind of shield was keeping her in place.

"Who is that?" I motioned at the water. "And why did you send for me? What do you know about Zeus?"

Hades stared at me, and I rolled my eyes. "What?"

He closed his eyes and looked up. Poseidon laughed.

"Well, who is she?" I demanded.

"Look at her. You can't tell what she is?" Poseidon replied.

I stared at the girl, her red hair swirling in the wind. I could tell she was a goddess, but knew he meant something more than that.

Hades narrowed his eyes and swore. "What has Zeus done?"

I gave the girl a closer look, but couldn't see anything different.

"You are new," Poseidon mused, looking me over curiously. "How old are you?"

"She's Zeus'," Hades explained, motioning toward the girl on the water.

"Yeah, I gathered that. So have you guys ever seen her before, or . . . " I trailed off at Hades' expression.

"No she's *really* new." Hades squinted his eyes against the setting sun.

"She appeared on the waves the day I sent for you," Poseidon added.

"And you kept her out there? What's wrong with you?" I demanded. I imagined spending two days in the ocean and shuddered.

"I'm not setting that thing loose in the world. If you can't see the level of charisma she's projecting, then I've severely overestimated your abilities."

"She's never seen another god with charisma," Hades interjected. "There wasn't an opportunity to teach her."

"So she has charm." I shrugged. "So do I, so does Zeus. What's the problem?"

"She doesn't just *have* charm." Poseidon laughed. "That's all she is. She's a full deity, but from what I can tell, she came solely from Zeus, and charm is all he gave her. He gave her an obscene amount." He went silent for a moment. "She wasn't created here. She rose from the sea near *Petra tou Romiou.*"

Hades swore. I looked at him in confusion. "What does that mean?"

"It's where Uranus fell," Hades explained.

Poseidon nodded, looking grim. "The resting place of a fallen god is always rife with chaotic power. I think he used Uranus' remains to help create her."

"What would that do?" I asked.

"She has the potential to become more powerful than us," Hades replied.

I realized what Hades meant, and my eyes widened. Uranus was Cronus' father. Cronus and Rhea had created my mother, Hades, Poseidon, Hera, Hestia, and Zeus. With gods, every generation is less powerful than the last. If Zeus had imbued her with charm and created her from Uranus' remains, there was no telling how much chaos she could wreak.

"So why send for me?" I managed to ask.

Poseidon looked surprised. "Isn't it obvious? You're the only one who's ever managed to kill a god."

Chapter V

"YOU WANT ME to kill her?" I exclaimed, my voice rising in shock. "She hasn't done anything!"

"I don't much care for your realm," Poseidon explained. "But the people in it have feelings of awe or fear regarding the ocean. It helps to keep me alive. So you'll understand why I have a vested interest in not allowing it to crash and burn."

I looked at Hades, and he looked back at me like *oh you want help now? What part of let me do the talking was too complicated for you?*

Crud. I was going to have to tread carefully here. I couldn't outright say no because someday I might be in a position where I had to kill this random girl, and I didn't want to be unable to do it because of something stupid I said today. "I have no intention of killing her at this time."

"That was carefully phrased," Poseidon mused.

I didn't like the way he was looking at me. I felt like a puzzle he was trying to solve.

I shrugged. I wasn't going to mention that I couldn't kill just any god. Killing Boreas had been a stroke of luck. He'd sworn allegiance to Zeus, pledging his powers behind Zeus' mysterious cause. Gods pass on a portion of their powers to their children. Since their children were once a part of them, gods are only vulnerable to their kids. A strange and messed up system that had allowed my mother's generation to kill the Titans. Since I was Zeus' daughter, Boreas had been as vulnerable to me as he'd made himself to Zeus.

"Hades, talk some sense into your young bride. You see what that creature is. You know how dangerous it can be."

"Creature?" I demanded. "It? That girl is one of us!"

Hades hesitated. "I can't justify her death for something she could do."

"Fine." Poseidon shrugged. "I wash my hands of this. She's your responsibility now." He met my eyes with a level stare. "If the world crumbles, you'd better hope Boreas wasn't a fluke."

Hades moved forward, eyes flaring. I grabbed his hand holding him back.

"Poseidon, you've lived this long, so you must have a healthy sense of self-preservation." I kept my tone light. "So let me get this straight. You're a god. You sent me a message to deal with this because you know I've killed a god before. You also know in the event of your untimely demise, my husband would determine where to send your soul . . . "

"Is that a threat?" Poseidon growled.

"As subtle as yours," Hades retorted.

Poseidon grinned at me. "You are spirited." He shook his head and stepped into the water. He made a sharp motion with his hand, and I saw the shield around the girl fall. "Enjoy the family reunion." He vanished before I could blink.

"On a scale of one to ten, how badly did I just screw up?" I asked.

Hades shrugged. "I'd never want that scumbag for an ally anyway. I forgot how much I hate him."

The girl in the water met my gaze and made her way toward us. I chewed my lip nervously. How were we going to handle this? If she was a danger to everyone around her, the safest place for her would be in the Underworld, but she couldn't go to the Underworld like I had. Hades had marked me as his bride to make it possible to travel between realms, but gods only get one spouse.

I bet he regretted that now. She needed to be down there more than I had. And she would make a much better queen. She was so regal, even dripping wet and trudging through waves.

She was prettier than me.

She was taller and thinner, looking every bit like a supermodel. Her hair was a gorgeous shade of red. She flashed Hades a beautiful smile, and I felt a pang of envy. It was a strange sensation. I'd never really experienced jealousy before. For all the trouble my appearance had caused me, I'd never felt ugly or plain like I did right now.

Hades watched her approach. Of course he would be watching her; she was a freaking vision of beauty standing before him. I bet he'd look past *their* age difference. When she reached the shore, he extended a hand to help her out of the water, and something in my mind snapped.

"Don't touch him!" I shrieked, flying at her.

Hades intercepted me before my clawed hands could reach her perfect face. She stepped back into the water, eyes wide.

"You whore!" I yelled. "Stay away from him!" I struggled to get out of Hades' grip, scratching and clawing at him, trying to get to her through the red haze of anger filling my mind. I was dimly aware that he was speaking, but couldn't focus on anything but her.

Hades swore and let me go, pushing me behind him as he reached for her. I gave a wordless shriek when he grabbed her arm, pulling her roughly onto the shore.

"Turn it off!" Hades snapped at her. At her blank stare, he swore again. Hades tightened his grip and pushed her toward the tree line. She cried out, some part of my mind heard the terror in her voice and registered that as important. "Let her go. Now!"

I fell to the sand, crying. He was talking to her! He was touching her. I could never compete with her. I'd never be able to measure up to her complete and utter perfection. My life was over! The waves crashing onto the sand filled my mind with an idea. I didn't know what would happen if I entered Poseidon's realm, but it was a safe bet I wouldn't be returning to bother Hades. I stood shakily and walked toward the ocean.

"Do not move," Hades told the girl in a threatening growl. He ran in front of me, grabbed my shoulders and gave me a small shake. "Persephone, snap out of it!"

I shook my head, sobbing too hard to respond.

"Damn it! This isn't you." He glared over my shoulder. "I said, don't move!"

"What's wrong with her?" she asked.

Gods, even her voice was perfect, light and melodic, like a freaking Disney princess.

"You're what's wrong with her!" Hades snapped. "Stay the hell back!"

"You deserve so much better." I gulped back tears.

"Gods," Hades muttered, rolling his eyes. He pulled me into a kiss. It was hot and frustrated, his anger radiating off him in waves. I felt power flowing into me, and gradually my mind stabilized.

I broke the kiss, staring at Hades wide-eyed, humiliated by the person I'd become. "What the hell was that?"

"She charmed you."

My mouth dropped open. *That* was what being charmed felt like? How could I have put anyone through that! The larger implications of the situation hit me, and I swallowed hard. If she could charm a god, we were in big trouble.

"I am so sorry." My voice was shaky as I turned to the girl.

"Don't you dare apologize." Hades crossed the beach with a quick, angry stride. The girl shrank back, eyes wide with fear. "What did Zeus send you for?"

"I—" Her voice shook, her eyes darting between us like a cornered animal.

I reached her before Hades. "I am sorry I tried to attack you." I gave Hades a level look, and he rolled his eyes and stepped back. "But I wasn't in control right then, you were. Do you understand how you caused that?"

She shook her head.

I kept my voice gentle. "That's okay. I've done the same thing to people without realizing it. It's called charm. Children of Zeus possess it."

"Are we sisters?"

I hesitated. "We're both daughters of Zeus," I said with what I hoped was a reassuring smile.

A beautiful smile grew across her face. "Sister!" she exclaimed, pulling me into a hug. Hades made a sharp noise, and she quickly let me go. "My name is Aphrodite."

I blinked, wondering where that name had come from. Gods suck at picking names. If I ever had a kid, they were getting a normal name, like Julie. "I'm Persephone, and this is Hades."

"Is this your realm?"

"One of them," I replied. "Will you answer a few questions for us? It's really important."

She looked back and forth from me to Hades, indecision clouding her face. Her gaze returned to me, and she nodded. "I'll answer anything you ask, Sister."

"Erm, thanks." I could deal with her calling me her sister—if I gritted my teeth. I looked to Hades for guidance.

"Have you ever seen Zeus?" he asked.

"Yes," she replied. "He created me, far from here. And then I saw him vanish."

"He didn't say anything to you?"

"No."

"Do you know anything else?" I asked, frustrated.

Aphrodite took a deep breath, and Hades quickly interjected, "Anything else about Zeus. Why he created you? What your purpose is? What his plans are?"

She shook her head. "He didn't tell me anything."

"Your question would have taken forever to answer," Hades explained. "She knows almost everything. She wasn't born; she was created. That's why she didn't have to learn to talk, or walk, and knew exactly who Zeus is."

"Almost everything, huh? How come she can't control her charm?"

Aphrodite flushed and looked down. "I . . . "

"He didn't want her to control it." Hades' voice was grim.

"What? Why not?"

"Aphrodite, did you swear fealty to Zeus?"

She looked at Hades, puzzled. "No. Why would I ever do that?"

Hades didn't answer, but I understood. I felt sick. We knew Aphrodite wasn't lying. Gods can't lie. She hadn't sworn fealty, and Zeus hadn't taught her to control her charm. Uncontrolled, Aphrodite's charm could drive people as crazy as I'd just been. And those feelings would be directed at her. Worship. Zeus was using her to gain followers. She hadn't sworn fealty yet, so I couldn't kill her. But, I'd wager anything he planned to come back to her later. And she'd be desperate for help. He could offer it to her in exchange for fealty.

I couldn't let that happen. Hades read my thoughts on my face and gave a slight nod. "Would you like to come with us?" I asked. "Get off this island?"

Her face broke out in a dazzling smile. "I'd love to."

Chapter VI

OF COURSE IT wasn't as simple as just leaving. Hades and I gave Aphrodite a crash course on charm so we could get back to the hotel without people attacking us or jumping off bridges or something equally crazy. She picked it up faster than I had, but I wasn't surprised. She had me to teach her.

Hades taught me to control my charm with guesswork and patience. He didn't have charm, and my charm wasn't strong enough to work on him, plus the souls in the Underworld were immune, so it was doubly hard to tell if I was doing something right. It had taken months to puzzle out some modicum of control. It was amazing I'd learned to control it at all. Aphrodite wouldn't have that problem. I knew how it worked now and knew how to communicate it in a way that made sense.

That seemed awfully convenient. Not only did Hades and I find Aphrodite, but we also just happened to be the only people who could teach her to control her powers. A glance at Hades told me he was worrying about the same thing. Had Zeus wanted us to find her? Could she be working with him without knowing it?

When we finally made it to the hotel, the morning sun had just begun to lighten the horizon. Hades unlocked the door and yawned. "She's going to need real clothes. We can't keep her shielded like this forever. It's a waste of power."

"Real clothes?" Aphrodite asked.

I smiled at Hades to show that I'd noticed his carefully averted gaze when the sea foam didn't cut it. I thought of the strange outfits Cassandra had packed and sighed. "Don't worry Aphrodite. I've got something." I started to close the door, but Hades caught it with his hand. I shot him a questioning look.

"I'm not leaving you alone with her."

I shrugged and let him in. I dug through my bag, too tired to care what I wore to sleep. I threw a green silk nightdress to Aphrodite.

When she disappeared into the bathroom and closed the door behind her, Hades turned to me. "Are you okay? You haven't said much since . . . "

"I went crazy?" I gave a bitter laugh. "I'll get over it."

I felt a flash of power as Hades dropped a shield around us and knew Aphrodite couldn't hear us.

"What are we going to do with her?" he asked.

"I didn't want Poseidon to know I couldn't kill her."

Hades nodded. "Of course, but now . . . "

"We have to protect her. She needs to learn how to fit into this world and to control her powers. We're the only people who can help her."

"Or that's exactly what Zeus wanted. What if he sent her out in the world to cause chaos and keep us occupied?"

"Keep us occupied for what?" I sat down on the bed. "And how could he possibly know Poseidon would send for us?"

He held his hands up in frustration. "Who else is left to send for?"

"But how did he know Poseidon would send for anyone at all?"

Hades shrugged. "Then she'd be wandering around collecting worshipers for Zeus. This is why I hate Zeus. He has back-up plans for his back-up plans. Any move we ever made always played right into his hands."

I folded my hands in my lap and looked around the room like it had answers. "What else can we do? We can't just leave her alone, and we can't kill her."

"There are ways to detain a god."

I thought of the smile on Aphrodite's face when she had hugged me, like I was some kind of hero rescuing her. "We can't just keep her prisoner forever. She hasn't done anything wrong."

"What do you suggest we do?"

I thought about it for a moment. "Help her." When Hades rolled his eyes, I spoke fast. "Use her? We don't have any weaknesses to speak of. There's nothing of value she could pass along to Zeus. If we can't hurt her, then she can't hurt us, and if she has any other purpose here, we'll be right there to stop her."

Hades shook his head. "I have a weakness, and you have many."

"What's your weakness?" I asked.

Hades gave me a significant look and touched my cheek softly. "Who do you think? And"—he continued when I blushed—"your people are vulnerable, remember?"

I sat down on the bed. Of course I remembered my people were vulnerable. Mom. Melissa. Her mother. I'd never forget watching Melissa die for no reason other than the fact that she meant something to me. I couldn't put her, or any of my friends, in danger again.

I yawned, exhausted. It had been a really long day in the hot sun, and we were no closer to answers than we'd been before we left. Worse, we had more questions. "This sucks."

"Why don't you get some sleep?" Hades suggested, dropping the shield when Aphrodite left the bathroom. "I'll think about it."

I was exhausted, but desperately needed a shower. I could feel the DEET burrowing into my skin. Thankfully, gods are immune to cancer.

I unclipped my necklace and hung it on the doorknob then hurried through my shower, toweled my hair dry, and slipped into a blue satin nightgown. The clingy material had me raising my eyebrows at my reflection, but at least it wasn't too low-cut. Not like Hades would even notice.

I moved toward the door, freezing when I heard Aphrodite's voice.

" . . . don't want to hurt her," Aphrodite said softly. "We're sisters. I can't use charm on her anymore, can I? Even accidentally?"

"No, she's immune to your level of charm now," Hades said after a moment.

"You must love her very much, to give that much of yourself to protect her." Her voice was wishful.

I hadn't thought of that. He'd done more than just snap me out of that craziness on the beach. He'd given me part of his powers.

"That's not really your business," Hades replied.

"You're very powerful, aren't you? Are you stronger than Zeus?"

I opened the door and walked to the bed, motioning for them to continue talking. Aphrodite lounged on the red couch, and Hades was sitting on the edge of the bed. I pulled the sheet over me, feeling self-conscious.

Hades greeted me with a smile. There was an awkward silence when Aphrodite realized he wasn't going to answer her question. How could he? We had no idea how powerful Zeus was.

"What do you think?" I asked finally. "You've seen Zeus."

"I was shielded. I didn't get a sense of power from him like I do from the two of you."

I gave Hades a puzzled look, and he inclined his head letting me know he'd explain later.

"I'm so glad you came for me." She beamed at me, and her smile was so beautiful my breath caught.

"I wasn't going to just leave you in the ocean." I shuddered, remembering those crashing waves.

I played her words back through my mind to find a loophole in her story, but I was too tired to think. I felt myself drifting off. Through the cotton sheet I could feel Hades' reassuring hand on my leg. I thought of the new word I'd chosen to close my mind to intruders. *Adios.*

When I woke up, Hades was slouched against the wooden headboard, reading a book with a blue cover. I could feel the warmth of him through the sheets and had instinctively snuggled closer during my nap.

I yawned, stretching, and glanced over to the couch where Aphrodite lay curled up, red hair cascading down the upholstery onto the floor. A look out the window told me it was dark outside, but I couldn't tell if it was early dark or late dark.

"How long have I been asleep?" My voice was hoarse.

"A few hours," Hades said softly, power blanketing the room so we couldn't be heard. I studied the shimmering shield and realized we couldn't be seen either.

"What time is it?" I asked, sitting up.

Hades glanced at the clock on the bedside table. "A little after two."

I blinked. I'd slept the entire day away. "Why—"

"There's a physical toll sometimes. Fighting that much charm, taking in that much power. You're not supposed to be doing any of this yet."

I nodded. There was a reason no one talked about child-gods. Before maturity, a deity's body just wasn't meant to handle much power.

I put a hand to my throbbing forehead and frowned. "Did you figure something out about Aphrodite?"

"I talked to her for a while after you drifted off. She's not privy to Zeus' plans."

"But she's a part of them," I reminded him, uncomfortable with the realization that I didn't want him to get too friendly with Aphrodite.

Hades shrugged. "She doesn't want to be. I think she's afraid of him. You're right. She needs our help, Persephone."

I pushed the blue spaghetti straps of my nightgown back up my arms from where they had fallen. "She needs to learn to fit in then. Right now she sticks out like a sore thumb."

"I taught her to do a glamour," Hades replied. "Socialization she'll have to learn from you."

"I thought she knew everything." I blinked at my snarky tone, but Hades didn't seem to notice. Was I still jealous? I'd thought that feeling fled with the charm, but hearing Hades say she needed help . . .

Gods, Persephone, he can't win for losing. If he doesn't want to help her, you think he's a jerk, and if he does, you get jealous? What's wrong with you?

"Not how to blend. It's natural for you because you were raised human, but for the rest of us . . . We're a different species. It can be hard, even for me, to understand humans all the time. She might be great with humans. Zeus is. But her attitude toward them may be different from what you're accustomed to. She needs to live in this world, Persephone. The Underworld isn't going to be an option for her."

"She can stay with me."

"Bad idea." Hades shook his head. "Your mother won't like that one bit, and I don't feel comfortable with her under your roof."

I suppressed a smile. Hades could be so overprotective. "I guess she can stay with Melissa then. Learn what normal girls her age do. I can count on Melissa to keep tabs on her."

Hades hesitated. "Is that wise?"

"I'll have her swear an oath not to harm Melissa, or her mother."

"No, have her swear an oath to protect Melissa and her mother from all harm," Hades corrected. "So she can't stand by and watch something happen to them."

"I'm going to have to work on the wording." I'd seen enough movies about angry supercomputers or robots to know better than to ask for protection from all harm. I winced and rubbed my temples.

"I was afraid of that." Hades traced my forehead with his fingertips. I didn't have the energy to ask—just waited for him to clarify. "I gave you too much power. Your headaches are getting worse."

"I'd rather have a headache than ever feel that again." I shifted so I faced Hades. "Have you ever been charmed?"

Hades opened his mouth then closed it, gaze going distant. "I'll never know."

He spoke so low, I wasn't sure I'd heard him correctly. "What do you mean?"

He leaned back. "Zeus is like you. He was born, not created. At the time, we hadn't seen anything like him. He was so much younger than us, so vulnerable. But as he grew into his powers . . . " Hades spread his hands in front of him in a helpless gesture. "We'd never seen charm before; it was something completely unique to him. We didn't have any resistance to it. He told us how terrible our parents were, and we believed him." Hades shrugged. "He wasn't lying. But, the rebellion . . . afterward, we were never sure whose idea it was. Or when exactly we'd agreed to it. Then suddenly he was King of the Gods, we had a mountain, and Hera was married to him. It all just happened out of nowhere."

"No wonder you hate him."

Hades looked up at me surprised. "For that? No. We'll never stop owing him for getting us out from under the Titans. It was horrible. No matter what he's done since, we all still owe him a debt of gratitude. I don't hate him for that. Just . . . everything after."

"But you think he charmed you?"

"We're not sure. And he was so young, I don't know that he could ever be sure either. Like I said, charm was new. But we worried, so we found ways to resist, and the others found ways to pass that resistance down so that no other gods could be controlled. It's too dangerous."

I blushed. "I think you would know. I was so . . . possessive. It was like it wasn't even me. I could feel myself going crazy. I just couldn't stop it." I shook my head. Dwelling on it wouldn't do anyone any good.

"In most cases, the charm will feel more subtle. People shouldn't realize they're bending to your will. That's the difference between controlled and uncontrolled charm. Uncontrolled charm is just a crazy mess. She was using too much to be effective. Had she known what she was doing, that would have been a show of power, or a fatal blow, though to my knowledge you're the only one who . . . "

He didn't have to finish the sentence. I was the only one who had ever used charm to kill someone.

Hades stifled a yawn, and I immediately felt guilty. "We don't have to do this tonight. You're tired."

He shook his head. "I'll be fine. As for sensing another deity's powers, that's just an instinct you're going to have to learn to trust. You need to master shields so she doesn't find out you're not fully vested in your powers."

"Okay." I already knew how to identify shields. Shields are pretty much just walls of power with thought behind them. They could keep a conversation private or make you invisible. Some shields could prevent teleportation, like the one Boreas used against me in the clearing last year. There were stronger shields, meant to block the use of any divine powers, such as the ones keeping the Titans in Tartarus and away from the other souls, but I was nowhere near powerful enough to cast that.

I practiced for a while, never tampering with the shield Hades had left up. My cheeks heated when I realized what conclusion Aphrodite would come to if she woke up and found our bed cloaked from her vision.

When I finished practicing, Hades channeled the excess power from me. When married gods shared any intimate contact, their minds were open to each other. Hades and I hadn't done anything beyond kissing, but channeling power apparently counted.

Marriage with gods was largely political. Love didn't often factor into the equation, but power did. An exchange solidified the marriage; the amount varied depending on the gods. Some gods kept as much of their own power as possible, others drained all the power from their spouse, and some chose equilibrium. The gods who chose to be equals were always connected, could always sense each other or hear one another, no matter how far away they actually were.

For the thousandth time, I tried to turn my thoughts to Thanatos. My mind threw up a wall to block the thoughts. I felt Hades respond to it. He was curious, and a little hurt, but he respected me too much to ask. I gave up and discretely searched Hades' mind for the slightest indication he'd thought anything about sitting so close to me, on a bed, at night, cloaked from view from anyone else in the room.

Not a single passing thought. Damn. That was almost insulting.

I bet he would think about her.

Hades snorted, breaking contact with me as the last of my headache receded. "Not likely." He paused. "You shouldn't feel guilty about charming all those humans," he said, incorrectly guessing what was bothering me. The humans he referred to included pretty much anyone I'd met between my sixteenth birthday and my time in the Underworld. Before I had control of my charm, I'd caused all kinds of problems. "Or Boreas. You didn't know what you were doing to the humans. I promise, they weren't as bad off as you were today. Boreas deserved it."

I frowned at Hades to show him I didn't appreciate him poking around in my mind. His raised eyebrow reminded me that I'd been poking in his mind first. I shrugged in apology. "I don't feel guilty about Boreas." Hades gave me a look. "I don't!" I protested. "I should, but I don't. I feel guilty that I don't feel guilty. Does that make sense?"

"No."

"What kind of a person kills someone and doesn't feel bad about it?"

"The kind who met his last victim, narrowly avoided her fate, and watched her best friend die at his hands. He doesn't deserve your pity."

"I know. He deserved worse than what I did to him, but not feeling even the slightest bit of guilt? That makes me a monster."

"You can't keep comparing yourself to humans. Gods have a

stronger sense of justice. We see a wrong and we fix it. There are not as many shades of grey for us." He put a hand on my shoulder. "You're the furthest thing from a monster I've ever met." He yawned and I turned around, shifting until I was lying down. "I can sleep on the floor," he said with another yawn.

"Don't be ridiculous."

He hesitated, putting his book on the nightstand. "I don't think—"

"I dream about that day all the time," I said, voice so soft he had to lean closer to hear me. "I see her die, over and over again, and sometimes I don't get away." I felt his reassuring arm wrap around me and leaned into him. "It's better . . . when I know you're here." I met his gaze, "I'm not afraid to sleep. I know when I'm with you, I'm safe."

His arm tightened around me, and he turned off the light without a word. I felt the shield drop away from us and fell asleep to the soothing sound of his beating heart.

Chapter VII

THE NEXT MORNING I woke to the sound of a shower running. Hades was still sleeping, one arm draped possessively over my middle. I smiled and let myself enjoy the feeling of his arm around me for just a minute before I slipped out of bed, careful not to wake him, and began packing. The water shut off, and I grabbed the extra outfit out of the unicorn bag for Aphrodite.

The door opened, and Aphrodite stepped into the room wearing a towel. I glanced over at Hades, glad he was still asleep, and handed her the outfit, motioning for her to keep quiet. The tank top and short skirt looked amazing on her, and I realized I'd need to have a talk with Cassandra later. The clothes fit her too well to be coincidence.

I ducked into the bathroom and slipped into a blue sundress and clipped on my necklace. I smiled and touched one of the pointed green leaves. I'd have to get Hades something. But what could I possibly get for the god who had everything?

By the time I was ready, Hades was awake. We ate breakfast before settling our bill and leaving the island. I made a quick phone call to the ferry company and left a glowing review for the captain I'd charmed into coming back for us then made Hades do the same from the hotel phone. It wasn't nearly enough, but it was all I could think to do. Then I called my mom when we reached the car and explained the situation. We filled Aphrodite in on our plan and had her swear an oath regarding the safety of the priestesses.

"Okay," she agreed in a cheerful voice.

"You don't have any questions?" I asked, surprised.

"You're trying to protect me. Why would I question you?"

"Imagine that." Hades gave me an amused look.

I narrowed my eyes at him, sure he was remembering the first time he rescued me.

"See how much smoother things go when you tell people you're trying to help them?" I poked him with my index finger and unlocked the car.

"Touché," Hades said. "On that note, whatever you do, don't piss off Demeter."

Aphrodite nodded, looking so worried I couldn't help but laugh. "Don't look so scared, my mom is really nice."

"To you, sometimes." Hades snickered. "And those who've sworn allegiance to her."

I frowned. "My mom is nice to everyone."

Hades shook his head, but didn't push the subject. "Just walk on eggshells," he warned Aphrodite.

It was dusk when we arrived at Melissa's house. The porch light shined like a beacon at the end of their long gravel driveway. I noticed Mom's car and drew a deep breath. I was still angry with her for lying about Zeus but returned her hug when we entered Melissa's home. No matter what, she was still my mom.

I hugged Melissa then introduced everyone to Aphrodite. She gave Melissa a cool appraisal, clearly not impressed with what she saw, and I winced. We'd have to talk about manners later.

"So you're Persephone's human?"

Or now. I grabbed Aphrodite's arm. "Excuse us," I told Melissa and dragged Aphrodite down the hall. "Don't ever talk to her like that again!"

"Like what?" Aphrodite asked, all innocence.

"Like she's beneath us. Like anyone is beneath us. She's not my human; she's a person—"

"Yes," Aphrodite agreed. "Of course she's a person. She's human. She is beneath us."

I gaped at her cavalier attitude and looked to Hades for help. He hadn't said a word since we'd walked into the house. I followed his gaze to Melissa's mother, crossing back and forth behind the half wall that separated the living room from the kitchen.

"Would anyone like cookies?" she called, putting a plate down on the bar. "They're just ready . . . " Her voice trailed off when she felt the power of Hades' stare.

"Minthe?" he breathed.

She met his eyes, and her face paled.

Melissa and I glanced at each other in confusion. What was this? "Treat her like you'd treat me," I told Aphrodite quickly. "And listen to what she says. She's your best bet at fitting in here. You can't just walk around like you're better than everyone—"

"But I am."

I rolled my eyes. I didn't have time for this. "Don't act like it," I snapped, moving away from Aphrodite and closer to Melissa.

"Hades, I wanted to tell you—" Mrs. Minthe began.

"But I thought it best she not further invoke Hera's anger," my mother interrupted in clipped tones.

"I thought you were dead." Hades' voice was careful, as if he was trying very hard to bury whatever emotions were at war within him.

"What's going on?" Melissa asked.

"She's *the* Minthe." I managed to work the words out of my dry throat. "Isn't she?"

Melissa knew the myth. We'd both heard it in Latin class, and then later, after my winter in the Underworld, we'd analyzed every facet of that myth to figure out what kind of girls Hades liked. Melissa met my eyes, looking pale and shocked.

"Hades and I used to see each other before I was a priestess of Demeter," Mrs. Minthe explained.

"Hera got jealous and turned her into the mint plant," Hades added.

"Why would Hera be jealous?" Melissa interjected. She blinked, seeming surprised at the sound of her own voice, and I knew that question had been the least important one on her mind. She'd just blurted it out without thinking.

Hades hesitated, but my mother had no problem filling in the gap. "Hades and Hera were a couple long before she married Zeus. Didn't he tell you, Persephone?"

I didn't bother to answer her smug question. No, he hadn't told me, but I'd already guessed. He'd always been unusually defensive on Hera's behalf. He'd been open with me about every other relationship he'd ever had. Obviously, that one was a sore subject, and I saw no reason to get upset about a relationship that had ended when dirt was new.

Aphrodite gave my mother a strange look and stepped closer to Hades in a show of solidarity.

"So you're nymphs," Aphrodite exclaimed, indicating Melissa and her mother with a wave of her hand. At Melissa's questioning look, she clarified, "It's easier to turn a nymph into a plant. Humans are easier to turn into animals. It's not impossible, mind you . . . "

"I'm a nymph?" Melissa asked her mom.

"Half," Mrs. Minthe replied. "Honey, the difference between a human and a nymph is so inconsequential it's hardly worth mentioning. We work well with nature. Unlike the human myths, turning into trees or rivers isn't typical of our race, unless cursed."

Melissa's shoulders slumped in disappointment. "Oh, so you got turned into a plant? Why?"

"It made sure even her soul was out of my reach." Hades' voice was bitter.

"Demeter rescued me. In return, I swore to be her priestess for all time."

I wondered how many of my mom's priestesses were refugees from other gods. I was about to ask when Hades interrupted. "Well, it's good to see you, Minthe. I'm happy that you're still alive." He turned to my mother. "I am grateful to you for that."

I fiddled with my necklace and studied Mrs. Minthe out of the corner of my eye. Her every feature should have been familiar to me, but too many conflicting images were vying for my attention. I saw the woman who babysat me since before I could walk. She'd baked every one of my birthday cakes. She was Melissa's mom, and that image didn't resonate with the youthful nymph I'd imagined from hearing the stories.

Words were being exchanged between Hades and Minthe, but I couldn't hear them. The words didn't matter anyway. Their eyes spoke louder, telling stories of regret and angst. I shouldn't be in here right now. Melissa gripped my hand, and I knew she understood.

"I'll . . . uh, I'll be back. Tomorrow. Can you . . . " I kept losing my train of thought, the right words slipping past me like water flowing through my fingers. "Aphrodite . . . "

"I will be fine." Aphrodite beamed. "You should have told me she was a nymph," she added, as if that made all the difference.

"Okay then, I'm going to show you to your room." Melissa kept her voice low, steering Aphrodite away. She met my eyes and quirked an eyebrow.

I nodded. We would talk later.

I made my way to the porch, gulping the fresh air as if I'd been suffocating. The door closed behind me, and I closed my eyes. "Which is it, Mom? Are you here to gloat or give me a cover story?"

"I deserved that," she said in a calm voice.

"Damn right, you did!" I snapped. She arched an eyebrow at my tone, but I was too angry to care. "You knew I was coming here with Hades, and you let me find out like this! Not to mention Minthe and Melissa. What do you think that did to them?"

"I spoke with Minthe before you arrived." Mom smoothed her skirt and sat on the porch swing. "We both agreed that it was best to get this over with. Hades was bound to run into her at some point if Aphrodite is going to be staying here, and you deserved to know about his past before you get any further involved in this relationship."

"You think he didn't tell me about her? He told me everything; he always does. He used her as cautionary tale for why we shouldn't be together. You didn't win here, you—"

"I wasn't aware we were fighting a battle."

"We're having a war, haven't you noticed?" I laughed. "And you've been fighting dirty, withholding information just long enough to sharpen the blow."

"Persephone." She gave me an annoyed look. "You can't believe I've been keeping things from you to hurt you."

"What other reason could there be?" I held up my hands in frustration. "I've told you I want you to be honest with me. I don't know how I can make it clearer to you. So yeah, I'm taking it personally. You've been against me and Hades from the start. It's not about the age difference. It's about power. As long as I'm in the dark, I'm easier to control, and he took that away from you."

She gave me a level stare. "You're upset right now, but when you calm down, we're going to talk about this attitude of yours—"

"So I can be better behaved?" I pushed off the wooden porch rail and moved toward my mother, furious with her deception. Her back stiffened, but she didn't move. "You know how this conversation would have gone a few months ago? You would have lectured me and ended by asking me to promise to have a better attitude. You took advantage of the fact that I couldn't lie and used it to bind me to your standards. But the secret's out. I'm not falling for it anymore, so you're changing your tactics. And you don't care who you hurt in the process." I pointed at the door. "That was ruthless, Mom, even for you."

She opened her mouth, but I cut her off before she could get a word in. "And I say that after finding out you let me believe my father was dead. After your refusal to be honest with me nearly got me killed last winter and actually did kill Melissa. After all of the half-truths and deceptions throughout the years." I shook my head. "Letting me plan for swimming and scuba diving on the Georgia coast trip, knowing I wouldn't be able to step one foot in the water. What is *wrong* with you?"

"Are you going to let me get a word in?"

"You've said enough." I crossed my arms, hands clenched so tight I was surprised my nails didn't draw blood. "If you love me at all, if you're even capable of it, you won't say another word. You'll go inside and leave me the hell alone. I can't take a single word my mother says to me at face value ever again, and you apparently lack the basic compassion necessary to understand how hard that is for me."

I spun around, facing the driveway. The porch light spilled over my shoulders, casting a shadow into the grass and gravel. The door creaked open, and Hades stepped onto the porch. I watched their shadows in the grass, still and silent. My silhouette was caught between theirs, blending us all into a featureless lump. I imagined the look being exchanged between the gods behind me. Was he mad? Grateful? Indifferent? For once I couldn't guess how he felt.

My mother retreated, leaving me with my shadows and Hades with his mysterious feelings. I breathed heavily, but didn't allow myself to cry.

It felt like eons later when Hades spoke. "You're angry."

I touched my necklace. "Not at you."

He fell into step beside me as we walked toward the car. "Are you okay?" I asked finally.

"I love that you would bother to ask that." He had a sad smile on his face. "I'm fine. I feel better, actually. I've felt guilty about what happened to Minthe for a long time. It's good to know she's okay."

"I guess it was nice of Mom to rescue her," I conceded.

"Strategic. Undying gratitude is powerful stuff for a god."

That explanation better fit my mood. We sat in the car for a minute. Dread filled the pit of my stomach, and I really didn't want to ask, but I had to. "Do you still love her?"

Chapter VIII

HE DIDN'T HESITATE. "No."

I let out a sigh of relief and started the car. We'd only driven a few miles when Hades told me to pull over.

"You shouldn't drive when you're so upset." He motioned to my shaking hands. "But I figured you wanted to get out of there."

He didn't ask for my keys, so I gathered he was too upset to drive as well. When I turned into a dirt lot behind an abandoned diner, he asked, "Why don't you tell me what's really bothering you?"

"Beyond the weirdness of you hooking up with my best friend's mom?" I laughed.

Hades winced. "I—"

I shook my head. "Way before my time, I know. This isn't you. It's me. I may need a day or two to get the idea of you two out of my head—" I shuddered. "Gods, Hades. She's so old!"

"She was thirty!"

"Yeah. That's old. I know it's stupid, but I always pictured the people you were with as my age, physically anyway."

Hades snorted. "No. You're absolutely the youngest person I've ever . . . " He trailed off, as if he wasn't certain what we'd done. What we were.

And wasn't that the problem?

"There!" He pointed at me. "That! Right there. You only get that look when something's bothering you."

"What look?"

Hades narrowed his eyes and scrunched up his nose. I stared at him, horrified.

"I'm not getting it right." He shrugged. "Just trust me. You have a look. So what's wrong?"

I opened the door and stepped into the parking lot, dust rising with my footsteps as I made my way to the front of the car. His door creaked open. I leaned on the hood, staring at the burnt-out shell of the old diner. "I'm so mad at Mom that anything I say to you right now is going to sound angry. And I'm not angry with you. I'm not . . . I don't know how I feel about . . . ugh." I shuddered again, thinking of him and Minthe. "There's just too much going on. I can't sort out anything that's going on in my head."

The car dipped down when he sat beside me on the hood. "I'll keep that in mind."

A solitary car drove by, the headlights illuminating the scrawling weeds that had taken over the foundation of the old diner. I bit my lip. "Do you really want to do this right now? Let's take a night. You've been through a lot. I'm all upset. Let's decompress—"

"That's exactly what I don't want to do!" Hades pushed off the car. "I don't want this to build up and become something bigger than it has to be. I'd rather clear the air, right here, right now. Get everything out in the open so I never have to think about her again."

I blinked, unsure of how to respond to that. There was a whoosh as another car drove by. Hades waited until the sound faded before continuing. "I've spent so long feeling guilty about what happened to her. But she's okay. Now I can put her behind me." His hands fell down by his sides. "So please, tell me what's bothering you."

I closed my eyes. "This is going to sound so petty."

"What?"

"You . . . and her . . . I mean you guys . . . " Gods, I didn't want to say it. I kicked at the dust, forcing the words from the throat. "Did you . . . ?"

"Does it matter?"

I gave him a look. "You're the one who wanted to go down this road. I was willing to drop it."

He grimaced. "You know the answer to that. I've always been up-front with you. I'm not going to spout some B.S. about how I've waited millennia for you. You weren't on my radar. I never knew . . . " He paused. "I didn't know I could feel like this about another person."

"And not just her," I whispered. "There were others. Hera?"

He looked up at me. "We could do this all night, Persephone." I winced. "But does it matter? Yes. There have been other women, but that doesn't matter to me because they aren't you."

"Why her? Why them?" My cheeks were so heated I thought they might burst into flame. "What's so different about them that you're not afraid to . . . You're barely willing to hold my hand, but with her—"

"That's what you're worried about?" Hades laughed then stopped when he saw my expression. "Persephone, there is no comparison." He reached out and grabbed my hand. "You're beautiful, you're smart, and you're so *good*. You see things in a way that—"

"Then why don't you want to kiss me?" I stared down at the ground, hair falling in front of my face.

"It's not a good idea."

"But kissing them was?"

"Did you miss the part where they got turned into plants?" He tucked my hair behind my ears, and his fingers traced my jawline, guiding my face up to his. "I always want to kiss you."

My breathing went shallow, and my pulse pounded in my throat. I stood on my tiptoes, lips brushing against his.

He stepped away from me. "That doesn't mean I should."

"You said you loved me."

"I do, but for the life of me, I can't figure out why."

My jaw dropped.

"That came out wrong." Hades said quickly. "Look, I've been around for a long time. I never bought into the whole love at first sight thing, but when I saw you, that changed. It didn't matter that being with you was going to make my life ridiculously complicated. It didn't matter that scum like Poseidon would see our age difference and do a double take, or that your mother was Demeter, of all people. I saw you, I wanted you, and nothing was going to stand in my way. I dragged you down there and bound you to me."

"We've been over this. It was either take me to the Underworld or leave me for Boreas."

"Probably, but I didn't even try to think of another way."

"Good! How many times do I have to tell you that I'm happy to be with you?"

"You don't know that!" He threw up his hands in frustration. "We talk a lot about how marriage is meaningless to the gods, how it's all political, but have you noticed how few of us are actually married? It might not be all about love, but being bound to someone, being a part of them, it changes you. It can mess with your perception, and I keep making it worse." He grabbed my shoulders and spun me to face him. "I saved your life, so now you feel indebted to me. I told you the truth when your mother wouldn't. So now you're mad at her and you trust me. She doesn't want you to be with me, and you want to get back at her—"

"You think I'm using you to rebel against my mom?" I stared at him, incredulous. "I could just get a tattoo."

"I'm in your head every night—"

"Which keeps me alive!"

"Exactly! I'll never know if you would have chosen me. Everything I do, every move I make manipulates your feelings about me. It's not intentional, it just keeps happening. I don't want to take advantage of you. That's not me. I would never do that. But I think I have, and that's—" His jaw tightened. "When I kiss you, I feel . . . guilty, and I don't enjoy feeling like the kind of slime that gets tossed into Tartarus."

"You think I don't know how I feel about you?"

"I think you're very young. This is your first serious relationship, and I'm not going to take advantage of you. I hated Zeus for what he did to Hera, but what I did to you is worse."

I rolled my eyes. Hera had given Zeus all of her power. She hadn't even left herself enough to stay alive. "Yeah, well sometimes I think you're stupid. Do you really think that I'm so weak that I'd let anything you've done define me? I am not Hera."

"She was not weak!" His eyes blazed with anger.

"Obviously, she was. Just not with you."

Fury overwrote his features. He took a deep, controlled breath. "I think maybe you were right."

I gave him a confused look.

"We shouldn't have tried to talk about this tonight. We've been through a lot today. We're tired." He took another breath, unclenching his fists, forcing himself to relax. "I'm going to stay tonight, maybe a few days. However long it takes us to sort this out."

Hades on the surface for a while? That would be fantastic. "But . . . what about the Underworld? Can Cassandra handle it by herself?"

"She's not alone. Thanatos is back. Between the two of them—Persephone, what's wrong?"

The world reeled around me. Thanatos was back in the Underworld, unsupervised. And I couldn't even say anything. I was a thousand times worse than my mother for keeping Thanatos' betrayal from Hades.

I took a deep breath to steady myself. "I don't think that's a good idea."

Hades' eyebrows shot up in surprise.

I closed my eyes, holding back the tears. I didn't want to do this. I thought of all the souls in the Underworld I'd come to count as friends. Who knew what Thanatos was capable of? Hades had to be there, to protect his realm, to protect his people. I had to convince him to go back but I couldn't tell him why.

I'd have to think of another reason. I closed my eyes and dug deep. When it hit me I almost winced against the pain. If I said it, it meant I felt it was true, and I didn't want *this* to be true. "I've viewed every kiss as a victory while you see it as a defeat, and that's wrong for both of us. Don't you get it, Hades? This, us, it shouldn't feel like a battle."

"Persephone . . . " He moved toward me, and I stepped away.

"Do you hear the way you're talking about me? I'm not supposed to be your responsibility. I'm supposed to be your equal, and you barely see me as capable of intelligent thought."

"That's not what I meant!"

"No, I get it. You're older, you know more, you're more powerful, and I've needed you for that. So until I don't . . . Until you can view me as more and trust my feelings . . . " I stammered trying desperately to find something that wasn't a lie. My heart thudded in my chest. I clutched at my necklace like it was a lifeline. Thanatos was in the Underworld, and it was completely defenseless. Hades had to get down there. If he didn't . . .

"I don't think we can work." I blurted it out before the thought had fully formed and immediately felt nauseated. I couldn't have said it if it wasn't true. Did I really not think we would work?

Hades stared at me, looking as confused as I felt. "So what are you saying?"

I closed my eyes. "I think you should go back to the Underworld and stay there. At least until all this stuff with Zeus is over. I don't want to be in a relationship with someone who thinks they need to protect me from myself."

"Persephone—"

"It's insulting and condescending, and it's not . . . " I struggled for words realizing the truth as I spoke it and hating myself for it. "It's not healthy. Best case scenario, I change your mind, which I shouldn't have to do, but worst I start to believe you. I don't want that. We need to take a break, as much as we can anyway." I would still need him to channel my powers.

Hades studied me for a long moment then nodded his head. "All right."

I forced myself to move my head in a way that could be taken for a nod and made myself a silent promise. I may not be able to tell Hades about Thanatos, but that didn't mean I couldn't stop Thanatos on my own.

Chapter IX

IT WAS NO USE. I clutched Eurydice's hand in mine, pouring all my energy into healing her, but I could tell it wasn't enough.

I tried to swing by the hospital every morning since my return from the Underworld to try to heal Orpheus' wife. After all, it was kind of my fault she was like this. I'd convinced Hades to allow Orpheus to bring her back from the Underworld.

It hadn't gone well.

"Don't overdo it." Mom's hand touched my back, and I stiffened. She made an offended sound but dropped her hand and moved it away from me.

The last few weeks had gone from bad to worse with us. Any time we talked, we argued. So now we didn't talk much at all. Which I wouldn't have minded one bit if it wasn't for the fact that she still wanted me to stick to the same training schedule she'd set up upon my return from the Underworld. Plant lessons all morning and then healing lessons on Eurydice. It was beyond awkward.

I let go of Eurydice's hand. "I've got to go," I said to Mom.

She nodded. I reached the door just as it opened and revealed Orpheus, balancing three paper cups from the hospital coffee shop. He started in surprise then grinned at me when I held the door open.

"Did it work?" Hope shone in his metallic gold eyes. I shook my head, and his shoulders slumped, dejected. "Thanks for trying again." He handed my mom a cup and held out the other for me.

I took a sip and smiled. It was my favorite. Blackberry pomegranate green tea. Long name, awesome taste. Had anyone told me a year ago that the famous rock icon Orpheus would bring me tea, I would have thought they were crazy. I had posters of him in my room, drawn to the features that marked him as a demigod, not that I knew that at the time. Demigods are gold. Literally. Their hair, eyes, skin, every feature that could be gold-toned, was gold. It had something to do with the ichor running through their blood. At least that's what Hades said.

"I'll see you tomorrow," I promised.

I swung by Melissa's for Aphrodite's goddess lessons then went to the park for a run. My feet hit the ground at a furious pace, the cross-country trail above Memorial Park passing beneath me in a blur. The Nike trainer app on my phone reported my progress as my playlist blared through my headphones.

I felt exposed in my short black exercise shorts and sports shirt. I didn't normally wear tops that showed my stomach, but I'd never run in hundred degree heat before this summer either. It was a far cry from the perfect weather of the Underworld, but Mom didn't like me spending all my time there. Running on the surface was a bitter compromise in our ongoing fight.

My thoughts kept pace with my feet. School started next week. I'd have to become "Kora" again. I'd gone by my middle name by choice my entire scholastic career, but now that people knew the name Persephone belonged to a goddess, Mom said it was too risky to even have my first name on paper. We'd charmed the school officials into forgetting my name was ever anything else . . . and suddenly, I didn't like going by Kora anymore.

She was someone else. A girl who had no reason to suspect she wasn't human. She had one best friend, a thousand frenemies, and a hopeless crush on the unobtainable cool senior transfer student, Joel. She'd never killed anyone.

My time in the Underworld had changed me. I knew what I was capable of, and I didn't tolerate backhanded compliments from petty girls anymore. I wasn't afraid to talk to Joel, who'd turned out to be a pretty nice guy and a good friend, but would never measure up to Hades. None of that mattered anyway because Persephone had bigger fish to fry than high school.

I didn't have time for Kora.

It was past three and this was my first free moment today. I still hadn't been down to the Underworld for court, self-defense, and goddess lessons. How in the world was I going to add an eight hour school day to that equation?

"Kora?"

My foot caught on a branch. I saw a flash of Joel's surprised face before my ankle twisted under me and I tumbled down the leaf-strewn hill. Branches scraped my skin. My breath whooshed from my lungs when I rolled to a stop.

Joel swore and tore down the hill after me. "Are you okay? Shit, you're bleeding!"

"I'll live." I raised my head and managed something resembling a grin. "Long time no see, Joel. How have you been?" My ankle throbbed in time with my pulse, and a shallow jagged hole had been torn into my thigh.

He laughed. "Oh, I could be better. Saw the first familiar face all summer and practically pushed her off a cliff. Can you stand up?"

"I think so." I shifted forward, and he grabbed my hands, pulling me to my feet. White-hot pain flashed through me when I put weight on my ankle, and I cried out, grabbing onto Joel's arm.

"Hey, hey, it's okay." He wrapped an arm around me and, to my surprise, swept me off my feet damsel-in-distress style and carried me to the nearest bench.

"Wow." I laughed when I got over my shock. "That was kind of epic."

"Epic fail you mean. Here, you're really bleeding." He pulled at his shirt.

"Gods, Joel, don't!" I raised my hands, laughing. "It's just a scratch. No need to strip."

He straightened his shirt. "Gods? Ugh, Kora, I knew you were a fan of Orpheus, but I didn't think you were a fanatic. I mean, what happened to his wife was sad and all, but I think the guy should have his head examined."

"Not a fan of the Greek gods?"

"The fewer gods I have to deal with, the better." He shrugged. "I missed you."

"Me too. Way to disappear after your graduation." I smiled at him to show I wasn't really upset.

"I know, jerk move. I've just been so busy. You know I almost didn't say anything? I saw you on the path, but it's been so long, I didn't . . . " He let out a self-deprecating laugh. "Are you sure you're okay?"

"Just a few cuts and bruises." I assured him. "How have you been?"

He sat on the bench. "Busy. Really busy. How about you?"

"About the same. It's been a pretty crazy summer."

He grinned at me, blond hair falling in his blue eyes. "Do you always wear jewelry when you run?" He motioned to my necklace.

I touched the small plant, feeling self-conscious. It bounced around a bit, but I hated to take it off.

When I didn't answer, he asked, "Still run every day?"

I nodded. "I normally come a bit earlier, but . . . " Aphrodite and

Melissa had gotten into an argument, and I'd had to help sort things out. "It's been a busy day."

"Guess that explains why I haven't run into you before. What time do you usually make it out here?"

"Three."

"I could do my run at three instead," he suggested. "We could run together."

"Do you have time for that? With college about to start and everything?" I didn't want to sound too reluctant, but I really enjoyed the solitude my runs provided.

"For you, I'll make time." He gave me an easy grin. "Just not right now. I should head out. Do you need help getting to your car? Or can you drive? I could take you home . . . "

I laughed at his hesitation. I lived a bit outside of town, and gas wasn't cheap. "I'm fine. I'm meeting someone later, so I should stick around."

"Great." He sounded relieved. He met my eyes. "Are we on for tomorrow?"

"Sure!" I needed to practice being human before school started, and Joel was about as normal as a human could get.

When he was out of sight, I teleported to the entrance of the Underworld. I let out a deep breath and looked around. This area was so drenched with life. A carpet of poppies surrounded the giant oak tree. It was difficult to believe that just last year I'd been fighting for my life under a mountain of ice and snow right here when Hades had burst from the ground to rescue me.

I touched one of the poppies and shifted until I was standing in just the right spot. I felt a brief sensation, like I was falling, and the picturesque park around me was replaced by the bleached red soil of Tartarus. I never stuck around here for long. As soon as my toes touched Underworld soil, I closed my eyes and teleported to Hades' chambers. The library materialized around me, and my feet planted firmly on the floor. I yelped, ankle folding under me, and grabbed the leather chair for support.

Hades was beside me in an instant. "What happened?"

"I fell down a hill." I collapsed into the chair with a groan. "How come I'm the only accident-prone god?"

"A mystery that eludes us all." Hades knelt in front of the chair and examined the cut on my thigh, summoning a washcloth to dab at the blood. "Sharp hill."

"It was full of branches and thorns." I felt a rush of warmth go through me as he healed the cut. "My friend saw the whole thing. He's going to wonder how I healed so quickly."

"Is he?"

Jealousy slashed through me, and it took a minute for me to place it as his. Hades' face was carefully blank as he brushed the hair off my forehead. He brandished the washcloth, dabbing at a cut I hadn't realized I'd gotten.

"Just charm him if he asks any questions."

I stiffened at the suggestion. The idea of charming anyone, much less Joel, was abhorrent.

"I told you before, there is nothing inherently wrong with using charm," Hades said with a sigh.

"It *feels* wrong."

"Use a glamour then. The souls aren't accustomed to seeing injuries."

A year ago, the suggestion that the dead were squeamish enough to be bothered by cuts and bruises would have seemed ridiculous. Now I knew better. The souls weren't used to seeing blood, no matter how mild the injury. They didn't have to worry about stuff like that anymore.

"Anywhere else?" Hades waved the washcloth in front of my face.

"My ankle."

I drew in a sharp breath when his fingers made contact, but the warmth that spread from his fingers stopped the pulsing pain.

Residual traces of his anxiety snaked through me. His heart beat just a little too fast in fear. "What's wrong?" I asked him.

"You worried me for a second, that's all." He straightened up and gave me a wry smile. "I didn't know what had happened to you."

I flushed. "It was just a few bumps and bruises. I think I'd be worse off if Zeus had gotten hold of me."

"I know. It just took a second. That made it out unscathed?" He motioned to my necklace.

"Lucky. Did you find out more about Zeus' plan? Or his whereabouts?"

Hades took the other seat. "No. I even tried asking Hera."

I kept my face neutral. "How did that go?"

"Zeus didn't tell her anything."

There was more. I could tell by the troubled look on his face, but I didn't press him. He would tell me if it was important.

"Is that what you run in?" His gaze lingered on my outfit.

"Yes."

He made a disapproving sound, and I gave him a look. "Do you really think it's appropriate for you to critique my wardrobe?"

He held up his hands in surrender. "No, it's not. I apologize for overstepping."

I winced. "Don't do that. You don't have to walk on eggshells around me."

Don't I? His sardonic thought sliced through my consciousness before he could stop it. I gritted my teeth against the wave of frustration that washed through Hades. He didn't know how to act around me anymore.

I stared down at the floor hard, blinking back tears. I wanted to tell him about Thanatos' secret. I wanted so badly to make everything okay again, but no matter how hard I tried, I couldn't get around the promise. We just kept drifting further and further apart. I still saw him every day, but he acted different around me. Stiffer, more formal. I was losing him.

What if it took me so long to find a way around my stupid promise that there was nothing left to fix?

Hades sighed and ran his fingers through his hair. "Persephone . . . "

I cleared my throat. "We should really get to court."

The muscles in his jaw tightened, and he motioned to the door. "After you."

Chapter X

AFTER HADES AND I finished orienting all the new souls, I dropped by Melissa's. I was exhausted, but I always made the effort to see her after Hades. I'd seen too many girls in our school disappear into their boyfriends and wander around like zombies after the breakup because all of their friends had moved on.

I didn't bother knocking. This was like a second home to me; I'd never needed to knock.

"Melissa?" I called, walking past the kitchen.

Minthe rounded the corner from the hallway, and her eyes widened when she saw me. "Oh!" she exclaimed. "Hello, Persephone. The girls are in their rooms."

"Thanks."

We stared at each other, awkward and uncertain. I opened my mouth to say something, anything, to bring us back to normal, but what could I say? It's cool you slept with my boyfriend eons ago. Let's move on? Talking about it was almost worse than not talking about it.

"Um . . . Would you like to stay for dinner?" she offered. Words I'd heard a million times, but never with so much stiffness. "I made chili."

"I'd love to." My voice sounded too cheerful. Fake.

Panic flitted through her eyes, and it cut me like a knife. She didn't want me to stay. Seventeen years of being like a second mom to me, and now the thought of spending an hour in the same room with me was panic-worthy?

"But," I added. "I really should be getting home soon."

Her relieved smile was like a punch in the stomach. "Well . . . I'll just leave you girls to it then. Can you tell Melissa I'm in the garage if she needs me?"

I nodded numbly and walked down the hall. I paused at the guest room. It was strange to see Aphrodite in what I considered to be my room. Mrs. Minthe had always kept a change of clothes for me in the closet and a spare toothbrush in the bathroom for my frequent overnight stays. Melissa had a similar room in my house for the same reason.

Now Aphrodite was curled up on my bed, entranced by a group of well-dressed teenagers yelling at each other on the television screen.

"Hey, Aphrodite."

She turned to me, eyes wide. "Persephone, we need to talk about school. I do not wish to attend."

"Aphrodite—" I sighed and fiddled with my necklace "—we talked about this. It's the fastest way you're going to learn how to fit in. School has a way of conditioning you . . . "

She twisted a ringlet of hair around her finger. "Is that what your school is like?" She motioned to the screen as the teenagers burst into song.

I laughed. "Not at all. I'm going to talk to Melissa. I'll see you in a bit, okay?"

Aphrodite nodded, turning her attention back to the show. I shook my head and smiled when I saw Melissa leaning against her door.

"We should sing next week; it would freak her out so much."

I flopped onto her bed. "It would freak *everyone* out."

"You could charm them into doing it. It would be awesome."

I smiled at the thought. "If only it didn't involve charm . . . "

She closed her door. "You're no fun. How was court?"

I shook my head. "Same old, same old. The souls are sad they're dead and want to come back to life. Failing that—" I dug a crumpled list out of my pocket— "can I check in on their loved ones?"

Melissa motioned for the list, but I waved her off. "I already divided up the names and texted them to all of the priestesses. We're off this week since we've got school starting soon. Oh! Speaking of school, Joel ran into me today." I laughed at my little pun. "Literally."

Melissa nodded, looking distracted. She usually perked up when I mentioned Joel. In fact, she'd been more upset by his absence this summer than I had.

I frowned. "Are you okay?"

"Promise not to get mad?"

I gave her a look.

She sighed. "I had my advisor appointment today. They looked over my grades, talked about my goals, and told me about this pro-gram . . . " She hesitated. "I want to go to the University of Iowa."

"Of all the random—er . . . I mean, why?" I couldn't understand anyone wanting to leave Athens. It was our home. We had plans. We'd live in the apartment above the shop and go to UGA. It was going to be perfect. Why give that up to move to Iowa?

"I like their creative writing program. It's the best in the country."

"You still write?" I asked, surprised. I sat on her bed, pulling my knees under me. "Since when?"

"I never stopped. Not since that creative writing class."

I grimaced. I'd hated that class. Creative writing was one of the few things I was bad at. For an agonizing month, I'd tried to put some kind of a story down on paper, but it had never happened. In retrospect, I realized it was because I can't lie. Storytelling requires lies, or, at the very least, exaggerations. For as many myths as the gods inspire, we couldn't tell one to save our lives.

Melissa had dropped out of the class the same week I had. I'd always figured her interest ended there, too. I winced and fought off the sudden urge to hit my head on the doorframe. Of course Melissa dropped out the same week I did. That had been her job. I'd always taken it for granted that we were always in the same classes, clubs, and activities, but she'd known the whole time that she was my priestess and so we were to share the same interests. Of course, we hadn't always done what I wanted. Melissa could talk me into just about anything, but creative writing was where I'd drawn the line.

I felt sick. My friend stopped taking a class that she'd been interested in because of me. How many times had that happened? How often had she missed out on something she wanted because of me?

Melissa was looking down at her green and white quilt, picking at stray threads while I sorted my thoughts.

"I'm so sorry," I said finally.

She waved a hand. "You didn't know. And it didn't bother me, not really. I hadn't thought about it in years, but after . . . " She trailed off for a moment and swallowed hard. "You know, the Boreas thing." When she died. "I just felt this need to write, you know? To get it all down. So I've been doing that." Her words came faster and faster, tripping over each other in their haste. "And I joined this writers' group online, and it's been really great and really fun, and they think my stuff is good. I want to learn more about it. Writing helps. With what happened, it helped so much, and they said this place is the best. So I was just wondering, did you want to go there?"

"To Iowa?"

Her thin shoulders slumped. "It's fine. UGA has a graduate program. I can just wait and—"

"Melissa, you should still apply."

She sighed, looking defeated. "Mom won't let me. My place is with you, remember?"

For a second I felt relieved. I didn't want Melissa to go away to college. I wanted her to stay with me. We were best friends. I needed her. But that was so selfish. Melissa wanted to go somewhere else. She shouldn't be stuck here because of some holy duty to me.

"And you're letting that stop you? You're the one who can lie. Apply anyway." I rolled my eyes for good measure. "When you get in, we'll find a way to make it work. Don't we have a whole bunch of priestesses in Iowa?"

She gave me a hug. "Thank you for understanding. I was so worried you would be mad. Mom might change her mind if I actually get in." She pulled away to look at me. "So, school starts next week, and I have a plan."

"What's that?" I sat on the bed.

"You should charm everyone into thinking we're there and maybe throw in good grades from the teachers. We could do whatever we wanted all day. No one would know."

I shook my head. "I'm not charming people if I don't have to. It's wrong."

"Oh, come on! You hate school!"

"It's not my favorite thing, but I don't hate it." I gave her an embarrassed smile and fiddled with my necklace. "I'm actually kind of looking forward to it."

Melissa leaned back. "Why?"

I leaned against the headboard and looked up at the peeling star stickers on the ceiling. "It's something normal. Not liking school is normal, being overwhelmed by homework assignments is normal. Not getting along with the other girls is normal." I shrugged. "I could do with a little normal."

"So is that why you want to go to UGA so bad? Continue the normal a bit longer?"

I scowled. "Now you sound like my mom. Ever since I found out I was a goddess, it's been this all-consuming thing, chipping away at my regular life. There's lots of good, and I'm not saying I want to turn back the clock or anything, but is it so wrong to want both?"

Melissa looked thoughtful. "No. You planned for life as a human. Every dream and thought you ever had went toward human goals. I think it would be weird to just switch that off one day. I mean, not that it would be wrong to want something else. That's normal too, right? To plan and prep for something and then decide you want something else?"

"If it were anywhere but Iowa," I teased. "I'd say that was normal."

"Oh shut up!" She threw a pillow at me. "Poor little Persephone. I'm a beautiful, powerful goddess. Pity me, pity me. All that will make my life better are boring-ass classes. Gosh, it's too bad I don't have anything better to do. Like my hot boyfriend." She batted her eyelashes dramatically, voice breathy.

I was laughing so hard I could barely catch my breath. "You can't think of him as hot!"

"I'm not blind." Melissa brushed her hair out of her face and stood, eyes twinkling. "When he walked into the kitchen . . . " She put her hand to her chest in an exaggerated swoon. "I'd break girl code for him. It's been nice being your friend and all, but gods!"

I threw the pillow back. "You'd be breaking more than girl code. The only thing weirder than me hooking up with someone your mother dated would be *you* hooking up with him. Had things gone differently, he might have been your dad."

Melissa cried out in disgust. "Why would you say that? I'm never going to get that out of my head now."

"Serves you right for fantasizing about my husband." I dissolved into giggles. "You should see your face."

"You jerk." She threw the pillow back. "Speaking of hot guys, did you say you ran into Joel?"

"WHAT'S YOUR GOAL?" Joel asked when I met him the following day at the park.

"Three miles in thirty minutes," I admitted, embarrassed. "I get the first mile in under ten, but it takes me longer and longer every lap."

Joel nodded. "Okay, so the key is pacing. You don't want to put all your energy into your first lap . . . " He trailed off as I shook my head.

"I need that burst of speed if I'm going to get away."

"Get away?" He leaned forward, face growing concerned. "Kora, who are you trying to run away from?"

A flash of fear passed through me as images of Thanatos, Boreas, and Pirithous filled my mind. "Anyone. I started taking this self-defense class last year, and Char—the instructor—made a good point about it all being useless if I couldn't run away."

Joel nodded, considering. "So that's how you started running? Breakneck speed all the way through?"

"Well, no," I amended. "I'd walk a little, jog a little, and work my way up to jogging all the way, and then run a little, until I worked my way up to running."

"Yeah, until you could maintain the speed. Same concept. You're practicing, not running for your life. Find a pace. Keep it steady. Next time you run, push a bit harder, and so on. You'll get faster. I'm surprised your teacher didn't tell you that."

"He doesn't really oversee my running habits anymore." I stretched to touch my toes.

We set out, keeping a steady pace. I was surprised to find I'd beaten my best time by the end of the third mile. When we finished, I collapsed onto the cool grass, breathing hard.

Joel's face hovered inches over me, a mischievous grin on his face. "You gonna make it?"

"Shut up," I gasped, pushing him away with a laugh. "Every step you take is like three steps for me."

"Not my fault you're short."

"Not my fault you're freakishly tall."

He pulled me to my feet. "Let me make it up to you. I'll buy you a smoothie?"

I hesitated and looked down at my hand, still locked in his. He followed my gaze and dropped my hand, his face going red.

"Sorry, Joel." I brushed the grass off my legs. "I should probably be going."

He caught my eye. "Aw come on, how long does it take to drink a smoothie?"

I found myself smiling. "Fine." I followed him to his car, a juniper Chevy Thunderbird that had caused quite a stir amongst the guys at Athens Academy last year.

He drove over to Smoothie King. I ordered a pomegranate punch and sat at one of the three tables in the tiny shop.

"Your mom's shop is right around here, isn't it?" Joel motioned out the window, though all we could see from our vantage point was the gravel parking lot and a steady stream of cars flowing down South Lumpkin Street.

"Yeah, just up the road. Don't tell me you've never been."

Joel laughed. "I've seen her work. You guys do all the centerpieces for school stuff, right?"

I nodded and fiddled with my necklace.

"But I haven't been to the shop. As much reason as I've had to buy flowers . . . "

I kicked him lightly under the table. I knew he didn't have a girlfriend, but flowers weren't just for couples. "What about your mom or aunts or something?" I didn't know if Joel had any sisters. None had attended Athens Academy, but he could be the youngest child.

Joel hesitated. "I don't . . . My mom's not . . . " He scowled at the table, rubbing at a spot with his thumb. "She was murdered. Forever ago."

I gasped. "I'm so sor—"

Joel cut off my apology with a wave of his hand. "Don't. I never mentioned it to you before. I just don't like to talk about my family. I'd send flowers to the extended members, but I don't think they'd appreciate the reminder I still exist." He shrugged and changed the topic. "If I were to get someone flowers, what would you recommend?"

"My favorites are daisies. But most people prefer something more elaborate."

He gave me an easy grin. "Daisies, huh? I'll keep that in mind."

A movement in the corner of my eye caught my gaze. A man stepped through the door of the Smoothie King. No one else seemed to notice his entrance, but that wasn't surprising. The light fractured around him, bending oddly and seeming to absorb into his black robes.

The Reaper met my gaze and stood behind Joel, hand hovering over his shoulder.

"Stop it."

Joel followed my gaze past the Reaper. "Stop what? What are you looking at?"

I smiled brightly at Joel. "Being such a shameless flirt. I'm not impressed."

"Still got a boyfriend?" Joel asked.

I eyed the Reaper, and he gave me a malicious grin.

I turned my attention to Joel. "I have . . . you know, it's kind of complicated."

Joel looked at me over his cup. "Is it exclusive?"

I did my best to ignore the Reaper's hand hovering over Joel's head. I had no idea what Hades and I were right now. Everything had gotten so weird. "I'm not interested in anyone that isn't him." I shrugged. "I'm flattered, really, but I don't want to lead you on."

Joel folded his straw paper into a tiny accordion. "It was worth a shot. Still running buddies?"

When I hesitated, he looked me in the eye. "I can date other girls. Friends are harder to come by. Plus, running alone is dangerous. I could fall and break my ankle, or some random stalker could push me off the path. You never know what kind of crazies are out there. Please?"

I laughed. "Yeah, okay. So what classes are you registered for?"

When he launched into his answer, I dropped a shield so Joel couldn't hear me and raised my smoothie in front of my mouth. "If his name was on the list, he'd be dead by now." I kept my voice calm as I addressed the Reaper. "Thanatos doesn't want to attract attention by taking the wrong souls, so you can cut the theatrics."

"Thanatos sends his regards," the Reaper said softly. His threat was completely undermined by his puppy-dog brown eyes. I frowned, trying to focus on his soul instead of the light bending around him. He was not much older than me. How long had he been dead? Why did he decide to become a Reaper instead of just spending his afterlife in the Underworld?

"Bring me to Thanatos," I demanded.

It was a long shot, but I was Queen of the Underworld, and that included Reapers. He might listen to me. I just needed one second of eye contact to charm Thanatos, and I could uncharm this mess. But so far I hadn't been able to get near him. Each time I'd gone to the Underworld, he'd managed to be elsewhere.

The Reaper gave me a cutting glare and meandered behind the counter. The brunette girl who'd made our smoothies shivered as though she sensed his presence. He touched her shoulder and she collapsed.

Joel swore and sprang from his seat, rushing behind the counter to check on the girl. I forced myself to stay in my seat and ignore the scream of rage and horror that threatened to erupt from my chest. I buried it and kept my face impassive as I stared down the Reaper. I couldn't show any weakness. Not to him.

"Your move, Queen." His lips curved in sarcasm as he gave a shallow bow and vanished.

Chapter XI

I WAS A NERVOUS wreck the following week when I pulled into the school parking lot. Change is unsettling, and over the last few years there'd been increasing tension between myself and the girls I'd once called friends. Apparently I'd been charming them, which led to all kinds of problems. Mostly their inexplicable hatred. But now that I knew what I was and had a handle on my charm, everything should have been fine.

Instead I was exhausted, angry, and unsettled, and it had nothing to do with school. It was the Reapers. For the past few days, they'd followed me everywhere I went, taking souls along the way. I knew those souls had to be on that day's list of the dead, otherwise Hades would notice, but it was happening too often to be a coincidence. Were the Reapers following around their marks and hoping to cross paths with me? Maybe they were taking them early. If so, where were they keeping the souls until they were supposed to die? Death runs on a tight schedule.

If they were, they'd have to keep the souls somewhere, right? If I could just find out where . . .

But I hadn't had any luck. Charon hadn't mentioned any unusual activity with the souls, and no souls had said anything about being left to wander around or mentioned anything suspicious. If the humans had noticed an uptick in the amount of deaths in town, they hadn't bothered to report it to the news.

I ground my teeth. This would be so much easier if I could just ask the souls or ask Charon instead of waiting for someone to notice something was wrong. But Thanatos was in charge of the Reapers so anything I said about them linked to him, and my stupid promise kept me from saying or doing anything about Thanatos or to help Hades discover him in any way.

"I won't tell anyone anything about you," I muttered to myself. "Hades won't get any help from me." I sighed, letting my head fall back on the seat with a thunk. "How could I have said that?"

I got out of my car, the effort exhausting me. I wasn't sleeping well.

Death shouldn't bother the Queen of the Underworld, but I didn't feel very much like a queen right now. I felt scared and powerless. It didn't matter that I knew they were supposed to die. It didn't matter that I knew the Underworld was a nice place and the souls would eventually be happy.

Death doesn't just happen to the person who died. It happens to everyone around them. The faces that haunted my dreams weren't just the shocked looks of the newly dead souls. No, I dreamed about the faces of their loved ones contorted with panic as they realized there was nothing they could do to bring that soul back. I dreamed about their futile efforts to revive the corpse while the Reapers laughed.

I felt sick. Weak. Powerless. *I'm Kora again*, I realized as I shouldered my book bag and made my way to the Media Center, keeping an eye out for Melissa and Aphrodite. They weren't hard to spot. A crowd of students surrounded Aphrodite outside the glass exterior of the building.

"Kora!" Melissa called, making her way through the crowd.

"Hey."

"You look exhausted! Are you okay?"

"How's she doing?" I asked, motioning to Aphrodite. I set my book bag down on the stone courtyard, too tired to carry it any longer.

"She's a natural. Everyone loves her."

I frowned at the bitterness in Melissa's voice. I opened my mouth to ask if she was okay when a commotion from the crowd cut me off. "Oh no, what did she say?" I stepped forward, trying to peer through the students to find Aphrodite.

"Kora?" Rachel asked.

I turned, surprised to find her standing behind me.

"One sec," Melissa muttered, edging her way closer to the crowd.

"Hi Rachel." I stood on my tiptoes trying to see between the book bags. There were days I hated being short.

"I have a message for you."

I sighed. "If it's about missing Jessica and Ashley's birthday, for the thousandth time I'm sorry. I've had a crazy summer and—"

"Swear fealty to Zeus."

I spun to face her. "What did you say?"

"The longer you wait, the more he'll take from you."

Rachel's hair was wrong, almost blindingly red. Her eyes shone brightly; the colors of her outfit were hyper realistic. Something inside me went numb as I realized what I was seeing. I felt a flash of power, and suddenly the voices of my classmates were no longer muffled. I heard their screams, cries, and frantic calls for help. I tore my gaze away from Rachel.

Now I could see what everyone was staring at. A shield had been crafted within the group of students so well that I hadn't even noticed it. Now I could see Rachel lying in the middle of the crowd in a crumbled heap on the concrete. Her eyes were wide open, staring straight at me, face frozen in a grimace of agony.

I turned back to Rachel's soul. I could fix this; I could put her back in her body . . . somehow. I'd make this right.

She was gone.

Something brushed my neck, and I hit the ground with a strangled yell. Fire flashed through my veins. I'd felt this before, in the Underworld when I'd shaken a Reaper's hand. The fire stopped as suddenly as it started. I spun to face my attacker, but no one was there.

"She shook my hand and just collapsed."

I jumped at the voice, breathing easier when I realized it was Aphrodite. "Did anyone else touch Rachel?" My voice quavered and for some reason my face was wet with tears. *Rachel's dead,* I realized. Of course I was crying.

"A man in black robes." Aphrodite twirled her hair nervously. "Persephone, no one else could see him."

A Reaper. No, *the* Reaper. Thanatos was the only one that could cast shields. *I'll kill him.* Once I would have been surprised at the coldness of that thought, but I just didn't have it in me anymore.

"I have to go." My voice sounded strange to my ears. Distant, like it was coming from the end of a long tunnel.

Melissa walked up to us, giving me an odd look. "Go? Go where? The police are on their way, not to mention all the teachers. I think they'll want—" She broke off when she saw my face. "Was this a god thing?" she asked in a whisper.

I nodded shakily, and something in her expression closed off.

"Go, we've got this."

Chapter XII

"WHERE IS HE?" I demanded, storming into the throne room. I couldn't say Thanatos' name. Just asking about him sent a wave of agony ripping through me. The three judges and Cassandra and Moirae looked up from where they were sitting on the side of the room in surprise. Only Hades didn't seem surprised at how I'd stormed in.

The judges exchanged a look and turned to Charon. "Should we ...?"

"Go? Great idea. Later Persephone." Charon waved.

They hastened across the white marble floors, footsteps echoing off the endlessly tall ceilings.

"Coward!" I called as the ornate wooden door slammed shut.

"Thanatos told me what happened." Hades pushed off his onyx throne in the center of the large, round room. "He didn't want to be around when you got down here—"

"I'll just bet!"

"Because there's nothing he could do. Zeus killed her in a crowd of people. It can't be undone."

That stopped me cold. "You think Zeus did this?"

"Who else could it have been? Rachel repeated the message she delivered to you," Moirae said with uncharacteristic understanding.

I sighed and shook my head, looking away from Moirae. It was hard to look at her long. She looked dizzyingly average—middle-aged with brown hair and eyes and ambiguously tan skin. Her eyes darted around like she was hearing things we couldn't.

Mostly because she could. The past, present, and future all warred for attention in the mind of this schizophrenic embodiment of the fates.

There was no explaining that Zeus had never been there. Moirae wouldn't have seen anything. She saw the past, present, and future of every human she encountered, unless they'd been touched by a god. Rachel would have been invisible to her when she died. I doubted Rachel knew who Thanatos was to accuse him. Even if she happened to spot him, it wasn't uncommon for souls to accuse the Reapers who collected their souls of killing them.

"Cassandra, did you see what happened?" I asked, fiddling with my necklace. Cassandra could see almost everything that was coming, including the divine.

"I didn't." She pulled on a strand of her dark hair, a nervous gesture.

"You guys think Zeus killed someone but Cassandra didn't see it? That doesn't seem weird to anyone?"

"There was a plane crash." Cassandra crossed her leg and leaned back, putting her hands behind her head. "I can only see one thing at a time. It's not often I see human actions rather than the divine, but it does happen."

"Isn't Zeus lord of the skies?" I asked pointedly.

"It was one death against hundreds." Cassandra's dark eyes flickered, but she kept her voice even. I could tell she wanted to be annoyed but was trying to be sympathetic.

I paused. What would it be like to see the things Cassandra saw? I'd gotten a taste of it in the last week with the Reapers killing people all around me, but those deaths, however disturbing, weren't violent. Plus, I knew on an intellectual level that they were already on the list to die that day. The Reapers couldn't afford to attract attention by taking someone who wasn't on the list . . . Or so I'd thought.

Rachel wasn't on the list.

My shoulders drooped; the anger that had been fueling me was spent. I was barely hanging on. Tears pricked my eyes. I hadn't liked Rachel very much, but I didn't want her to die.

"I know it's frightening to think that Zeus may have been so close to you." Hades moved close to me and clasped my shoulder. "Thanatos has generously offered up some of his Reapers to act as guards."

You're supposed to protect me! I wanted to scream. *Not throw me to the wolves.* How could he be so blind to Thanatos' betrayal? Why hadn't he figured out what was wrong and fixed it?

Some of my rage must have shown on my face because Hades drew back in confusion. "It's a great solution. Only gods can see them, so they shouldn't interfere with your day-to-day activities. They can keep an eye on Aphrodite as well, and any of your friends or family."

"No!"

"If Zeus wants you to swear fealty, he'll stop at nothing—"

I threw my hands up in the air in frustration. "Why would he want me to swear fealty? He had my powers; he gave them to me."

Anger flashed in Hades' eyes, quickly doused. He didn't like being yelled at, but my friend had just died so he was going to let it pass.

I glowered at him. He had *no* idea why I was upset, and in this moment I almost hated him for it.

Hades took a deep breath. "He had a *third* of your powers. I don't think he's coming after you for your charm. But having control of the Earth and Underworld would have *some* appeal to him."

I narrowed my eyes at the sarcasm he'd let slip through. "I don't have control—"

"You have a legitimate right to both realms. With you, Zeus could gain access to both. He doesn't need much in the way of permission to enter the living realm, but my realm . . . "

My heart gave an uncomfortable thump. "He could come here?"

"I would ask you to stay down here, for safety, but . . . "

"We don't know how long Zeus will be a threat," I finished. Zeus wasn't restricted to a single season like Boreas. I couldn't live my whole life in the Underworld. And I couldn't tell Hades why I didn't want Thanatos' Reapers shadowing me. I sighed and sat down on my throne. I felt a hand touch my shoulder and looked up to see Cassandra's concerned face.

"Was she your friend?"

That was complicated. Rachel and I had been friends until I'd accidentally charmed her. I'd managed to undo the charm, but nothing could make up for the months of time we'd had to grow apart. Now that I had control of my powers, everyone was friendly to me again, but no one was close. "I don't have many friends."

"She'll be fine down here," Moirae said. "After a brief period of adjustment."

"Thank you." I stood, brushing off my dress. "I should get back to the surface. Mom'll be freaking out."

"Moirae, Cassandra, can we have a moment?" Hades asked. They nodded and left the throne room. "I think you should stay just a few days."

"No. I'm not hiding again."

"Then let me come with you."

Panic flooded my chest. "You can't leave the Underworld unprotected."

A muscle jerked in Hades' jaw. "He can't come here, but he can come after you! Look, I know you want space, but if anything happened to you . . . "

I couldn't stop shaking my head. "I have to go." I stumbled away from him. "I can't-you can't, just . . . Stay. Please, stay."

Frustration flickered over his face. "I don't think the Reapers are going to be enough to protect you. I know you're still upset with me, but this is bigger than us."

I searched desperately for a reason, any reason, that didn't correlate to Thanatos. "You don't have my mom's permission—"

"She wants to protect you as badly as I do. I'm sure she'll allow it."

"Just take a hint, would you! I don't want you protecting me, and I don't want you in my realm." The words burst out of me. "Just stay here!" I didn't wait for a reaction. I teleported to Tartarus and left the Underworld.

I'd barely surfaced in Memorial Park when I heard Joel calling my name. "Kora!"

I stared at him as he crossed the wooden bridge. I felt disoriented, out of place. I didn't belong in this park, filled with life. The sky was too blue. The cherry blossom trees were too vibrant. Children laughed and played on the playground behind me. Their laughter was jarring; it felt wrong.

"Where did you come from?" Joel asked.

"I . . . " I looked behind me, toward the parking lot.

Joel caught my hand. "Is it true? What happened to Rachel? I didn't know her well . . . But she . . . I mean, I knew her." He looked upset. "What happened? Are you okay?"

I burst into tears. I couldn't take this anymore. If one more person asked if I was okay . . .

"Hey, hey . . . " Joel said soothingly. He drew me to him in a tight embrace.

I clung to him, crying for everything I'd lost and everyone I was probably going to lose.

Chapter XIII

"IT'S DISGUSTING," Melissa said.

"Huh?" I asked. I was supposed to be shopping. That's why we were at the mall, but all I could concentrate on were the Reapers. They followed me everywhere. But at least in public, they didn't touch me.

I shuddered at the thought and clutched my necklace. I was defenseless against the Reapers. Their touch tore at my soul. If one of them so much as brushed against me, the pain was bad enough for me to bawl my eyes out.

"That!" Melissa motioned to the food court where Aphrodite sat on a table surrounded by a bunch of guys. "I think some of those guys even have girlfriends."

I eyed the glowering girls scattered around the food court and had to agree. I turned my attention to the As Seen On TV store. Maybe I would buy some pajama jeans. It wasn't the type of thing I normally wore, but I wasn't sleeping much anymore. Anything pajama sounded comfortable to me.

"Persephone, you have to do something about this. It's like date rape."

I fought to keep the irritation out of my voice. "For the thousandth time, she's not charming them."

"Sure, they just drop everything and follow her because she's pretty," Melissa snapped.

"Pretty much."

She snorted and walked toward Macy's.

"Melissa, where are you going?" I hurried after her. "Aphrodite's still back there, we can't just—"

"She doesn't need a babysitter. She's perfectly capable of lifting one of those well-manicured hands to call your cell phone. She might even deign to follow us. Isn't that a crazy idea? Instead of waiting around for her all day, we could actually get our shopping done."

"You make it sound like a chore. Shopping is supposed to be fun."

"*Supposed to be* being the key words." Melissa stopped at the pretzel stand. "Hey, I have a buy one get one free thing. Want one?"

"She's next," a redheaded Reaper said, pointing to an elderly woman sitting on the bench. "Five grandkids. See the youngest one over there?"

I followed the Reaper's outstretched hand to where a little girl was putting a quarter in a gumball machine.

"She gets to watch," he added in a snide voice.

"Grandma, look!" She held up a pink gumball with triumph. "My favorite!"

"I'm not hungry," I told Melissa. I watched the little girl run to her grandma, still chattering.

"Are you sure you don't want anything? I didn't see you eat lunch."

It's hard to eat with death breathing down your neck. "I'm sure."

Melissa shrugged and ordered a pretzel.

"Look!" The little girl squealed in excitement. "A train!"

"Ugh." Melissa grabbed her pretzel and a drink and started walking again. "Why do people let their kids shout like that inside?"

I stared at the little girl as she and her grandmother boarded the train that circled around the mall every few minutes. "Leave them alone." I glared at the Reaper when I said it.

"Huh?" Melissa asked, turning around.

"They're spending the day together, having fun. Who knows how often they see each other?"

"What are you even looking at?" Melissa waved her hand through the Reaper. "Fine, let her yell. Gods, no need to get so upset about it. You look like you're about to cry."

I started to explain about the Reaper then stopped. What was the point? I couldn't explain they were stalking me without drawing attention to Thanatos, and even if I kept it to the usual business of Reapers, what would telling Melissa accomplish except to get her upset? Why burden anyone else with the knowledge of that grandma's impending death. "Sorry," I muttered, as we set off for Macy's.

"Anyway," Melissa continued. "Shopping is supposed to be fun. But nothing is fun with her around." She paused at a display of boots and motioned for a salesperson. "Size eight, please." She turned her attention back to me. "What's the point of shopping for clothes when Miss Perfect over there could make a paper bag look good?"

I made a noise that could be taken for assent and slid my necklace back and forth on the chain. Melissa narrowed her eyes. "What? No impassioned speech on how I should be more patient or something?

What's with you, anyway? You've barely said a word since school started."

"Sorry." I feigned interest in a pair of heels I wouldn't be caught dead wearing.

"Don't apologize. Tell me what's wrong." Melissa snatched the shoe from my hand and looked me in the eyes. "I'm worried about you, okay?"

"Believe me, if I could tell you, I would."

Melissa raised an eyebrow. "If you *could*? What do you—?"

"Hey, guys!" Aphrodite called. She hurried over to us. "Ooh, cute boots."

Melissa slammed the boot back down on the display and stormed off toward a nearby rack of dresses.

"What's up with her?" Aphrodite asked. She beamed at the salesman who'd brought out the shoes. "Size eight. How did you know? Oh Persephone, I met the nicest people!"

"Call her Kora in public," Melissa snapped. She thrust a hanger at me. "You have to try this on."

I lifted the hanger and stared at the white dress with a lacy flower pattern. "Um . . . okay?" I slipped into a dressing room and pulled it on. It was too loose. The neck gaped and it threatened to slide off my shoulders. When I walked out to show Melissa, she frowned.

"Aphrodite, go play with your new friends. Persephone and I need to talk."

"You're supposed to call her Kora in public," Aphrodite reminded her.

Melissa shot her a murderous look.

"Fine." Aphrodite shrugged, completely undisturbed by Melissa's mood. "I was going to meet Jessica and Ashley for a movie anyway. They'll bring me home."

I watched her go with a sinking heart. She could see the Reapers, which kept them in check. If she noticed them behaving oddly, she could tell Hades or my mom. Then this would finally be over.

"What is it?" I asked Melissa as the Reapers swarmed around me.

"That's a size two."

"So?"

"You're a four."

I struggled to understand the significance of this through the Reaper's taunting.

"Persephone." Melissa gripped my arms, looked straight into my eyes. "What's going on? You have circles under your eyes."

I'd forgotten Melissa could see through my glamour. All the priestesses could.

It's hard to sleep after watching someone die, I wanted to snap. I knew I'd be having dreams about that little girl tonight. It's impossible to sleep knowing there is something in your room that wants to hurt you.

"You're not dressing like you normally do," Melissa continued, indicating my jeans and short-sleeve T-shirt. "Come on, Persephone, spill."

Why couldn't Hades see what Melissa saw? Did he? Did he just attribute it to Zeus? Our "breakup"? What did he think was causing this? Did he even notice?

"I'm sorry, Melissa." I cast my eyes down to the floor. "I can't tell you."

"Of course you can't," she muttered. I couldn't see her face, but her voice sounded hurt. "It's god stuff, isn't it?"

"Yes, but it's not like that. I can't tell you—"

"No, no, I understand. I'm just some human. What do I know?"

"Melissa—"

"Melissa? Kora?" Joel walked over from a display of leather wallets. "Hey!" He gave Melissa a hug and she flushed. "It's been awhile."

"Not for all of us. I hear you ran into Kora the other day." She smiled at him, but it didn't reach her eyes. "Did you forget how to use the phone?"

"Ouch." Joel frowned at her. "I've been pretty busy." He shifted closer to me, a smile lighting up his face. "But I've got some free time now. Want to go to the movies?"

"Sure!" I answered quickly. Aphrodite was at the movie theater. If I stayed close to her, the Reapers would leave me alone for a little while.

Melissa was looking back and forth between the two of us. "You know, I'm not feeling well. I think I'm just going to head home. Have fun."

She didn't sound like she meant it. I threw her a questioning look. Being annoyed with me, I got. Best friends shouldn't have secrets, but what had Joel done to piss her off?

All thoughts of Melissa fled my mind when a child's scream pierced the air.

Chapter XIV

THE FAMILIAR feeling of fire coursing through my veins woke me up. A hand clapped over my mouth, cutting off my scream. Two Reapers glared down at me, savage grins on their cruel faces.

"Knock it off guys," Zachary scolded. He towered above the other two Reapers. His eyes were so dark they were almost black. Of all the Reapers I'd ever met, he was the one who most looked the part.

The pain stopped abruptly, and I scrambled away from the Reapers, breathing hard. "Zachary," I gasped. "Long time no see."

Zachary was the first Reaper I'd met. I'd shaken his hand and felt the pain of my soul ripping free of my body. The same pain I'd woken up to this morning and every morning since Hades had agreed to let the Reapers be my guards.

"Thanatos told us to make her suffer," a female Reaper pointed out.

"Did he happen to mention how to avoid Demeter ripping us limb from limb if she finds us torturing her daughter while she cooks breakfast downstairs?" Zachary asked.

The Reapers stepped away from me.

I read the apology in Zachary's eyes, and my shoulders loosened a little. The Reapers weren't all evil. Thanatos was putting them up to this. I was sure he'd chosen his most aggressive Reapers for guard duty. I wondered how Zachary had made the cut.

I skipped breakfast and headed to school. I arrived early, but enough students were milling around to prevent another attack from the Reapers. They might not be able to see the Reapers, but even humans would notice if I hit the ground screaming in pain. There was no fighting back. Anytime I touched them, it hurt me ten times more than I could possibly hurt them. And they weren't corporeal to anything but deities and the dead, so I couldn't throw things at them or charm them. I was helpless, and that was really starting to piss me off.

I had small victories. I'd told Moirae I needed to take more of an interest in the day-to-day running of the Underworld. Every night she gave me a schedule of the next day's events. I made it a point to be in the palace anytime Thanatos was supposed to be there. He dodged me easily, always managing to be somewhere else. Hades was getting really annoyed at Thanatos' "new work ethic." All my time in the Underworld was cutting into my schedule quite a bit, but all I needed was a second's worth of eye contact with Thanatos to end this. If I could charm him, I could kill him.

The thought made me feel sick but it was my only option. I'd promised not to help Hades find out about Thanatos, so it wasn't like I could charm Thanatos into turning himself in. I'd never promised not to hurt Thanatos. 'Course I'd never be able to explain to Hades why I killed his best friend, but I'd cross that bridge when I came to it.

"There you guys are. What took so long?" I asked the moment Melissa and Aphrodite stepped out of Melissa's gold Civic.

Aphrodite yawned and pointed to Melissa. "She spent forever in front of the mirror getting ready."

I glanced at Melissa, surprised to see she was wearing a brown satin skirt with a maroon blouse. "You look nice. What's the occasion?"

"Picture day," she reminded me. She walked toward the white school buildings, heels clicking on the sidewalk.

"It's picture day?" I followed Melissa.

"What is picture day?" Aphrodite asked.

"You forgot?" Melissa shook her head. "You're wearing yourself too thin, Persephone."

"I forgot because we took senior pictures over the summer. I thought we were done."

"They're still going to do the club pictures."

I groaned and plucked at my necklace. "I look terrible. Ugh, I can't believe I forgot!"

"So they're going to take our picture . . . why?" Aphrodite asked while we walked to the classroom.

"To put in the yearbook," Melissa explained.

"Which is what, exactly?"

I searched my mind for a way to explain that wouldn't lead to more questions while I opened the classroom door. A high-pitched squeal caught me off guard, and suddenly I was bombarded by the girls in my class.

"Oh my god! Aphrodite! Kora! You look amazing!" Ashley exclaimed.

We stepped into the classroom. "Thank you," Aphrodite said graciously.

"Your hair looks so nice and this dress!" Jessica touched the floral material of a dress I'd worn a thousand times without inspiring comments and turned to her twin sister. "Hey Ashley, do you remember that dress we saw in Macy's the other day? The white one with the flowers. It's about this cut. We should run by the mall after school and get it, Kora. It's so you."

"Uh—" I began.

"It's so daring!" Ashley exclaimed over Aphrodite's blue ensemble. Aphrodite had slid right into the social circle in school effortlessly filling the void Rachel had left. The twins followed her around campus like lost puppies. It annoyed Melissa to no end, but I'd made sure they weren't under charm. What else was I supposed to do?

Melissa made an offended noise behind me, and I turned to see her rushing out the door.

"Melissa, wait!" I cried, following after her.

My sandals slapped at the concrete sidewalk. I caught up to her on the bamboo "Causes Bridge" the art teacher had created. Signs dangled from the arches of the bridge, different problems written on each. I slowed as the weight of the problems settled on my shoulders. As a goddess, shouldn't I be doing something about issues like world hunger? Instead I was stuck dealing with Zeus, Thanatos, and the Reapers.

Melissa leaned over the bamboo rail, staring down at the canopy of greenery between the beams for overpopulation and war.

"Melissa, I'm sorry no one said anything. You look amazing—"

"It's not enough." She swiped angrily at her eyes. "I'm just the mere mortal."

"Don't let her get to you. Aphrodite was created to cause a stir, it's—"

"The fact that she was intended to be perfect doesn't make standing next to her any easier. Look, I'm not proud to admit that she gets to me, okay? Yes, I'm being shallow and overdramatic, but I'm telling you, my self-esteem can't take this anymore."

"Melissa . . . "

"It's not just her, it's you, too. You're both so freaking perfect." She made a gesture of frustration with her hands. "No one notices me if you guys are in the room. How could they?"

I blinked, surprised by her anger. "This isn't just about what happened back there, is it? You've never cared what those girls think."

Melissa sighed and sat on the bridge, feet dangling through the rails. "It's everything. It just builds." She was quiet for a moment before adding, "I had a fight with my mom."

"What about?" I sat next to her. The wood caught on my cotton dress. I could only imagine what it was doing to Melissa's skirt. She must be really upset not to notice.

"I got accepted at Iowa State."

My heart froze in my chest, but I shoved my selfishness aside. "That's great!"

"Mom said I couldn't go."

"So we'll work it out. I'll tell her I said it was okay—"

"I shouldn't need your permission Persephone!" Her eyes glittered with rage. "I died last year, and you know my first thought when you brought me back?"

I shook my head, but she was already continuing.

"That could have been it. My entire life, and I'd never done a single thing for myself. Every decision I've ever made had to be weighed against what you wanted. You think you have mom issues, Persephone? Mine wouldn't have even had me if she hadn't been ordered to. You're the entire reason I exist and, sorry, but that's pretty screwed up."

I'd been afraid of this ever since I found out she was my priestess. Maybe back in ancient Greece people hadn't had issues with being born subservient, but modern-day society didn't allow for that kind of thing. I'd never treated her like a servant, but if it was me instead of her, that would be a cold comfort.

"You've felt this way ever since you came back?"

She shook her head. "Like I said, it builds. At first I was just grateful, you know? I figured things could go back to the way they were, but you changed."

"Me?"

"Before, everyone at school kind of hated you, and you couldn't deal with that, so I helped you."

"You fought my battles for me," I corrected. I was proud that I'd started standing up for myself. That was the one good thing that had come with facing Boreas. I wasn't afraid of confrontation anymore. I'd fought for my life: standing up to a few high schoolers paled in comparison.

"Well, you don't need me anymore. And you have these cool powers, and you're confident and self-assured and have an awesome guy—"

"Who dated your mom . . . "

Melissa shuddered. "It may be gross, but at least someone is interested in you. And as if that wasn't enough, you're stringing Joel along—"

"We're just friends!" I protested.

"He doesn't want to be your friend and you know it, but you still hang around with him. It used to just bug me, but I could deal. You're my best friend after all. I should be happy for you. Even if you do look freaking perfect."

I stared at Melissa, stunned. In my entire life she'd been the one person who'd never cared what I looked like. She'd never made me feel guilty, or superior, she just accepted who I was. "I didn't know I was bothering you."

"It was fine. I'm allowed to be jealous, okay? It's stupid and petty of me, but I'm only human, remember? I thought I could handle it, but then you dropped *her* into my lap, and I just can't. She's completely perfect. I didn't think prettier than you *existed*, yet there she is. And . . . I know this is shallow. I'm not saying I want to be in the center of attention, okay? It just hurts not to be noticed at all. And then this college thing . . . "

"We'll work it out."

She laughed, tears chasing each other down her cheeks. "And you're so damn nice about it that I can't even be mad at you. That's the worst part. *You* understand! You get how incredibly screwed up this is. It's my mom who doesn't. She just keeps telling me that you saved me, and I'll live forever, and I should be grateful, but she doesn't mention how I shouldn't have been killed in the first place. She doesn't mention how screwed up it is that I was used as a divine bargaining chip, and the only person who protested was *you*. They were going to let me die, Persephone! She had already accepted it because you are so much more fucking important than me."

I was silent for a moment, unsure of what I could possibly say to that. "What can I do?" I asked finally, unable to bear the thought of my best friend being so miserable.

"Keep her away from me. I'm not asking you to choose between us, or anything that petty. I know helping her is important. I just don't want to have to look at her."

I nodded, my heart beating uncomfortably hard in my chest. "Did you want me to stay away from you, too?"

She didn't answer, but there was pain etched across her face. Seventeen years' worth. I turned away, unable to face what I'd done to my best friend.

"I'll go," I croaked, my voice hoarse. I stood and took a step backward. "I'll take Aphrodite and just charm the teachers into thinking we're finishing out the year. Our parents don't have to know. At school at least, you'll get to lead your own life. And I promise, I'll work out the college thing. You don't have to be around me to be my priestess. Mom has hundreds of them all around the world. There's no reason I can't do the same."

"Yeah, thanks for that." She stared hard at the ground beneath her feet.

My already frayed temper snapped. "I didn't ask for any of this, you know! Do you honestly think if I had the chance to just go back and make it to where we were both just normal that I wouldn't? I don't want you for my priestess any more than you want to be my priestess. I just want to be your friend."

I wanted to throw in some witty retort like "apparently that's too much to ask," but that was the problem with not being able to lie. You can't be too dramatic. Whatever else happened, Melissa had been a great friend. I just hadn't returned the favor. Instead, I settled for a dramatic exit. I spun on my heel and stormed off.

Each step felt progressively harder to take. By the time I reached the classroom, I felt so heavy I worried I'd sink through the earth. I grabbed Aphrodite's arm when I got into the classroom and looked my professor full in the eye, for once not even feeling a pang of guilt for using my charm. I was past caring. "You think we stayed for the whole class."

"Yes," he agreed.

"Great, and you'll say we were here every day, right? Turning in every assignment and making straight A's."

He nodded, starstruck.

I hesitated, fiddling with my necklace. Me getting straight A's would be nearly as conspicuous as failing for non-attendance. "Oh fine. Just average me out to a low B."

I turned to Aphrodite. "Charm the students with the same message. I'll get the rest of our teachers."

I stormed out of the classroom, tossing my nametag in the trash as I left. So much for normal.

Chapter XV

"GET *AWAY* FROM me," I snapped to a Reaper as I made my way to the parking lot.

The Reaper took one look at me, and the smirk faded from his face. He stepped back.

"Persephone!" Aphrodite's heels clacked on the cement as she hurried after me. "What's going on? What happened?"

Just let me get to my car, I thought in desperation. One look at Aphrodite's concerned face crushed what was left of my composure.

"A minute," I gasped. "I just need a minute. I'll tell you everything in—" I cut off before a sob broke through my voice and threw up a shield. I gave myself thirty seconds to cry, scream, and beat out my frustration against the shield. I spent the next thirty seconds regaining my composure.

"Is it Zeus?" Aphrodite asked when I dropped the shield. "Has he come for me?"

I closed my eyes against the wave of guilt that rushed through me. "No, I just . . . I'm sorry. I didn't mean to scare you. Melissa and I . . . I just—"

"Okay, that's it." She started back toward the school.

"Aphrodite, what are you doing?" I grabbed her arm and pulled her back.

"She needs to be put in her place. She bosses me around, she dared to upset you . . . " Aphrodite took a deep breath. "I'm sorry if I'm overstepping. How you deal with your worshipers is your business, but Persephone, she made you cry."

"You don't understand." I explained as best I could, but Aphrodite wasn't having it.

"You risked your own well-being for a nymph, gave her immortality, and treat her as a friend—no, family—and Melissa has the audacity to complain about it! And you! You not only let her get away with it, but you allowed her to upset you? Why do you care what she thinks? You're a goddess!"

"I wish I wasn't!" I exploded, throwing my hands in the air. "I've lost my best friend. I can barely look at Hades. I'm not even on speaking terms with my mom. This time last year I was *normal*." My voice broke. "I can't . . . I can't *do* this anymore. I've got nothing left."

"You have me." Aphrodite draped an arm around my shoulder and steered me to a wooden bench. "I know you feel like you've lost something, your normal life, or whatever, but that life was a lie. The harder you try to hold onto it, the faster it's going to slip away. You're never going to fit in with humans. They can tell what we are. Look at how the children at this school treat you. They're polite, sure, but they whisper. They know you're different."

"*You* seem to fit in just fine."

If she heard the bitterness in my voice, she ignored it. "That's because I don't pretend to be something I'm not. Humans understand their place. There are leaders and there are followers, and then there's us. It makes them nervous when you act like their equal."

I didn't believe that for a minute.

"Persephone, I'm not friends with those girls. I don't pretend to be, yet they follow me and they respect me. They would do the same for you if you just stepped up and behaved like a goddess." She laughed. "It's really terrible what Demeter has done to you. You're not *just* a goddess. You rank. There are four major deities left. You're the child of two of them and wife of a third. These humans shouldn't have any power over you. If you'd been created like me, you'd know all this. She took the knowledge that was your birthright."

"My mom wanted me to be able to fit in."

"How's that working out for you?"

I stared at the concrete. I wanted Aphrodite to be wrong. I wanted to keep my human life, to believe I still belonged here. But the knot in my stomach told me that wasn't going to happen. And, really, what did it matter? I put my hand to my forehead and closed my eyes. I couldn't think. I was too tired.

"Come on." She pulled me up from the bench, voice gentle. "It's time you learned how to behave like a true goddess. If you're to rule with Hades then—"

I balked at that. "I don't need to change. Not for you, and not for Hades. He likes me the way I am."

"Does he? You just said you can barely look at him. What's going on with you two?"

"We're taking a break." Her sympathetic nod made me defensive. "It was my idea."

"Oh good!" She looked relieved. "I was afraid he'd fed you some crap about your age difference."

My eyes shot to hers. "Why would that be bad? We're like millennia apart."

"He was one of the first beings created, so it's not like he's ever *not* dated anyone significantly younger than him, with the exception of Hera, I suppose." Aphrodite met my eyes with a frown. "She would have been his equal in power and knowledge as well, wouldn't she? Meh." She waved her hand in a dismissive gesture. "Doesn't matter. I'm just glad it was your idea. If the age difference really did bother him, then that would mean he's looking for something he could only possibly have had with one person. And being his rebound is beneath you."

I couldn't breathe. It felt like someone was sitting on my chest. Could that be true? It sounded reasonable.

Oh gods, was that all I was? Rebound?

"Anyway," Aphrodite's voice was a thin buzzing in my ear. "I'm sure you're right. He loves you just the way you are. But, you are naive. And while I'm sure that's endearing, isn't it a bit of a security risk to his kingdom?" Aphrodite met my gaze.

I thought of the promise I'd unwittingly made to Thanatos. I'd endangered the whole Underworld with my ignorance. *Guilty*, Hades' voice echoed in my mind. I touched my necklace and swallowed hard. That was how he felt when he kissed me. Like he was taking advantage of a child.

Maybe Aphrodite had a point. Maybe I was naive. I'd never fit in at school. Only with Melissa. *You've changed*, she'd said. What exactly had changed about me? I could stand up for myself. She'd rather me be helpless, just like my mother did. If I was helpless, then I was easier to control.

Rebound? He was the love of my life, and I was just rebound?

Maybe I was too naive.

I didn't want to be helpless. I didn't want to be controlled.

I broke away from Aphrodite's gaze with a sigh. "What did you have in mind?"

She gave me a bright grin. "Let's leave humanity behind, shall we?" She motioned to the parking lot. "It's time you learned to behave like a true goddess."

Chapter XVI

"THIS IS BEHAVING like a true goddess?" I asked dryly as Aphrodite tried on yet another dress.

"No. This is *dressing* like a real goddess. We're going out tonight." She put the dress back on the hanger and approached the saleswoman. "I'll be taking this with me when I leave."

The woman's pupils widened as Aphrodite's charm erased any objections she may have. "Would you like me to put it in a bag?"

I caught the woman's eye and handed her my credit card, praying it hadn't maxed out. Aphrodite had gone on quite a shopping spree.

"You don't have to do that." Aphrodite pointed out.

"Yes. I do. Otherwise it's stealing."

"Everything humans make is because we created them to make it. Don't think of it as stealing. It's like . . . an offering."

I rolled my eyes. "No, it's like mind control. This—" I snatched the dress "—costs money. Money keeps the store open so you can get more dresses. That woman gets paid money, which means she doesn't starve. If she lets you walk out of here with a dress, she could lose her job."

Aphrodite waved a dismissive hand. "You're no fun." She caught my eye. "Live a little. Pick out something. It's fun."

A flowing peasant skirt caught my eye. "I don't need anything. I can just get clothes from the Underworld."

"So what if you don't *need* it? You're a goddess. You should want for nothing." She grinned at me and caught my eye.

Her smile was contagious. I picked up the skirt. Maybe I was being too uptight. After all, if it weren't for me, this store would probably still be covered in snow. This city kind of owed me one.

Of course if it weren't for me, Boreas would have never set his sights on Athens. So maybe I owed them.

I put the skirt down. "I'm hungry. Are you almost done?"

She wasn't. Once she finished picking out clothes, she moved on to shoes. Then purses, then accessories, then clothes and purses and shoes for me. We were stumbling under the weight of the bags by the time we made it to the food court.

"We need our own place," Aphrodite announced. "I'm not living with that stupid nymph any longer, and you really should move out from under your mother's thumb."

"There's an apartment above the shop." I picked at my salad. "You can move in there. I may stay over sometimes, but it's really not worth arguing with my mom over. As is, I only go home to sleep."

Aphrodite's eyes sparkled. "We'll have to buy stuff for the apartment. That'll be fun." Something behind me caught her attention, and a smile spread across her face. "That guy is checking you out."

I followed her gaze to a group of men a few tables away. A cute guy, who looked to be in his early twenties, met my gaze with a grin.

"So?" I returned to my soda.

"So?" Aphrodite raised an eyebrow. "I guess he's not really much compared to Hades. Still fun to look at."

I frowned at the mention of Hades. "I'm not . . . I wouldn't feel right dating anyone else."

"Who said anything about dating?" She smiled at me. "Look, we're here, we're having fun, and we turn every head in the building. If you see something you want, just take it. There's no reason to feel guilty. I doubt he'd complain." She glanced over and giggled when she saw the man was still looking at us. "Or are you seeing Joel?"

"No. We're just friends." I stirred my drink with my straw. "You really think that's okay? You see something you want, or someone you want, and you take it? Isn't that kind of taking advantage?"

"Taking advantage of what? We're goddesses. You need to stop feeling guilty for having the upper hand. We were created to rule this strange little lot. Anything the humans make is ours for the taking. Including some of the hotter humans."

"That sounds a lot like the way Zeus feels about us."

Aphrodite fell silent. "I guess it does."

I immediately felt bad. She had just been trying to cheer me up. She'd been going about it all wrong, but that didn't change the intent. I tried to change the subject. "I think the apartment is going to look really nice."

She brightened. "And it's super close to all the bars and clubs. So I can walk home."

I stared at her. "Bars and clubs?"

"Yeah! You should come with me tonight. They have some of the nicest people. Course it would be easier if your mom would authorize me to teleport."

I ignored that last bit and focused on the important part. "Aphrodite, we're not old enough to go out drinking!"

She laughed. "Oh come on, Persephone. You can't think those rules apply to us. We should go out tonight. Just the two of us."

I considered for a moment. It was better than being tortured by Reapers. "I'll think about it." I took a look at my phone. "I've got to get to the park to run then head down to the Underworld. But I can swing you by the shop and get the keys to the apartment for you."

Aphrodite brightened. "Sounds great." She caught the eye of the guy at the other table. "You want to carry all this for us, right?"

He nodded, tripping over his feet to get to her. I started to protest but changed my mind. I didn't want to carry all these bags.

IF MOM HAD ANY objections to Aphrodite staying above the shop, she didn't voice them. I dropped Aphrodite off and left her my credit card. I'd have a hard time explaining the bill to Mom later, but it was better than the alternative.

I felt a pang of guilt flash through me when I saw Joel waiting for me at the bridge. Melissa was right. I was leading him on. I wasn't sure how it had happened. We'd progressed from our daily jog, to a daily jog and smoothie. Then to a daily jog, smoothie, and occasional dinner. Now it was a daily jog, smoothie, occasional dinner, and occasional movie. We weren't going out, and I had no interest in dating anyone other than Hades, but every time Joel suggested something and looked at me with those big blue eyes, I found myself agreeing. It was just so easy to be normal around him. For those short bits of time, I could forget about Hades and Thanatos and the Underworld.

"I gotta say, I liked your other outfit better." Joel motioned to my Disney princess running shirt and pink shorts.

I laughed nervously. I hadn't switched into different running clothes because Hades had made that comment, but because the way Joel looked at me sometimes made me want to wear a shapeless sweat suit. But this was Georgia. Sweating to death was a distinct possibility.

Joel grinned at me, and I forgot all about that. He was too nice to lead on. I needed to end this.

"You ready?" Joel asked, eyes searching mine.

"Yup!" We could talk after the run.

I ran faster than I ever had, beating Joel and my goal. I collapsed on the grass when I finished my third mile, grinning like an idiot.

"You're in a good mood," he noted.

I pushed myself up on my hands. "Hanging out with Aphrodite, running with you, it's weird, but . . . " I struggled to explain it. "I feel like I get to be me again, for just a few minutes. It's really nice."

"Who else have you been?" He sat beside me, eyes lingering appreciatively on my legs. He caught my reproachful look and gave me an impish smile. "You can tell me anything you know. I won't tell anyone."

And suddenly I wanted to tell him. Not everything, but Joel was so easy to talk to, I bet he'd understand what I was going through better than most of the gods. "What the heck," I said catching his eye and waiting for the charm to catch. When his pupils widened I said, "It's not like you're going to remember this anyway."

"No," he said slowly.

I slid my necklace back and forth on the chain, trying to think of the right words to say, "A year ago, I didn't know about any of this, and I was fine, happy even. And now I know everything, but it's like I became this completely different person. And I don't know if that person is me, just more somehow, or if I've lost who I was completely. I look at the decisions I've made lately, and I wonder if the girl I was a year ago would have made the same ones."

"Everyone goes through that," Joel assured me. "It's just a sign you're growing up."

I laughed. "Is that so, oh old and wise one?"

"I'm serious. It's a rare adult who'll admit they're the same person they were at sixteen. It's completely normal to want to hold on to who you were, but you need to give yourself space to grow into who you'll be."

"I just don't want to disappear into this stuff that I'm dealing with. I did something today that I thought I'd never do, and I didn't even think twice. I'm losing myself."

Joel touched my cheek. "I don't think you give yourself enough credit. You're stronger than you think."

He met my eyes, leaned closer, and I knew he was going to kiss me. I thought of stopping him. I shouldn't have led him on this long. But . . .

I let him kiss me, releasing him from the charm that would compel him to forget this conversation. His lips on mine were warm and eager. Completely different from a kiss from Hades. Hades was always fighting a battle with himself, trying to hold back. Joel had no such reservations.

My stomach turned at the thought of Hades, and I pushed Joel away. This was wrong. I didn't want to do this. Why was I doing this? I knew it was just kissing, but I didn't *want* to kiss anyone else. I just wanted Hades.

"What's wrong?" Joel's bright blue eyes searched my face.

I stared at him wondering that myself. What was wrong? Joel was a perfectly nice guy, and I liked him before. No, he wasn't Hades, but Hades was never going to be happy with me. Even if he managed to forgive me for the Thanatos thing, he would always feel guilty for being with me. He would always wonder if he was taking advantage of me. Didn't I deserve a guy who wasn't filled with regret for kissing me?

I shook my head, breaking free of his gaze. "I should get going. But . . . " Here I was, leading him on again. "I'm going out with Aphrodite tonight, maybe you could come? You should meet her. You kind of remind me of her."

Joel gave me an odd look. "How so?"

I laughed. "Not like . . . physically. There's just . . . " I frowned, try-ing to put my finger on it. "You're both very confident, comfortable with yourselves." I stood up, brushing the grass off of me. "To be honest, I'm kind of jealous."

He smiled at me. "You'll get there. I'd love to hang out tonight. I'll give you a call later, all right?"

I nodded and walked toward the parking lot. When I was sure I was out of his sight, I teleported to the Underworld and went to find Hades.

He was in the library, as usual, reading a book that he quickly stashed cover down, something about the gods Mars and Venus. "You still run?" His gruff voice sounded surprised. His gaze caught on my necklace, like he was surprised I still wore it.

I touched the plant. "Every day. Why?" I sat down on one of the cushy brown chairs.

Hades hesitated, like he wasn't sure how to answer, his dark gaze watching me warily. "You don't . . . erm." He paused as though he wasn't sure how to continue. "You don't look like you have enough energy to stand for more than two minutes. How exactly are you running every day?"

I scowled at him. "Can we just get this over with? I'm supposed to meet Aphrodite at her place when I'm done here."

He jerked his head and his gaze sharpened. "Isn't she still staying with Melissa?"

My mood darkened. I'd forgotten about my fight with Melissa.

When I didn't explain, Hades took my hands and channeled away the excess power. His grip on me stiffened, expression going dark as bits and pieces of my day flashed through his head. I felt a flash of anger go through him when he saw Joel kiss me. My stomach twisted with guilt. I watched him watching me, his dark lashes lowered to conceal his eyes from me. I couldn't feel a single thing from him. It was like he'd thrown up a wall.

We didn't say anything for a few minutes. The silence felt like it dragged on forever. Hades finally cleared his throat. "We need to talk."

I stood and walked to the door. I couldn't look at him. How could I have kissed Joel? "I'm sorry. I don't know—"

"Not about that." His voice was much too calm for the torrent of anger running beneath it. He took a deep breath, as though he was forcing himself to calm down. "Are you ever going to tell me what's bothering you?" He ran his fingers through his hair and caught me in a piercing stare. I felt like I did the first time I'd seen him. Like he could see everything in me, everything I'd ever done and would ever do.

And he wasn't impressed.

"What do you mean?" I pressed my hand against the frosted glass on the French door leading to the library.

"We're gods. It takes a lot for us to look as worn down as you do. You've lost weight, and you feel anxious and worried all the time. You've been like this since you found out Zeus was alive, but it's gotten worse since . . . "

That night. I finished the thought for him.

Hades moved in front of me. "This isn't you. You used to tell me everything. Something's happened. What's going on, Persephone?" His voice dipped, entreating me to respond.

The warmth of his nearness reached out to me, but this entire conversation hurt. My heart thudded uncomfortably in my chest. I felt dizzy, sick. I needed to get out of here. I shoved past him. "I can't tell you."

I made it as far as the door before he got in front of me again, blocking me with his body. "It's not just Zeus. I kept thinking maybe it was just . . . " He gave a helpless shrug. "I know you've been through a lot—"

My temper flared. "A lot? Oh, you mean finding out that everything I knew about my life was a lie? Or were you referring to having to hide in the Underworld from a psychotic rapist until I *killed* him, then discovered my sociopathic father sent him after me and is now killing students at my school to send me messages. Gee, Hades. You think I've been through a *lot?* Wow, you're like, observant."

Hades shook his head. "That's not it. I watched you deal with all of that, and none of it affected you like whatever this has." He gripped my shoulders, his gaze pinning me. "I can help you."

"You're not listening to me!"

"Then *tell* me! You know one of the things I like about you? I've never had to sit around and try to decipher the things you said. You're different than the other gods, Persephone, or at least you were."

That stung. "You mean I wasn't like Hera."

His grip tightened. "I mean that you used to trust me. I don't know what I did to screw that up, but whatever it was, I'm sorry." His blue eyes met mine, full of concern. "There is nothing I wouldn't do for you. Do you get that? Whatever it is that you're keeping from me, it can't change that. I can help you." He stooped down so his face was level with mine. "So whatever you're hiding, whatever you've done, I promise—"

"Don't! You don't know—you can't promise that it won't change the way you feel about me."

"What are you talking about?"

For the thousandth time I tried to tell him about Thanatos. My stomach clenched, my throat closed, trapping the words. My head spun. I couldn't breathe. I felt as if I was about to fly into a million pieces, but I couldn't break my promise.

"I—" The single word cost me. The pain that wrenched through my body was unbelievable. I saw stars. My knees buckled beneath me, and I found myself clinging to Hades. "You'll hate me." I drew in a sharp breath, hiccupping around a sob.

"Never." Hades' arms wrapped around me, pulling me even closer to him, pressing me hard up against his body. "I could never hate you. It isn't in me."

I wanted so desperately to believe him. There had to be a way to tell him. I stood on my tiptoes, twining my arms around his neck, and poured my feelings into a kiss. I couldn't think about Thanatos directly, couldn't think about anything that would help Hades to figure it out, but the promise couldn't block my feelings. Hades knew *something* was wrong. I could only hope the pieces fell into place before it was too late.

To my surprise, he kissed me back. One hand looped around me, pulling me to him, the other cupped my face. His body crushed against mine, and I bumped into the door, shifting so the doorknob didn't dig into my back.

"Wait," I gasped.

Hades stopped immediately, taking a step back for good measure.

"Gods," he gasped, breathing ragged, his face dark and intense.

My lips longed for his, but I shook off the feeling. "I shouldn't have kissed you. I still need . . . "

What? What did I need? The issues that seemed so pertinent had vanished, taking all my reasoning skills with them. What did it matter he'd dated Minthe, or that Thanatos was probably plotting to overthrow Hades at this very moment? None of that mattered compared to *this*. This felt right.

He's going to hate me.

So what? I argued with myself. *He's going to hate me anyway, but we have now. Why am I letting Thanatos take him from me?*

If you see something you want, just take it! Aphrodite's cheerful voice echoed in my thoughts.

I looked back up at Hades, bridging the distance between us with a single step. "Never mind." I leaned forward to kiss him again, but he drew back.

"I think—" He broke off, staring into my eyes.

"Stop thinking," I whispered, pulling him into another kiss.

Suddenly things were moving fast. My brain seemed to fog over when he took me into his arms again. There was a different quality to his kisses. Desperate, almost forceful . . . yearning. We stumbled back toward his bedroom.

Chapter XVII

I LIFTED MY HANDS over my head, breaking contact for a minute to get my shirt off, but then he was kissing me again. I pushed his shirt up, but he was too tall for me to get it over his head. We broke apart again while he stripped off his shirt. Words fell out of my mouth in a whisper as I pulled him back to me.

Wait, what? What did I just say?

A moment of crystal clarity burst through my brain. What had I just said to Hades? What was I doing? I replayed the last few seconds in my mind to the place where I'd looked Hades in the eyes, and he'd kissed me.

No!

He was already whispering back. "I swea—"

"Stop!" I pushed him away from me, reeling with horror.

"Seriously?" His hair was disheveled. The expression on his face was a combination of confusion and frustration. His pupils were so wide that his eyes were practically black.

What had I done? He'd almost sworn fealty. I broke off the charm so fast I got whiplash. Hades blinked, startled.

"Persephone, what—"

"I'm sorry!" I stumbled away from him, backpedaling toward the door. I snatched my shirt off the floor and clutched it to me. "I'm so sorry. I didn't mean to. It was an accident."

"Wait, what?" He followed on my heels, his breath warm on the back of my neck. "What was an accident?" He turned me around, his grip tight on my upper arm, then rubbed it, as if he was afraid he'd bruised me. His gaze, even darker than normal, lingered on my lips.

I shook my head, unable to face his questions. I stared at his bared, hard chest. It hadn't been me. Something, someone else had been calling the shots.

Charm's subtle, Hades had said. *It should feel like it's your idea.*

Aphrodite's voice echoed in my head. *If you see something you want, just take it.*

I gasped for breath setting the room spinning around me. What had she done? What else had she asked me to do? It wasn't possible! Hades had given me enough power to withstand her charm.

"Persephone, look at me!" Hades gripped my shoulders and stooped until his gaze was level with mine. "What just happened?"

I'd been tired. So tired. Resistance to charm should be innate, but what if I'd been so worn down that I didn't have the energy to resist?

But why?

I'm not working with Zeus. Aphrodite had promised.

Glamours. The gods could look like whatever, whoever, they wanted. She might not be working with Zeus, but we'd forgotten a question. Such a basic question.

Hades had almost sworn fealty. What would I have done to him next? What had I been *programmed* to do to him next?

"How?" I whispered. "You said it wouldn't work on you. On other gods. I'm the exception because I haven't come into my powers yet. How did I use it on you?"

Realization dawned in his eyes. He stepped away from me, pulling his shirt back on. Something flickered in his expression. Fear. "You've grown more powerful since then. We're married." His voice was tight, drawn. "I'm vulnerable to anything you can throw at me and vice versa."

Inexplicably my mind turned to Hera. Was that what had happened to her? Was that why she had given Zeus so much of her own power that she hadn't been able to sustain her own life? No wonder they all hated Zeus so much. That was despicable.

And I'd just done the same thing to Hades.

"I didn't mean to." My voice broke.

"Persephone." He reached for me, and I twisted out of his reach, practically falling out of the library door.

"Don't! Don't touch me. Don't even look at me. I'm dangerous." I was shaking, trembling. What had I almost done?

"Wait a minute. Look, I know it was an accident. We just need to work more on your control . . . " I didn't hear the rest of what he'd said. He didn't realize what had almost happened. How he'd almost sworn away his free will.

I had to get away from him! Without further thought, I teleported back to Tartarus. Shaking, I pulled on my shirt and reentered the living realm. Tears blurred my vision. I collapsed onto the grass and retched, but could only manage dry heaves. I clutched my knees to my chest and waited for the shaking to stop.

"Hey, there you are!" Aphrodite's voice sent chills up my spine. I looked up and saw her approaching from a distant picnic table.

Joel was with her. He waved one finger at me and grabbed two cups from the table, heading off toward a nearby trash can.

"I've been waiting for hours!" Aphrodite called. "We're supposed to go out, remember? But look who I ran into? I recognized him from that picture of the three of you that Melissa has on her desk. You know, the one where you—" Her features shifted to something resembling concern when she got closer to me. "Persephone, are you okay?"

"How could you?" I whispered. I stood shakily, drawing as much of my power to myself as I could.

I didn't have much to work with. Hades had just channeled it all away.

Her head tilted, and she gave me a confused look. "What?"

An image of Hades, eyes wide with charm, flashed through my brain. A torrent of anger ripped through me. "How *could* you? I trusted you!"

Her eyes widened in alarm. "Uh—"

My vision was tinted red with rage. "Did you really think it would work? That you could charm me into hurting him? *How could you?*" I lunged toward her. I wasn't sure what my plan was. I just really wanted to hit something. I was so mad and angry and humiliated and horrified. So many negative emotions swept through me in a nauseating whirl, why not add violence to the list?

Two Reapers grabbed me, holding me back. I gasped as the pain of their touch lanced through me, but the pain only fueled my anger.

"Everything okay?" Joel asked.

Aphrodite's gaze flicked between the Reapers, and then landed on Joel.

"Leave him out of this!" I glared at Aphrodite and turned my charm on full force. "Joel, don't worry. You're not going to remember any of this. You should go home now."

"Okay." Aphrodite's voice was measured, even. She approached me slowly, using the type of caution typically reserved for wild animals, or crazy people. "I'm not going to hurt him. But I'm going to need you to look at me—"

"No!" I shut my eyes and tilted my head away from her. I couldn't let her charm me.

Aphrodite shushed me, a cool hand gripping my chin. I felt the edge of her sharp nails digging beneath my jawbone, forcing my head up to her.

I lashed out, kicking as hard as I could. I struggled against the Reapers' hold, but their grip only tightened. "Let me go!" I shrieked, jerking my head free from her grip. "I won't do it! I won't be used against Hades. *Never.* I will never charm him! I will never act with the intention of hurting him! You can't make me!"

Aphrodite clapped a hand over my mouth, but it was too late, the words were spoken. "Do you have any idea what you've just done?"

I laughed. "Do you really think I don't know what it means to make a promise after all this? I know exactly what I'm doing."

"Oh, Persephone . . . "

Was that pity in her voice?

The Reapers tightened their grip. Pain slashed through me, and I cried out.

"Look at me," she demanded.

"Please!" I gasped. I jerked my head, but her nails dug into my flesh, holding me tight. "Please, don't do this! *Stop!*"

One of the Reapers grabbed my neck. Pain ripped through my body, traveling from my spine to the end of every individual nerve. My eyes flew open as an entirely new wave of agony tore through me. My screams echoed through the park.

Blue eyes stared into mine, and everything went black.

Chapter XVIII

"SHE DID WHAT?"

A jolt of adrenaline shot through me when I recognized Thanatos' deep voice. All I needed to do was look at him. But however hard I tried, my eyes wouldn't open. I drifted just beneath consciousness. I was lying on something soft. A fan whirred overhead. The cold air gave me goose bumps.

A man with a voice as smooth as silk replied, "She swore she wouldn't be used against him. We can't count on her to obtain his fealty. It's time to move on to the next plan." He sounded like he was standing near my feet.

"She bound herself. Intentionally?" Thanatos' voice was incredulous. His footsteps echoed as he walked closer to me. The hair on my arm prickled, he was standing so close. If only I could open my eyes!

You are *outnumbered.* The rational part of my brain pointed out.

Right. It was probably best I didn't wake up just this second. I needed a plan. I focused on listening instead.

"It's unfortunate," said the man. "But there's no sense dwelling on it. Of course had you done your job, Hades would already be in our grasp."

"My job? Zeus—"

I stiffened. Zeus? Zeus was here? *Oh gods.*

Thanatos was still talking. "Come on! It's nothing short of miraculous that Demeter hasn't caught on to the Reapers—"

"I can keep Demeter occupied. We need to take this to the next level."

"The next level? Persephone barely eats or sleeps. Frankly, I don't understand how she's retained her sanity. Over the last few weeks she's endured physical and psychological torture every hour of every day. She's as isolated as we can get her. I don't know *how* she broke free from your charisma, but the fault was not mine."

"She's strong." There was something akin to pride in Zeus' voice. "I had hoped to avoid using her for the next step."

"She'll die."

"That upsets you?"

"Hades deserves anything we throw at him, but *her*? She's just a kid."

Zeus snorted. "Gods, you're half in love with her too, aren't you?"

"She doesn't deserve to die for *him.*"

"Collateral damage," Zeus' voice was dismissive. "If I'm going to use her, she needs to have enough power to be worth it. I can generate some more worship for her, but Hades would be an ideal source. How much do you think he'd give her if the situation were to turn dire?"

"Everything," Thanatos said without hesitation.

Zeus laughed. "I doubt that."

"You haven't seen the way he looks at her. He'd do anything for her."

"I can work with that," Zeus mused. The floorboard creaked as he shifted. "I can almost see why. She's incredible." His fingers touched my thigh, and I jerked away.

"Oh good, she's coming to." Zeus leaned so close I could feel his hot breath on my face. "Look at me, sweetheart. There's something I need you to do."

"I'M SO GLAD we went out!" Aphrodite giggled.

I blinked and looked around. We were on Clayton Street walking toward Five Points. It was dark. I glanced down and saw I was wearing a short black dress and heels. Not my usual look.

"Um . . . yeah. Fun." I murmured, trying to get my bearings. A sign advertising a Halloween party "tomorrow" gave me pause. "Is that right? Halloween's tomorrow?"

"Geez, Seph, can you say lightweight?"

"Ugh, no! For the thousandth time, unless you want to go by Phro, you cannot call me that."

She rolled her eyes. "You are no fun. Anyway, um yeah. Or I guess today, if you want to get technical."

Halloween? That was weeks away. I frowned trying to recall the last few days. Brief snippets flashed in my mind. Hanging out with Joel during the day, Aphrodite at night. It was the only way to avoid the Reapers. Some club, 8E's, or something. Random guys buying us drinks. Lots of dancing. "My feet hurt! Why can't we catch the bus again?"

"Bus service stops at three a.m." Aphrodite's voice was patient.

"But wasn't that fun? Next time, tell Joel not to bail. He's pretty hot, you know, as hot as humans get anyhow."

"You say that like you've seen *so* many cute gods." I kicked off my heels and scooped them up. It wasn't like I could get tetanus.

"Well, if they all look like Hades—"

I shot her a murderous look, and she burst into giggles. "Oh he's so not my type. But he's nice to look at. You know, you're right. Forget walking. I just found us a ride."

She stepped into the crowded street without warning. A horn blared, tires squealed. A silver two seated convertible stopped just short of hitting Aphrodite.

"What the hell!" The man driving it exclaimed.

"Gosh, sorry to scare you." Aphrodite giggled. "But my friend and I need a ride."

The man's eyes widened as he took Aphrodite in. "Uhh . . . okay. But um . . . I only have room for one."

"Oh that's fine, you can walk," Aphrodite said brightly.

The man unbuckled his seatbelt and fumbled for the door handle. Aphrodite tapped her foot until he got out of the way.

"Thanks!" She slid into the driver's seat. "Come on, Persephone."

I got in the other door. Something about this was . . . off. I put my hand to my forehead trying to get my befuddled brain to think clearly. There was something I was forgetting.

Meh, it probably wasn't that important.

Chapter XIX

I WAS STILL hungover the next afternoon, but I forced myself to go on my run. Joel was waiting for me at the park.

"So you're sure you can't go to the Halloween party tonight?" he asked when we finished our jog.

I sat on the carpet of orange and red leaves, watching the sunlight sparkle on the lake. "I told you I have a thing tonight." I'd been avoiding Hades as much as I could, but there was no getting out of Halloween in the Underworld. It was a pretty big deal to the souls, and, like it or not, I was still the queen. "We can do something tomorrow if you want."

Joel sat beside me on the leaves, hand wrapping around my waist. "Like what?"

I moved away from him. "I'm all sweaty."

"I don't mind." He leaned in and gave me a kiss, pushing me down onto the leaves.

"Joel!" I pushed him off me with a laugh. "We're in a public park . . . And leaves are really uncomfortable."

"No one's watching," he murmured. He looped his hand behind my back, protecting it from the scratchy leaves. His other hand ran up my leg.

I grabbed his hand, frowning. When had we gotten to this point? This didn't feel right. I vaguely remembered Aphrodite saying something about loosening up and having more fun.

"Everything okay?" He caught my eye and gave me a concerned look.

"Um . . . yeah, everything's fine. I'm just . . . I've been really disoriented lately."

"You're probably spending too much time with that Aphrodite girl. Every time I text you, you guys are out. Ever considered staying in for a night?"

"You don't like her." I brushed a leaf out of my hair. "Why?"

"I don't know. You act different around her. You've been . . . really different lately."

I shrugged off his concern. "I'm not going out with her tonight. I've got . . . kind of a family thing. Happy?"

"Almost. Come on, can't you get away for a little while? Orpheus is playing at Terrapin tonight."

I laughed. "Wow, what's next, volunteering to take me to the new *Dusk* movie? It's at the dollar theater, you know. I think that's in your budget." I pushed myself up on my arms, giving him a look of mock concern, that familiar lightheadedness returning. "Why are you trying to gain brownie points? Is there something you need to confess?"

"You want the long list or the short list?" Joel nuzzled my neck. "Maybe I just want to spend more time with you."

I pushed him away. "You're sweet, but I still have to go."

Joel sighed. "It was worth a shot. Why is Orpheus playing in Athens anyway? Isn't he too big for this town?"

"Athens has a rich musical . . . " I stifled a giggle at Joel's look. "His wife is here. He wants to stay near her." Orpheus still had to travel more than he liked, but he was never out of Athens for more than a day or two.

"Why is his wife here? Atlanta has better hospitals, and there are probably hospitals that specialize in whatever's wrong with her."

"Don't knock St. Mary's." I pushed his shoulder playfully. "I was born there."

Joel's expression sobered. His blue eyes turned thoughtfully to the lake. "Do you think she's happy? Being kept alive like that? I mean it's been months. She's got to be on life support or something, right?"

I shrugged uncomfortably. "He's in love with her. He doesn't want her to die."

"What if her soul has already moved on?"

"That soul is half the problem," I muttered, fiddling with my necklace. At Joel's confused look I added, "Well, what if that's all comas are? Or maybe not all the time, but in this case, what if her soul and her body aren't talking?"

Joel fell silent while he mulled my question over. I liked that about him. Half the stuff I said to him had to sound crazy, but he never laughed at me. He took everything I said seriously, thinking it over from every possible angle.

Like Hades.

"There's a myth about broken souls," Joel said finally. "I'm surprised Orpheus hasn't heard it. As crazy as he is about all that stuff."

I leaned against Joel, and he draped his arm over my shoulder. "What is it?"

"When the gods created humans, they didn't look like us. They had four legs, four arms, two faces, and one soul. They were complete and happy. But they were too fulfilled. Too powerful."

"They were a threat," I murmured.

"Exactly. Zeus split them in two saying that men would never amount to anything if they spent half of their lives searching for their other half." He gave me a significant look. "Some people get lucky and find their soul mates, but the rest will always be searching to fill that void in their lives."

"Do you think the gods have soul mates?" I winced at the wistfulness in my voice.

"Why would they need them?" He leaned down and gave me a quick kiss. "Since I was willing to listen to Orpheus, does that mean I get to pick the next movie?"

I grinned at him. "Deal. Now get out of here or you'll be late to class."

I SWUNG BY MY house after I left the park. I didn't spend much time at home anymore, but I had to drop by at some point, otherwise Mom would get mad. I was so exhausted from my night out with Aphrodite that I almost forgot my book bag in the car. I hurried back to my trunk and grabbed it. If she figured out I wasn't in school anymore, she'd be furious.

"Mom, I'm home!" I dropped my book bag on the floor by the door. I didn't have a lot of time to hang out at the house. I was due in the Underworld soon.

"Mom?" I rounded the corner into the kitchen, anticipating my after-school snack. Sure, she couldn't be trusted to tell the truth, and she was scheming and manipulative, but she always made a good snack.

A Reaper was sitting at the table in her place. I came to a surprised stop, aware of two other Reapers slipping behind me. "Where is she?" It took more effort than I cared to admit to keep my voice from trembling.

The Reaper picked up a note from the table and read in a ridiculous falsetto voice. "Persephone, went to Buford with Minthe to shop. Cookies are in the oven. See you in the morning."

I threw a quick glance at the oven to make sure the house wasn't going to catch on fire. It was off. She must have left them in there just to keep them warm.

Shit. Buford, Mall of Georgia, the Melting Pot, and outlet malls. Mom would be home late. Again. She'd been out almost every day lately. *It's all our fighting*, I realized with a sudden clarity. She was avoiding me too, just like everyone else.

"Looks like we have you all to ourselves," the redheaded Reaper said with a grin.

I shrieked in pain as one of the Reapers grabbed me from behind, fingers digging painfully into my ribs. Something in their touch was different. I actually felt it. Not just a tearing feeling at my soul, but actual hands on my actual flesh.

It hurt like hell.

"Happy Halloween," one of the Reapers hissed.

I screamed as they dragged me through my house. One of the Reapers bumped into a chair and knocked it down. That never happened. Were they corporeal?

"Let me go!" I lashed out and landed a blow on one of their shoulders. It hurt me, I was still touching him after all, but for a second I thought I saw the Reaper wince.

"Swear fealty to Zeus."

I shook my head, and he wrapped his hand around my neck, sending shock waves through my body. I couldn't breathe. I clawed desperately at his hand, and his grip tightened. The world spun around me in a dizzying wave. He released his hand and slammed me into the wall. "Swear fealty to Zeus!"

"No!"

His fingers dug into my jaw, and he lifted my chin until I was staring into his eyes. "You think this hurts? We're just getting started."

His lips found mine in a cruel, bruising kiss, tearing at my soul. There was no desire in his kiss, no attraction at all. It was just supposed to hurt. I struggled against the pain, trying to kick my way free, but the other Reapers shifted, one grabbing me roughly by the arms, the other taking hold of my legs so I couldn't lash out. I couldn't even throw up a shield since they were already touching me.

Light sparked in the redhead's fingertips. I wasn't sure what that meant, but it couldn't be good. Suddenly his fingers passed through my flesh. My screams ricocheted off the walls, and one of the Reapers clapped his hand over my mouth. With strength I didn't know I possessed, I wrenched free. I was out the door in a flash and halfway to the driveway, car keys in hand, when I smacked into a solid wall of flesh. I shrieked and fell backward, scrambling away.

"No! Please! Don't!" I lashed out, blind with panic.

"Persephone! Stop, it's me!" Hades pulled me to my feet, and I threw myself into his arms.

Hades! Hades was here. The Reapers wouldn't touch me with him here. I wouldn't have to feel that horrible pain again.

"What happened?" Hades held me at arm's length and looked me up and down. "You're as white as a sheet! Are you okay? Persephone, talk to me!"

I tried to answer, but couldn't stop gasping for breath. Horizontal lines zigzagged in my vision. A high-pitched whine sounded in my ears, and my knees gave way. Hades caught me before I hit the ground. He glanced toward the house then back at me and swore.

"Okay, I'm here now." He kept his voice soothing, but I could hear the panic beneath his words. He pushed my hair off my neck, fingers fumbling for a pulse. "What the—" Hades jerked me toward him and traced something on my neck, shifting my necklace to the side.

"Is she okay?" The redheaded Reaper emerged from the house, trying and failing to sound concerned.

My grip tightened on Hades, and I glanced around for the other two Reapers.

"Is the house clear?" Hades demanded. When the Reaper nodded, Hades hoisted me into his arms and walked toward the house.

"No!" I tried to get free, but a wave of dizziness pushed me back into Hades' arms.

"It's okay." He flung open the door and looked around before laying me down on the couch. The Reaper followed on his heels, eyebrows pinched together in fake concern.

"Put your feet up," Hades demanded, grabbing the sofa pillows and stacking them under my feet. He pulled the blanket off the back of the couch and draped it over me.

"What's wrong with her?" the Reaper asked.

"She's in shock. Where's Demeter?"

The Reaper indicated the note on the kitchen table. Hades snatched the note and made a disgusted noise. "What happened?"

The Reaper shrugged. "She was sleeping and freaked out. Must have been a nightmare or something."

I glared at the Reaper, cursing their ability to lie.

Hades turned to me. "Is that what happened? Did you forget to shield your dreams again?"

"No." I barely managed the one word answer, my voice was so hoarse.

"So you're trying to tell me this was just a run of the mill nightmare?" Hades asked the Reaper, his voice dripping with skepticism. When the Reaper shrugged, Hades asked, "Where are the others?"

"They went to get you. I stayed behind to protect her."

"No one else was here? You're absolutely certain."

"Not that I saw."

"Persephone, was anyone else here beside the Reapers?"

I shook my head.

Hades knelt and pried the car keys from my grip. "So when she woke up hysterical, grabbed her keys, and ran out of the house, your plan was to let her get behind the wheel of a *car*?"

The Reaper narrowed his eyes. "What did you expect me to do, restrain her? In case you've forgotten—" He waved his hand in my direction. I flinched. "I can't touch her."

Hades' hand shot out, snapping the Reaper's wrist. "Do *not* lie to me." He tightened his grip. "What really happened?"

The Reaper gasped, face paling. "I told you, she woke up and went nuts—"

Hades twisted the Reaper's arm, using it to steer him into the wall. "Then why are there bruises around her *neck*?"

The Reaper's eyes went wide. "I . . . I don't know. Someone must have . . . " He trailed off, noticing Hades had gone very still, gaze riveted to the Reaper's arm.

A single strand of my hair clung to the Reaper's sleeve, shining like a golden beacon against the dark material. Hades yanked the Reaper's sleeve back, exposing the scratches decorating the Reaper's wrist.

"What did you *do*?"

"I can explain."

"Did you touch my wife?" Hades' voice was low and dangerous.

"Yes, but—"

Hades' fist slammed into the Reaper's face. A shield dropped. I blinked, staring at the place where Hades and the Reaper had been. My vision was swimming. I felt lightheaded, a wave of dizziness overwhelmed me, and my eyes rolled shut.

"No you don't." Hades was beside me in a flash. I bolted upright, looking behind Hades for the Reaper. He was at the table; a shield had formed around him, gluing him in place. His face was puffy, like Hades had used it for a punching bag.

"It's okay." Hades' voice was soothing. "It's going to be okay." He gently kissed my forehead, searching for echoes of pain and panic. His fingers traced a sensitive spot on my neck. I flinched, feeling the network of bruises laced around my throat from the Reaper's grip. He pushed my sleeves to the side following the red impressions left by the Reaper's fingers. His jaw clenched when he found the handprints on my side.

Healing warmth spread through his palms, erasing the pain wherever they touched. His fingers brushed the bruises on my leg. His gaze went dark. I could feel the rage coursing through him. He was like a powder keg, ready to explode. When his fingers traced my bruised lips, he took a deep breath, struggling to maintain his temper. He clasped a hand to my cheek, probing further. For a second I could feel my soul as solid and certain as any other part of me.

"Gods," Hades swore as he assessed the condition of my torn and battered soul. I felt a flash of power, and it fell back into place, whole and unharmed.

Behind him, the Reaper gasped for breath. He looked different. The light wasn't bending around him the same way it usually did. "What's happening to me?"

Hades stiffened and pulled away. He studied me for a moment, and I knew he wanted to make sure I was okay before he dealt with the Reaper. I nodded and Hades stood and pivoted toward the Reaper.

"I've brought you back to life." Hades' voice was cold.

"What?"

"Don't get too excited. The condition is temporary." Hades gave the Reaper a dark grin. "You seem like the type of guy that likes to experiment. You got real creative tearing my wife's soul to bits. Surely at some point you must have wondered what it felt like."

"N . . . no." The Reaper looked like he wanted to say more, but couldn't. Thanatos must have found some way to bind him. He looked to me, eyes wide in desperation.

Sucks, doesn't it? I sat up on the couch, flashing the Reaper a savage grin.

He read my thoughts on my face and gulped. "You don't understand. It wasn't just—I didn't—There's more—" His voice gave to an anguished cry when Hades reached out and grabbed him by the shoulder.

"Please! Stop!" he screamed, writhing in agony.

"How many times did she say that?" Hades demanded. "How many times did you make her beg?" His hand turned white, and it plunged through the Reaper's neck.

The Reaper let out a guttural cry.

"How long could a normal human soul survive this? Did you ever wonder that?" Hades shook the Reaper; he moved limply, like a rag doll. "Let's find out."

There was a bright flash of light, and the Reaper was gone.

Chapter XX

HADES DUSTED off his hands and turned to me. "You okay?"

I nodded numbly. "Why . . . What are you doing here?"

Hades glanced at me, surprised. "Why do you think? I haven't seen you in over a week! I was worried sick. When I felt your pain and panic, I thought your powers—" He waved his hand at me and sat wearily at the kitchen table. "Anyway, there's a new entrance to the Underworld in your backyard. Hope you don't mind."

"A week?" I stared at him, incredulous. I tried to remember the last time I saw Hades and drew a blank.

He nodded. "I know you're still . . . embarrassed, or whatever, over that whole charming thing—"

I blinked. What was he talking about?

"But it really is okay. I know you'd never do that on purpose. I trust you. We just have to work on your control. Okay?"

I nodded, even though I was still confused.

He looked at me for a minute, then took my hand and channeled away my excess power. Images from my mind flowed to his, but they weren't anything I remembered. Drinking with Aphrodite, dancing with random guys, dark corners, and a really intense make-out session with Joel. The images flew like barbs, attacking Hades. He drew back, staring at me in surprise.

"What the hell, Persephone!"

"Hades, wait." I tried to say something, tried to explain, but I didn't know how to explain. I didn't remember *doing* any of that stuff.

He shook his head and stood abruptly. "It's not my business."

"But—"

"No really, Persephone, I don't want to hear it." There was a bitter edge to his voice. A muscle twitched in his cheek. "And for the record, you don't have to avoid me if there's something you don't want me to see. I've been around for a while. I can handle it."

"I wasn't—"

"Are you ready? We should probably be getting back to the Underworld."

"Wait, Hades!"

"Actually, I think I'm going to head down." He walked to the door. "I'll see you later tonight."

"Stop! *Please!*" My voice broke. "I don't remember any of that!"

"Yeah, that's generally a sign to lay off the liquor."

Tears sprang to my eyes. "No, I wouldn't . . . I didn't . . . I don't—" I broke off with a curse. "I can't even form a complete thought! I don't know what that was, but it wasn't me."

He stopped, his hand still clasping the doorknob. I caught my breath. I could fix this if I could just get him to stay.

"I'm sorry. I'm so sorry. And I don't . . . I don't know what charming thing you were talking about, but I'm sorry about that too."

Hades turned slowly, an expression I didn't recognize on his face, his blazing blue eyes intense. "You don't remember charming me?"

I stared at him. "Hades, I would never—"

He crossed the room before I could blink. "Drop your glamour and look at me, right now."

"What? Why?"

"Just do it!"

I dropped the glamour, and his eyes searched mine, gaze intent then let out a string of curses as he turned for the door.

I grabbed his arm. "Hades what is going on?"

"You've been charmed." He stared at me again. "And it's already gone, isn't it? I wonder how many times a day you figure it out. Gods, no wonder you've been so out of it. There's a physical toll."

"What's already gone?" My head was spinning with confusion. "What are you talking about?"

Hades shook his head. "She's strong, but she isn't this good." He ran his fingers through his hair. "I'm missing something."

I couldn't answer, but Hades didn't seem to expect me to be able to. "We've got to get you immune to this. When's the last time you slept?"

"I don't remember."

Hades' nodded. "Hypnos taught me a new trick, to help with your nightmares." He snorted and shook his head. "But that was never the problem, was it?"

I shook my head, feeling dizzy. This conversation was on dangerous ground. My mind felt like it was split into three, each side fighting the others.

Hades sat on the couch. "Can I use your phone?"

I raised my eyebrows at the odd request, but dug my phone from pocket and handed it to him.

"Thanks, now lie down."

I curled up on the couch. I was practically in his lap. Part of me felt awkward, but a larger part of me was too exhausted to care. I felt drained. Emotionally and physically exhausted. Hades stroked my hair, a steady current of power flowing from his fingers. I was drifting off in seconds . . .

He muttered something I didn't catch. A few seconds later I felt him fumble with my phone and heard a distant ringing sound.

"Demeter." His hushed voice was full of disdain. "So glad you took a break from *shopping* to answer your phone. Yeah, we need to talk."

I CAME TO FEELING like I'd gotten a year's worth of sleep in what couldn't have been more than an hour. I felt like a fog had lifted from my brain.

"'Bout time you showed up," Hades muttered.

I jumped, but he wasn't talking to me. I was still stretched out on the couch, but I was shielded. I studied the shield and shot him a questioning look. He was leaning against the kitchen table with his arms crossed. He looked pissed.

"Why is there an entrance to the Underworld in my backyard?" my mother demanded, dropping her purse on the countertop. "Where's Persephone?"

He glanced up in the general direction of my room, the motion seeming to be involuntary. "She needed rest before the thing tonight."

I did my best to stay still so I didn't disrupt the shield. Hades obviously wanted me to hear this conversation, and I didn't want to screw that up.

"She's asleep?" She sounded relieved. "Good. I haven't seen her sleep in—"

"From what I gathered you haven't seen her much at all."

Mom's eyes narrowed. "You still haven't told me what you're doing here." She pulled back the wooden kitchen chair and sat, crossing her legs and staring at Hades expectantly.

My eyebrows shot up at her tone. I'd never heard her sound like that. She'd been mad at me before, but this was different. There was danger in her voice. She was staring at Hades like she'd tied him to a stake, soaked him with gasoline, and was playing with a lighter, just waiting for a spark to "accidentally" catch.

"There was a . . . situation with one of her guards. One of my Reapers went rogue."

"What kind of a *situation?*"

Hades sucked in his breath, looking more unsettled than I'd ever seen him. "He um . . . " He ran his fingers through his hair in a nervous gesture. Mom's eyes widened in alarm. I somehow doubted she'd ever seen Hades rattled. "Yeah, there's no good way to say this."

"What. Happened."

Hades let out a deep breath. "He attacked her."

"What?" My mom bolted from the chair.

Hades intercepted her before she reached the staircase. "She's okay. I handled it."

"I'll just bet you did." Mom's eyes were blazing. "Get out of my way!"

I tensed, ready to teleport to my room.

"You really want to wake her? Do you have any idea how long it's been since she slept? *She* doesn't. In fact, there are some pretty significant gaps in her memory lately. Now normally, I'd ask you to help me fill those in, but you haven't exactly been around—"

"Are you seriously accusing me of being negligent? You told me she'd be safe with those . . . things, and now you're telling me one of them attacked her?" Fury still laced her voice, but I noticed that she'd lowered it.

Hades clenched his jaw. "What have you been up to, Demeter? And I swear by the Styx, if you say shopping—"

"You'll what?" She drew herself up to her full height, challenge sparking in her eyes. "This isn't your realm. I'm not one of your subjects. I don't answer to you."

Hades glowered at her, and my mom sighed.

"I went by a store. I purchased an item." She indicated the single shopping bag on the counter. "It counts. And then I followed a lead."

"A lead on what?"

Mom made her way back to the kitchen and sat down, fingers drumming on the wooden table. "Have you spoken to Orpheus lately?"

"Ugh, Orpheus again? No. Once was enough."

I rolled my eyes. Hades worked hard to make the Underworld a paradise for the souls. So when Orpheus showed up, determined to take his wife back to the living realm, he took it personally.

"Some of the Muses have gone missing."

Hades raised an eyebrow and sat down at the opposite seat. I leaned forward, listening intently. This is what Hades wanted me to hear. "Missing?"

"I don't suppose they've passed through the Underworld?"

Hades shook his head, leaning back in his seat. "Thanatos knows to bring all deities to me. Demigods too."

I ground my teeth together. For a second I toyed with the idea of searching the Underworld for the missing Muses. Thanatos would have a tough time explaining it if they were down there. I dismissed the idea. The Underworld was huge. I could search forever and never find them. Even if I succeeded, it wasn't like I could tell Hades where they were.

"Thalia contacted me. Some of her sisters are missing as well. And what do they all have in common?"

Hades sighed. "They're all Zeus'."

"Exactly. There's been an upswing in missing persons lately." Mom reached into her purse and pulled out a stack of missing person's flyers. I couldn't see much more than gold hair. "Demigods. I'm willing to wager they're Zeus' as well. Since his kids are the only ones that can kill him, it seems logical that he's taking them out before they can be used against him."

"The only ones he can kill are the demigods."

"Unless he can get the others to pull a Boreas. Give Zeus all of their power," my mom pointed out.

Hades mulled that over. "Have you warned Athena?"

"Of course."

"If Zeus is hunting down his kids, that's even more reason to stay close. You should have told me. I could have followed up on this, and she deserved to know. Did you even tell her what was going on?"

"There was no reason to." When Hades groaned, she continued. "Nothing's changed. We still know Zeus is after her—"

"You know the definition of insanity is doing the same thing over and over again and expecting different results, right? You need to tell her—"

"Hades, we're not even on speaking terms." She propped her elbow on the table and massaged her forehead with her hand. "I haven't seen her for more than five minutes in passing since the night she found out about Minthe." My mom gave Hades a sad smile. "You won, okay. She's completely turned against me. So why don't you two go live happily ever after? She'll be safer in the Underworld—"

"Demeter, we aren't together."

I winced, the pain of that statement shooting me straight through the heart.

Mom looked up. "Then where's she been spending all her time?"

"Apparently making out with random men in clubs."

Mom's mouth dropped open. "What?"

"Oh, yeah, and her new boyfriend. Did she tell you she quit school? She's not on speaking terms with her priestess, either. She spends the bulk of her time out drinking and charming random shopkeepers with Aphrodite. I'd tell you more, but remember those significant gaps in her memory I told you about?"

"That's not—" Mom stared at him, shocked speechless. "She wouldn't—"

"No. She wouldn't. Significant. Gaps. In. Memory." Hades enunciated each word. "Remember the last time we saw those?"

Mom paled.

Hades continued. "I went through every stray thought in her head while she was out." He shot an apologetic look in my direction. "I've seen every milestone with her new boyfriend, every dark corner of every nightclub, every lapse in judgment, but you know what I didn't see? That Reaper torturing her earlier this afternoon." He gave her a significant look. "I still don't have a clue what's been bugging her for the last few months. There's a wall there, and I can't break it."

"Zeus is using her to get to you." Mom's voice was strained.

Hades nodded. "Exactly."

"Aphrodite?"

"Do you think I would have left her here with Aphrodite if I wasn't completely certain Persephone had enough power to resist her charm?"

My mom considered that, and then nodded. "Someone else then."

"It's not likely anyone I've seen in her head. He's covering his tracks too well. She's figured it out before, and today I point-blank told her she's been charmed several times. She doesn't remember." He shot me an apologetic look. "She's not going to remember until we can break her free of the charm."

I frowned, pushing my necklace back and forth on the chain. What was he talking about? Mom spoke, breaking my concentration and washing whatever Hades had just said from my mind. "Your Reapers would know who she's been spending time with."

Hades shook his head. "I'll ask, but I think we need to assume this was all taking place on the rogue Reaper's shifts."

"Did you interrogate him?"

Hades sighed and indicated the pile of dust on the kitchen floor. "I got a bit carried away. It was before I knew—"

"I would have done the same thing. I can talk to Melissa."

"They haven't spoken in weeks. Our best bet's Aphrodite, but I'm not sure we should tip her off that we know anything."

"How about her boyfriend? He may know where else she's been spending her time. If you talk to him—"

Hades gave her a level look. "I just watched what feels like half the men in this city get to second base with my wife. Do you really want me in a room alone with one of them?"

Mom snorted. "Fine, I'll talk to him. It's probably a dead end anyway. If Zeus is putting out enough energy to maintain a hold on her, he's not going to leave witnesses."

Hades hesitated. "That's actually what I wanted to talk to you about. He's got to be using a ton of energy keeping her under. Persephone isn't weak. Thanks to Orpheus, she almost rivals you and me. If we found Zeus now, we might actually be able to end this thing fast."

Mom narrowed her eyes. "You want to use her as bait?"

"Hell no. She's completely vulnerable to him right now. If Zeus catches wind we're on to him, he could just have her swear fealty and give him all her power. Then he'd have access to the Underworld, and she'd be gone. I want to keep her in the Underworld until this is over. If we both know she's safe, we can put all our resources toward finding Zeus."

My mom's shoulders relaxed. "Good. I don't know how you're going to convince her to stay down there, but it's good we're on the same page." Her eyes widened as if a thought had just occurred to her. "What if she's already sworn?"

Hades shook his head. "I'd know."

Mom nodded, her lips pressed in a firm line, expression troubled. "I wonder what he's waiting for?"

I drew my knees to my chest. *Good question.*

Chapter XXI

"THANKS FOR LETTING me listen in," I told Hades as we made our way down to the Underworld. "Mom never would have told me what she was up to."

Hades nodded, looking distracted. "Do you remember anything else from that conversation?"

I gave him an odd look. "Weird question. Yeah. You two argued. A lot."

"Nothing else?"

I shook my head. "Why? What did I miss?"

He took my hand, and we teleported to the hall right outside my room. The hallway was huge and looked like it was carved from ebony. Not a single fingerprint marred the gleaming surface or silver trim. Hades changed that by planting his hand on the wall behind me and pulling me into a kiss. A surge of power rushed through me, and I pulled away, staring at Hades in surprise.

"What was that for?"

"You tell me." He studied my eyes for a moment, and then, as if I wasn't confused enough, kissed me again.

The door swung open. "Whoa!" Cassandra said. "Sorry to inter-rupt, but do you have any idea how late you are?"

Hades ignored her, but I pulled away. There was something . . . my mind flashed back to a half-remembered conversation between Thanatos and . . . someone.

"How much power would he give her if the situation turned dire?"

"Everything."

My breath caught. Who had said that? Who had said what? Damn it! It was slipping away!

What was slipping away? I blinked and tried to remember some-thing . . . important?

I looked up at Hades. His gaze was locked on mine.

"Almost," he murmured. "Cassandra, do you mind?"

"Yes, actually. She should have been here hours ago. You, too! Go get ready."

"She's right," I said quickly. "I need to get ready."

Cassandra gave him a triumphant smile, and I stepped into my room. "Bye, Hades."

He clenched his jaw. "You've got one hour."

"See you in two." Cassandra laughed and closed the door. She turned around to face me. "Hey!"

I'd already changed into my costume—a white, Greek-styled tunic. I added heavy gold jewelry crafted to look like leaves to the ensemble. I touched the crown and adjusted the necklace until it felt comfortable. I let a glamour settle over me instead of bothering with makeup.

"Take all the fun out of it, why don't you?" Cassandra muttered.

"Sorry, you said we were in a rush." My thoughts were racing. Hades hadn't caught on to Thanatos yet, but he had to be at least suspicious of the Reapers. I needed to push him further in that direction, but in the meantime I'd actually touched a Reaper today. Physically. It probably had something to do with Halloween, but if I could touch them, could I charm them? Normally souls were immune, but they weren't typically corporeal either. It was like all the rules had just changed. Maybe, just maybe, I wasn't completely helpless today.

I needed to hurry. "Say, Cassandra, could you do me a favor?"

"Might as well," she grumbled. "Not like we have anything else to do." She stood in front of the mirror and tapped her shoulder. Her costume appeared on her—some anime-style fairy thing.

"That looks great." I smiled at her as she yanked her black hair back and twisted it into an up-do.

"Save the flattery. What do you want?"

"I didn't want to bother Hades with this, but I was wondering if you could send me a few of the Reapers." I moved aside the sheer canopy and plopped down on the bed.

Cassandra's eyes narrowed. "Why? They should all be off now that you're here. It's Halloween, Persephone. It's like their biggest holiday."

It was still weird to me that Greek gods celebrated Halloween. I knew Hades wasn't *just* Hades. He was the god of the Underworld in every culture. He had thousands of names, but the Greek names stuck, so that was how I thought of him.

I plucked at my necklace. "I know it's typically their night off, but I wanted a few of them to keep an eye on my friends and family on the surface. If Zeus was going to do anything, he'd do it tonight, wouldn't he?"

Cassandra frowned. "Yeah, actually, that makes sense. Hang on; I'm sure there are a few of them wandering the palace."

She vanished. A few minutes later she popped up with three Reapers. The light fractured around them. I'd never seen the one in the middle before; he had hair so blond it was almost white. "This enough?"

I pretended to consider. "I don't know . . . "

"Hang on." She vanished again.

I smiled at the Reapers when she left. Their pupils widened as my charm took hold. "I want to try something."

"Okay," one of them said. The others nodded, grinning like idiots.

"Swear fealty."

They hit their knees.

IT TOOK ALMOST all night to find and charm the rest of the Reapers. It wasn't easy slipping away from Hades at the party, but bit by bit I managed to corner every single Reaper alone. Fealty was weird. I could feel each Reaper tethered to me. It felt strange, unnatural.

It was nearly midnight when Zachary found me in the banquet hall. "What have you done?"

"I fought back." I grabbed a glass of water from a passing soul and sat at the large table. "Don't worry. I'm not going to charm you."

"And what do you think Thanatos is going to do to you once he figures out what you've done?"

"What more could he possibly do to me?"

Zachary gave me a sympathetic look. "You have no idea." He knelt on one knee. "I swear—"

I held up my hand to stop him. "You don't have to! You helped me. I trust you. You don't need to swear to me to prove anything."

"Yes, I do. What do you think Thanatos would do to me if he realized I was the only unsworn Reaper?"

I grimaced. I hadn't thought of that. "I won't keep your power," I promised. "As soon as Hades finds out what's going on, as soon as he deals with Thanatos, I swear I'll release all of you."

Zachary shrugged. "The dead always serve someone. I'd rather serve you than Thanatos. You make me remember . . . "

I frowned. "Remember what?"

He gave me a sad smile. "Being alive. The first day we met, I hurt you. And I felt something. Guilt, shame, fear—nothing good, but all the same, it had been so long since I'd felt anything."

I titled my head and studied him. "How long have you been dead?"

He narrowed his eyes in thought . . . "Forever. In any case, I swear fealty and protection."

The power that flowed through me would have knocked me off my feet had I not been sitting down. I gasped, pushing it back to him before it could burn through me, but I could still feel it, tethered to me like a beacon of energy. Burning and bright. It wasn't just the power of a Reaper. It was the power of a god.

"There you are!" Hades rounded the corner. He glanced between Zachary and me. "Everything okay?"

"Yup," Zachary replied. He stood and walked toward the archway. "I heard about what happened. I wanted to apologize on behalf of the rest of us." He glanced at me. "You need me for anything, don't hesitate."

Hades looked at me. "Persephone?"

I nodded, wide eyed. "Yeah, everything's fine." I shot Zachary a questioning look. "Thank you."

Hades stared after Zachary for a minute then turned to me. "Would you like to dance?"

I smiled. "Sure."

We walked into the main hall. I took his hand and let him lead me into a waltz.

"I've really missed you." I let myself relax in his strong arms and laughed. "That sounds so weird, but I feel like I've been asleep for like . . . months."

Something flickered in his eyes. "Yeah, I get that."

I hadn't expected Zachary to have so much power. Between that, the added strain of the Reapers, and the extra power Hades kept giving me for some reason, my head was buzzing. My plan might work sooner than I thought. Hades was going to wonder why all the Reapers had sworn fealty to me. When I couldn't explain, he'd have to connect the dots to Thanatos.

I brightened. I hadn't considered that, so it didn't affect my promise. I couldn't ask Hades to channel the extra power away now, but he knew all the signs, conscious and otherwise.

I winced and put my hand to my forehead. *Gods, it hurt.*

"You okay?" Hades led me through a turn, his hand tight and warm around my waist. Souls danced around us, smiling and waving when they recognized us.

When I didn't respond, his fingers brushed my forehead. "Ah. Let's try something different. We should see how much you can take. The more power you can hold onto, the better."

"What? Why?"

"You won't remember even if I tell you. Just trust me. I'll keep an eye on you to make sure you don't—"

"Die?" Desperation colored my laugh.

Hades frowned, steering us away from the other souls. The music softened as we reached the edge of the ballroom. "You're here. I can make sure that doesn't happen."

"It hurts."

An emotion I couldn't identify flashed through his eyes. "Yes. But it's better than letting him use you as his puppet. I don't know what he's asked you to do, I can't risk—" He raked his fingers through his hair. "You still have no idea what I'm talking about do you?"

I gave him a blank stare. He'd said something, and . . . something about what he'd said seemed important, but for the life of me I couldn't grasp what he'd said. The words and meanings slipped out of my brain like . . .

What had I been thinking about again?

Hades clenched his jaw and flagged down one of the passing souls. A brunette with a far-away look in her eye, common to the souls that drank from the Lethe, offered Hades two champagne glasses from the tray she carried. Hades wasn't going to change his mind about channeling my powers unless I could explain why. Since my promise prevented me from doing anything to help Hades learn about Thanatos, I was out of luck.

Hades took a cautious sip of my drink. "Sparkling grape juice?" He offered, no doubt remembering the time I'd accidentally drunk ambrosia and made a fool of myself.

I took the glass, rethinking my plan. It would still work, just not the way I'd envisioned it. He'd know something was going on with the Reapers the second he channeled my power. If I didn't die before he got around to it . . .

I felt like the floor dropped away beneath me. I could really die. I could die before making things right with Mom, or with Melissa, or with Hades. "I love you."

Hades' eyes widened. He opened his mouth, but I rushed on before he could interrupt.

"I've tried not to. I know your life would be easier if I didn't. There are other guys. Guys with less baggage."

Hades raised an eyebrow and drained his drink.

"Guys who aren't using me as a placeholder for someone else—"

"What?" Hades set his glass down with a thunk.

"Hera." My voice was so low that, at first, I thought he hadn't heard me.

He looked confused. "You think I have feelings for Hera?"

I set my glass down and liquid sloshed over the top, covering my hand in sticky grape juice. "They all looked like her didn't they? Laurel, Minthe? Everyone else?"

"You don't."

His non-answer confirmed my suspicions. "I'm the exact opposite. You keep saying how much you love that I'm not like the rest of the gods, but in the next breath, you can't be with me because I'm not enough like them. I'm naive and young and not powerful enough—" I broke off with a frustrated sigh. "You want an equal, but you've only had that with one person, and it's not me."

"Where is this coming from?" Hades' voice was incredulous.

"Aphrodite—"

Hades groaned. "I should have known."

"You're the one who reads the self-help books," I protested. The whole theory came out in a rush. "It would make sense that Hera hurt you so much that you think you want the exact opposite of her. But really you're just sabotaging yourself because you're not over her, so you find fault in the very attributes that attracted you to me because they are so fundamentally unlike her."

Hades gave me an incredulous look. "I'm sure Aphrodite can twist the facts and rationalize her theory all day, but that's not what this is. That's not what we are. I'm not using you to replace her or self-sabotaging or any other nonsense Aphrodite can come up with."

"Maybe not consciously, but there are so many factors here. How could I ever be sure your feelings for me are real?"

"I love *you*. That's real. And if you can't . . . " He raised his hands in a helpless gesture. "I can't lie, Persephone. I'm not really sure what else I can do to convince you. Can't you just trust me?"

I raised my eyebrows. "Can you grant me the same courtesy?"

Hades drew back, his expression guarded. I could almost see him going over the conversation and linking my words with his. His mouth dropped open. "Oh."

"You tell me that I'm too young to know what I want, or that my feelings might not be real because you saved me, or you're in my head, or it makes my mom mad. You twist the facts and rationalize my feelings away. It's insulting and frustrating and condescending, but I love you anyway." I paused to let that sink in. "And I just . . . I need you to hear that tonight. I need you to know that I care about you, and I'd never knowingly do anything that would hurt you, and that no matter what I've done—" My voice broke. "No matter what happens, I just . . . I need you to know that I love you, and I'm sorry—"

Hades grabbed my shoulders. "Nothing he's made you do is your fault. You're not going to remember this now, but when we break his charm it should all come back. You aren't responsible for any of that. You don't need to apologize to me, and I don't think any less of you for it."

I stared at him. "What are you talking about?"

He kissed me on the forehead, and I winced as a pinprick of power surged through me. "I miss you too," he whispered.

It didn't occur to me to wonder why he'd said it in present tense. I allowed myself to relax in his embrace, laying my head on his chest, feeling the reassuring beat of his heart beneath my cheek as we swayed with the music.

We danced late into the night, neither wanting to let the other go. I think we both felt like we'd been granted a reprieve of some kind, and we didn't want to waste it. By some unspoken mutual agreement, we didn't mention Zeus the rest of the night.

We were both yawning when we finally left the ballroom. He stopped outside of my room, looking like he wanted to say something, but instead, leaned in and gave me a chaste kiss on the forehead.

I touched my hand to my forehead, smiling to myself as I closed the door.

Now to get to work.

Chapter XXII

I DIDN'T HAVE much time. My head was already hurting from the added strain of the Reapers' powers. I figured I had until morning before Hades either realized what was going on with all the Reapers or their power burned through me. Before that happened, there was something I needed to fix.

My mind replayed the conversation between Joel and me while I changed. What if he was right about humans having soul mates? If Orpheus and Eurydice were two parts of the same soul, that would completely change how I'd been trying to heal her.

I teleported to Tartarus and then stepped into Memorial Park. It was late. The moon was shining over the lake, casting an eerie light to the rest of the park. I swallowed hard. I was safer in the Underworld, but I needed to set something right. My life had spun so far out of control in these last few months that I didn't even recognize it as mine anymore. But it could be over in the morning. The very least I could do was make amends where I could.

My eyes closed as the park swirled around me. The breeze hardened and shifted, the scent changing from flowers and moonlight to gasoline and asphalt. Music filled the air, pulsing with a steady beat. I opened my eyes and found myself staring at the front door of the local restaurant and brewery, Terrapin.

I pushed open the door, gaze intent on the stage. Orpheus saw me through the crowd, and held up his index finger to indicate he'd be down in a minute. I put a hand to my forehead and took a deep breath. It was hard to focus, my vision kept swimming.

My gaze caught on a flash of red hair. Aphrodite. She was dancing with some guy in a way that bordered on pornographic. My jaw dropped when I recognized who her partner was.

"Joel."

I didn't think I'd said his name very loud, especially against the sound of Orpheus singing and the noise of the crowd pressed around me, but they both turned when I said his name.

"Persephone!" Aphrodite broke away from Joel. "What are you doing here?"

"Persephone?" Joel looked at Aphrodite with confusion. "Huh?"

"Right. I meant Kora." She laughed. "Don't remember that I called her that. In fact, just ignore us."

Joel's expression went blank, and he turned to stare at the stage.

I glared at Aphrodite. "You charmed him into dancing with you, didn't you? How could you, he's my—" I frowned, not sure what to call Joel. But no matter what he was, I was *not* okay with Aphrodite charming him.

"What? You can join in." She grinned at me. "This is fun. Loosen up. Grab a drink, we can—"

"Manipulating people like puppets isn't fun," I snapped. Aphrodite drew back, looking at me with surprise. "Let him go, now."

"You charm Joel all the time!"

"I'm not charming him into *doing* anything. I'm covering our tracks. It's different."

"And our teachers and all your friends at school, was that different too?"

"Yes! I'm not forcing people to do anything that matters, anything they care about." I was beginning to understand why my mom raised me as a human. She'd never had to explain things like this to me. I could identify the lines that shouldn't be crossed, maybe even better than she could.

"So why couldn't I charm the people in the mall into giving me free stuff?"

"Because that's stealing!"

"I'm a goddess. Accepting offerings is my right—"

"It's not an offering if it's not voluntary."

"Right." Aphrodite rolled her eyes and threw her hands in the air. "To think I went almost a whole day without getting a lecture from you on the moral high ground. Do you have any idea how annoying you can be? Look at me." She grabbed me by the shoulders and glanced over at Joel. "Grow a backbone some other night okay? For now, have fun. Go dance with Joel." Her grip on me tightened. She looked into my eyes, and everything got blurry for a moment. "You can come by my place later, and we can hash this all out. Sound good?"

She pushed me toward Joel. He looked up, as if surprised to see me.

"Stop," I muttered, disoriented. I put my hand to my forehead, wincing at the splitting pain.

"You okay?" Joel stared at me, concern flickering in his blue eyes.

"Just . . . " I pushed him away from me, trying to think. I'd come here for a reason. What . . .

Orpheus.

My eyes flew to the stage, but he wasn't there anymore. I rubbed my eyes and glanced around. I finally spotted him making his way toward us.

"Kora, you're not looking so good. Did you want me to take you home?" Joel put his hand on my shoulder, and I flinched away from his grasp.

"Don't." My head buzzed with the power from the Reapers. I touched the plant on my necklace. It felt warm, like it had too much power running through it to. What was I doing here? Memories of other nights in other bars came flickering back to me. I stared up at Joel, feeling sick. I heard Hades' voice whispering, *"I swear."*

Oh gods. What had I done?

"Kora?" Joel looked alarmed now. "I'm sorry about dancing with Aphrodite. I don't know why . . . It wasn't what it looked like."

A hand touched my shoulder. I spun around, heart in my throat, expecting to see Aphrodite.

Why was I scared of Aphrodite?

Orpheus removed his hand from my shoulder. "Sorry it took me so long to get away." His brow furrowed when he saw my face. "You okay?"

"Can you leave?" I asked, finally remembering my purpose. "I want to try something."

Hope flickered in Orpheus' eyes. "Absolutely."

He led me to the door, ignoring a stunned-looking Joel. I caught a glimpse of Aphrodite and quickened my pace.

A camera flashed, and for a second I was blinded by the brightness. Orpheus' jaw tightened. I gave him an apologetic smile as he pushed open the door. Poor guy couldn't get any privacy.

Chapter XXIII

ORPHEUS KEPT shooting me expectant looks while he drove, but I didn't say anything. I was too busy cradling my head in my hands and taking deep breaths. When the car stopped, I fumbled for the door handle without looking. It wasn't until gravel crunched beneath my feet and not asphalt that I looked up and realized we weren't at the hospital.

"Um . . . Orpheus?" I glanced around the abandoned parking lot then looked at him, alarms going off in my head. "This isn't the hospital."

He gave me an odd look. "I figured we'd teleport there. Visiting hours are over, but if you'd rather charm the nurses . . . " He opened the car door. "I know you're not a fan of charming people—"

That ship's sailed, I realized.

"But it would be a bit more convenient to have my car there."

I let out the breath I'd been holding. Orpheus took me being a goddess into stride almost too well. He knew how to act around gods since his mother was one, and he sometimes forgot I hadn't been raised with the idea that I was all powerful. I doubted Aphrodite would have thought twice about the unexpected detour to a creepy abandoned parking lot with a mere mortal, so he didn't expect me to. "Teleporting is fine."

"Can I ask what's changed? I mean, with my wife, why you think . . . " He trailed off, as if afraid of getting his hopes up.

"I heard this myth . . . " I leaned against the car and explained it as best I could. "I can't promise trying to heal her like this will work, but it's worth a shot."

Orpheus nodded. "I thought you'd given up on us." He let out his breath slowly. "Your mom kept telling me you hadn't, but when you stopped coming by the hospital . . . I thought you were avoiding me. That maybe there was nothing else that could be done." He looked at me, gaze full of apology. "And all this time, you were doing research, tracking down obscure myths . . . I . . . " His voice cracked. "Thank you. Even if this doesn't work, I owe you everything."

"Stop," I whispered. I couldn't look at him. When was the last time I'd been by the hospital? I couldn't remember. I took a shuddering breath, blinking back the tears that threatened to brim over. "I haven't done anything yet. You can thank me if I heal her."

Orpheus shook his head. He reached out to grab my arm then seemed to think better of it, touching the hood of the car beside my hand instead. "But you have done something. You spoke up for us in the Underworld. You bothered to try healing her, and when nothing worked, you kept looking for solutions. My whole life, I thought all the gods were as cold and distant as my—" He cleared his throat. "You're different. You care, and you're a good person."

I burst into tears. "Sorry," I gasped, holding up a hand as if I could ward off Orpheus' concern. I tried to dry my eyes, to compose myself, but the tears just kept falling. I didn't feel like a good person anymore. My skin crawled with half-remembered memories, and my stomach twisted with guilt. "This myth, I didn't track it down with research. It was complete coincidence. Before tonight, I can't think of the last time I thought of you or her at all. I'm not good. I'm keeping something from the one person—" I broke off with a sob. "I'm going to lose everyone. I miss my mom and Melissa, and I don't know what I'm doing or why or who I've become, but it's like my life is spinning out of control, and all I can do is watch."

Orpheus hesitated then pulled me into a stiff embrace. I sniffled and tried to catch my breath. I hated this. I felt like all I'd done lately was worry and cry. I needed to act. That's what tonight was supposed to be about, and instead I was sobbing into Orpheus' shoulder.

"Oh gods." I pulled away from him and scrubbed at my eyes with the back of my hand. "I'm sorry. That was—"

"It's fine," Orpheus reassured me.

"No, it's not. You're in a hurry to see your wife, and I'm—"

"I'm actually stalling," he admitted with a shrug. "Got more than I bargained for, but yeah. Stalling."

"Why?" My voice was still quivery.

He gave me a look, like he was trying to gauge how close I was to crying again. "I'm scared. What if it doesn't work? I mean . . . Should I . . . The Underworld didn't seem so bad, and it has to be better than this limbo." He raised his hands in frustration, freezing when I patted him on the shoulder.

"We can cross that bridge when we get to it. But I really think this has a chance of working."

"And what if it does?" His shoulders slumped as though he were exhausted. "All I had to do was not look at her. I couldn't do that, and she's been stuck, for months! She's going to hate me."

"No she won't! You went through hell and back to save her. You've been by her side every day. She's so lucky to have you!" I grabbed his arm and he jerked back.

"Sorry," I muttered, stung.

He sighed. "It's not that. I appreciate what you said. Really, it makes me feel a lot better. I hope she sees things the way you do." He hesitated. "My mother—erm, Calliope, taught me how to behave around gods at an early age. There are rules and mannerisms and things that protect me from ending up dead or a puppet."

"You think I'm dangerous." My hands dropped to my side, and I turned away from him trying not to show how hurt I was. Orpheus had been my idol. When I met him, I'd been giddy and exited and stupid, and I'd been so proud that I actually knew him. I'd never imagined he viewed me as some kind of monster that might attack him at the slightest provocation.

"You're different. I don't worry that I'll say the wrong thing, offend you and end up a constellation." He gestured up at the stars. "But you're still dangerous. Hades is a loose cannon, and your mom is scary as hell. It's just best to avoid any misunderstandings. I don't know how to act around you. How to treat you."

"Treat me like I'm a person."

He gave me a level look. "But you're not."

I closed my eyes. "I don't know how to be anything else. I tried being a ruler like Hades, and I put the whole realm in—" I broke off, unable to go into specifics. I shook my head and continued. "I tried Aphrodite's way, and it's just not me. I can't disconnect like my mom does. But I suck at being human too. I drove Melissa away, and I just don't connect with other people. I just . . . I'm not cut out for this. I feel like I don't belong anywhere."

Orpheus gave me a wry grin. "I get that." When I gave him a doubt-ful look he laughed. "I'm a demigod. I know more about trying to strad-dle that line between the human and the divine than you ever will."

I flushed and slid my necklace back and forth on its chain. I'd never considered that either. I just figured my struggle between the realms was unique. There was an entire species that shared my confusion. They actually had it worse than anyone. I was a goddess. Like it or not, I firmly belonged to that world. Demigods didn't really fit in anywhere . . .

No, I could think of some who had it worse. Normal humans who knew about the gods. How many books had I read, or movies had I watched, where some normal teenager discovered they were special or had some ability that set them apart? Mortals craved that distinction, that power. They dreamed and wished and wondered. How much would it suck to realize all those things you'd dreamed of and hoped for were real, just not for you?

"I'm no expert, but if you tell me what's going on, I can offer some perspective," Orpheus offered.

I shot him a look. "You really are stalling."

He shrugged. "You sound like you could really use a friend right now. Least I can do."

I didn't tell him everything. I couldn't. But I did tell him what had happened between my mom and me and about my fallout with Melissa. I couldn't stay still, so I walked while I talked, making odd orbits around Orpheus and the car.

He blinked when I finished, and I laughed. "Didn't know what you were signing up for, huh?"

"I figured there would be a lot, you're a goddess. I forgot that you were a teenage girl, though."

"Oh, thanks." I grinned to let him know I wasn't really offended.

He looked up at the sky and took a deep breath. "I can't give you a lot of advice about your mom. I do believe she had your best interests at heart, however misguided."

"I don't. I think she likes to keep me in the dark so I'm easier to control."

Orpheus' eyebrows disappeared into his bangs. "You think she's trying to control you? *Your* mother?"

I clenched my jaw. "Why is that so unbelievable? She would make me promise things before I knew I couldn't lie. She didn't tell me about Zeus, she—"

"I've already heard your list. And like I said, misguided, but she doesn't want you under her thumb."

"How do you know?"

"She gave you spring."

I must have looked dubious because he continued.

"Persephone, the fact that she risked her very existence by giving you enough power to come to life says a lot about how she feels about you. But she didn't just give you enough to get by, like most gods do. Like Zeus always does. She gave you the best of herself. Spring is all about rebirth and new life." He caught my eye and made sure I was looking at him before he continued. "You've got more going for you than growing flowers."

"I can't even grow food."

"By rights you should be able to, but she kept that. She gave you all the power associated with that new life and kept all the responsibilities. She provided you priestesses and actually raised you instead of just throwing you into the world. She's continued to give you support when I told everyone about you and you gained your own following. That's unheard of among your kind. She doesn't want to overpower you. She's given you everything you need to become her equal."

I blinked. I hadn't considered that. "That's . . . nice. Wonderful even. I'm not denying I'm lucky. But I want to be able to trust her. I can't risk being clueless anymore. Too many people have been hurt."

"I agree. You should talk to her. But do everyone a favor, Persephone. Once you two work out some kind of agreement, move on. You're not doing anyone, least of all yourself, any favors by hanging on to this."

I leaned against the car. "You're not bad at this whole advice thing."

"Oh, I've got more. You need to make a decision on whether or not you want Melissa to be your priestess or your friend."

"Friend," I replied without hesitation. "I never asked her to be my priestess."

"Maybe that's the problem. No one did."

I nodded. From what I'd heard, all my mom's priestesses had been asked, or had asked to join her. Melissa had been born into it. "Her mom isn't just going to let her—"

"It's not up to her mom who you choose to be your head priestess. It's up to you."

I swallowed hard. "But she's going to move away." I winced at how whiny I sounded. "I mean . . . I need her. She's my best friend, without her to talk to . . . "

Orpheus laid a hand on my shoulder. "It's okay to tell her that. She's your friend. Of course you'll miss her. But you can't let her stay because of an obligation to you and still call yourself her friend. She can be your priestess, and you can keep her around, or you can let her go and keep her friendship. It's not like you'll never see her. You can always teleport."

That was true. "But why can't she just be both? Mom is friends with her priestesses. And I'm not just saying that," I said responding to

Orpheus' incredulous look. "I've seen them together. They're friends."

"Well . . . " Orpheus sounded doubtful. Gods! First Hades and now Orpheus. Did my mom really come off that cold? "It's possible, but they had a choice. I mean, I consider myself your friend, and I follow you."

I flushed. It was still strange to me that Orpheus had created a cult-like following in my name after his trip to the Underworld to re-trieve his wife's soul. I'd practically worshiped him for years before I knew what I was. He was still my favorite singer.

"Fine. I'll talk to Minthe," I acquiesced. I leaned against the car.

"So . . . That boy? Do you like him or . . . "

"He's a friend, mostly. I don't know." I pushed my hair out of my face with a sigh. "I keep thinking about breaking things off with him, because I'm not really interested in anyone but Hades. But when I actually see him, my resolve just vanishes. He's nice. He's really nice, and he's actually interested in me without all these crazy hang-ups—"

Orpheus held up his hands. "I don't want to know all of that. Sorry, I forgot what a loaded question 'do you like someone' is to teenagers. I just mean, do you care about him at all? Would it upset you if he got hurt?"

I gave Orpheus an incredulous look. "Of course I'd be upset if he got hurt. I'm not in love with him, but he is still my friend."

"Then you need to be more careful. Because however you feel, he's clearly not just interested in your friendship. And had anything hap-pened between you two, and your mother or Hades learned that your judgment had in any way been compromised, what do you think would happen to that boy?"

I paled. "Oh."

"Oh is right. She would have killed him. And after he suffered whatever horrifically painful death your mother inflicted on him, he would have to deal with Hades."

"I didn't even think about that." I fiddled with my necklace and bit my lip.

"You need to. And even without them in the picture, you're not the first god to use a human as a distraction from complicated divine prob-lems or relationships, but you're new at this, so I'm going to tell you how it generally ends."

I looked up at him.

"Badly. Very, very badly. The humans suffer for it, Persephone. They're never the same. If you care about him at all, I'd suggest you follow through on breaking things off now, rather than later."

"You're right." I realized. I'd been so stupid leading Joel on like that. What had gotten into me?

The horizon lit up with lightning. "That's odd." Orpheus shielded his eyes at the sudden brightness . . . "No rain or anything."

"The weather's always so weird here," I complained. "This one time I was driving on Epps Bridge Parkway, and it was perfectly sunny. But then when I turned onto Atlanta Highway it was pouring, and later when I turned on to Alps Road, it was sunny again—"

"Persephone?"

"I mean you could see the line where there was rain over here, but not over—"

"Persephone watch out!" Orpheus crashed into me, throwing me off balance and knocking me to the asphalt.

The air whooshed out of my lungs. There was a cracking sound, and the pungent smell of burnt ozone in the air. The ground shuddered. Orpheus pulled me to my feet, and we stared in disbelief at the cracked asphalt where we'd been standing just a moment before.

The hair on my arms stood straight up. Lightning lanced down from the sky. I threw up a shield. It shattered with the next strike. Orpheus and I sprang away from each other as lightning struck between us. I shrieked as successive strikes drove us to opposite ends of the parking lot.

"Teleport!" Orpheus shouted. "Get out of here!"

I wasn't going anywhere without Orpheus. Yet another human I'd put in danger just by association. Orpheus was right; I needed to be more careful.

"Enough!" I shouted when a dozen bolts rained from the sky. "That's enough! Stop hurting people to get to me. I'm right here! What the hell are you waiting for? You want me so bad, either come and get me, or kill the light show and move on!"

A bolt strong enough to rip the lot in half answered me. I stared at the gaping chasm of stone, eerily reminded of the day Hades had rescued me. But Zeus couldn't dig or tear deep enough to get to the Underworld.

I skirted around the gap, running to Orpheus. If Zeus wanted to hit either of us, he would have. My reflexes were good, but even I wasn't faster than lightning.

A bolt hit just behind my heel, and I stumbled forward, losing a layer of skin to the rough stone of the parking lot.

I regained my balance, saw Orpheus rush toward me, and then the sky opened up above him. Blinding light shot down from the heavens. I dashed forward, throwing myself in front of Orpheus.

Chapter XXIV

THE LIGHTNING stopped a hair's breadth away from my forehead. I stared into the white-hot molten light cross-eyed and let out a nervous laugh.

"What the hell?" Orpheus murmured behind me.

I threw up a shield and felt behind me for Orpheus' hand. The second I made contact I teleported to the hospital.

"What *was* that?" Orpheus demanded. "You got in front of me." He grabbed my arm as I made my way down the hall. "Persephone, what was that? Why would you do that?"

"I can't die. You can."

"Still!" He shook his head. "It stopped! It just stopped." He looked around as if noticing his location for the first time. He searched the room until he found Eurydice, and emotion flickered in his eyes. Fear? Hope? Both?

"If this works, you two need to leave Athens." I crossed the small room and stood by the bed.

"Wait, what?" Orpheus followed on my heels. "Persephone, I appreciate the effort, but shouldn't we be getting you down to the Underworld, or telling your mom what happened? That Zeus attacked you! We should—"

"I'm not telling them anything, and neither are you."

A nurse in pink scrubs pushed open the door, startling with surprise when she saw us.

"You can't be in here," she said. "Visiting hours are from—Oh, it's you," she said when she saw Orpheus. She gave him a sympathetic smile. "I'll just go finish my rounds."

"What do you mean you're not telling them what happened?" Orpheus demanded when the nurse left the room. "And what do you mean get out of Athens? What's going on? What did I miss back there?"

"He wasn't after me. He was after you." I yanked the heavy wooden chair away from the window and shoved it next to the bed, motioning for Orpheus to sit on the mauve cushion. "Hitting you would send a message, the same threatening, intimidating messages he's been sending all along. So I'm getting you out of here before he can try again."

"And *why* aren't we telling your mom or Hades what happened?" Orpheus lowered himself into the seat and took his wife's hand.

"Because I'm done playing his games. I'm not going to let the only two gods who actually have a chance against Zeus—"

"Three, you've forgotten Poseidon."

I dismissed that with a snort. "Two gods who actually have a chance against Zeus waste any more resources protecting me. He's not going to hurt me, because if he goes too far, they'll take me to the Underworld, and Mom, at least, will be able to devote all her resources to finding him."

"If he's just using you to distract them, wouldn't it just be better to hold you hostage so they won't interfere?"

"No way. Mom and Hades would never stop looking until they found me. He'd have to be constantly on his guard against them. It's not like I'd stay willingly, so he'd have to watch me to make sure I didn't run off. This is much more efficient. He throws a few lightning bolts, kills a few bystanders, and Mom and Hades circle the wagons, keeping me safe when they should be throwing everything they have at him."

Orpheus nodded, considering my theory. "And if you're wrong?"

"What else could it be? If he wanted to hurt me, nothing is really stopping him. If he wanted to take me, he could."

"What if he's herding you?"

"Herding me?" I touched the glass pomegranate on my necklace.

"What if he needs you for something, but you haven't gotten where he needs you to be yet?"

"What could he possibly need from me?" I asked, frustrated.

Orpheus shrugged. "Think about it. You're becoming more and more isolated. You're on the outs with Hades, your mother, and Melissa. You've even quit school! You think I'm his next target so he can send a message. What if I'm just his next target to keep you alone? Who's left that you spend time with?"

"Joel and Aphrodite."

"I'd bet money that Joel is next on his list, and you already know he wants Aphrodite. So you two are constantly keeping each other company? The two goddesses he needs for . . . Whatever it is that he needs you for?" He gave me a significant look. "I'll go wherever you want me to, but what if you're wrong?"

I met his gaze. "Then I'm wrong. Do you want me to try this, or not?"

Orpheus' gold eyes turned on his wife then back to me. He seemed conflicted. "Promise me you'll be careful."

I gave him a level look and he sighed, his gaze going back to his wife. Her frizzy hair was damp with sweat. Freckles stood out against her sallow skin. She'd lost weight despite the efforts of my mother and me.

Orpheus laid a golden hand on her cheek and leaned down to kiss her forehead. The first time I'd met Orpheus and Eurydice I'd wondered how a guy that looked like him, the ultimate golden boy, had ended up with someone so plain. Then she'd smiled and I'd gotten it. She had a beautiful soul. It sounded cheesy, but that didn't make it any less true.

Emotion glittered in Orpheus' metallic gold eyes as he searched her face, seeming to look for some sign of that inner light, some sign of life in his wife, but there wasn't one. She looked like an empty shell.

"Bring her back to me." His eyes met mine, and I swallowed hard. There was so much hope, so much desperation in his gaze. What if I couldn't do this? What if I made it worse?

My hand gripped his, and with power borrowed from the Reapers, I touched his soul. He shuddered, knuckles turning white around my hand. I winced, hoping my fingers wouldn't break.

This was my last chance. What I was trying was dangerous for him and Eurydice. If this didn't work, I'd be sending Eurydice's soul to the Underworld. And if I messed up too badly, Orpheus would be joining her.

But what else could I do? I had to get Orpheus away from Athens, away from me, before Zeus came after him again. Of course Zeus could come after them anywhere, but why make it easy?

If any couple I'd ever met could be described as soul mates, it was Orpheus and Eurydice. I fumbled for Eurydice's limp hand. I could sense her soul buried further within her and difficult to reach. It sat loosely within her body, unbound and unattached. Thanks to my power borrowed from the Reapers, when I touched her soul it practically leapt into my hands. I winced. She really was more dead than alive.

Through daily healing sessions, Mom kept her off life support and all but the most basic tubes or wires the hospital might otherwise require. But I'd heard her say it had been getting harder every day. I just hoped Eurydice wasn't too far gone.

Orpheus and Eurydice's souls poured into my hands. They felt the way candlelight looked. Tenuous and flickering, but aglow with energy that, left uncontrolled, could destroy everything in its path. They resonated with one another. Two parts of a whole, reunited as one.

Joel had been right, or rather, it seemed his long lost myth had been accurate. My mother hadn't been sure of the origins of that myth. She had little to do with the creation of humans. Her energy had been focused on sustaining them. The souls had been Zeus' department.

I used Orpheus' soul as a guide to mold Eurydice's renewed soul back into her body. His soul flowed effortlessly into her to fill in the missing connections. The souls merged easily, the trouble was getting them to split apart. I pulled more power from the Reapers, shoving each soul back to its rightful place.

The power from the Reapers came easily, but the power from Zachary had a different flavor to it. It was stronger. Wild. It tore through me. When it left my body for Eurydice's, I felt like I had an open wound. I gasped, winded.

I won't be doing that again. The Reapers' power was filtered through Thanatos; Zachary was something different altogether. I set my mouth in a grim line. I was going to have to ask him about that later.

I let their hands go. Orpheus looked at me then grabbed at his wife's hands, clutching them to him as though she was the only thing tethering him to the world. He leaned close to her, nose brushing against her cheek. "Please," he whispered into her ear.

Eurydice gasped, eyes fluttering open.

Orpheus gave a wordless cry, gathering her to him in a tight embrace. My knees gave way under me. Orpheus' hand shot out, and he guided me to a chair without letting go of her. "Are you okay?"

"I'll manage," I replied. I really shouldn't have drawn on so much power from the Reapers. My vision was spinning. "We've got to get you two out of here."

"What happened?" Eurydice asked without taking her eyes off Orpheus. "Where am I?"

"Oh my god! She's awake!" A nurse exclaimed from the doorway.

"We'll go," Orpheus assured me.

I nodded and stumbled past the surprised nurse.

Chapter XXV

I MADE IT TO the entrance of the hospital before I realized I didn't have a way to get home. Teleporting was out. I couldn't even charm anyone for a ride. It was all I could do to stay shielded. My powers had been completely depleted.

The pavement slid sideways and met me with a painful smack. I struggled to my knees and crawled out of the doorway, leaning against the stucco wall for support. My skin felt funny, disconnected. It was like my foot was asleep, but it was my whole body prickling painfully every time I moved. I'd used way too much power. Exhaustion forced my eyes shut. I focused on making my ragged breathing even.

It was okay. Orpheus was going to leave. He had his wife back. I'd made something right. For once, I hadn't screwed up.

A startled swear jolted me from my reverie. A black-robed figure prodded me with a foot, and a familiar oval face filled my vision.

"Zachary?" My eyes struggled to focus on his blurry form. "What are you doing here?"

"You drew on my power. Warn me next time you do that, okay?" He looked as haggard as I felt.

"I didn't realize—" I began, but he cut me off with a wave.

"We need to get you out of here. You're a sitting duck." He leaned forward as if he was going to offer me a hand and stopped short when I flinched away.

"Right, sorry. I'll go get Hades."

"No."

Zachary swore again. "I wasn't asking permission. I need to get you help." When I shook my head, he knelt beside me. "Do you have your phone?"

I managed a weak nod and pulled it from my pocket. My fingers slid across the screen, dialing on autopilot. I wasn't fully aware of what number I was dialing, but I wasn't surprised at who answered.

"Melissa?" My voice was so soft, I was afraid she couldn't hear me. "I need you." She asked me something, but I couldn't focus. My eyes were so heavy. I was so tired. I felt hollow, empty.

A hand on my shoulder startled me into consciousness. My eyes snapped open. How long had they been closed? I followed the arm to its owner and blinked with confusion when I recognized Melissa's arm sticking out of Zachary's body. He gave her an irritated look and moved out of her way. She, of course, didn't notice him.

"Persephone? Is that you?" Her eyes darted to the security guard at the entrance. She touched my shoulder again, blindly groping down my arm. She swore, pulling on my arm. "I can't see you. Can you drop the shield?"

I was still shielded? I blinked and lowered the shield. Melissa fell backward in surprise. "It is you, good! What happened? You look awful."

"How did you find me?"

Melissa pointed at the automatic door opening and closing of its own accord. "You sat on the sensor."

"Oh."

"Come on, get in the car."

I braced myself against the wall, trying to stand. "I healed Eurydice. But I guess I overextended myself a bit."

Melissa wrapped her arm around me and helped me to her car. Zachary followed behind us like a shadow. "That's not how it works. You either have the power or you don't. You shouldn't be able to burn more than you have."

"I had to borrow some power from the Reapers."

"Some?" Zachary barked the word. "That was more than *some.*"

Melissa pulled me away from her to look at my face. "You did what?"

I cleared my throat. "I channeled—"

"Are you stupid? You can't even use your own powers without endangering yourself, and you channeled someone else's? What? Is immortality like a challenge to you? Are you trying to find a way to die?"

Was I? I'd jumped in front of Orpheus when the lightning struck. I'd challenged Zeus, and then I'd channeled the power of the Reapers. I furrowed my brow in thought. "I don't . . . think so."

Zachary muttered something uncomplimentary under his breath, and I shot him a look. He rolled his eyes and vanished.

"Is that alcohol I smell?" Melissa demanded. "And smoke? Gods, Persephone? What have you been doing?"

I tugged on the hemline of my skirt to make it longer. "It's not smoke. It's burnt ozone."

"Burnt ozone? Wait, like lightning?"

"What are you doing here?" I asked, touching my forehead.

"You called," Melissa reminded me, sounding worried. "Don't you remember?"

"Right." I shook my head, trying to clear it.

"Though I'm not sure why you called me instead of Aphrodite," Melissa prattled on, not even trying to hide the irritation from her voice. "Afraid to interrupt her beauty sleep?"

I blinked, too drained to deal with her anger. "I shouldn't have called you. You can't be here. It's not safe to be around me. Sorry, I'll just call Aphrodi—"

"Oh, get in," Melissa snapped, throwing the door open. "I can't die remember? You took care of that."

"There are worse things than death."

Melissa gave me a look. "What's happened to you? You're different."

"Of course I'm different, Melissa!" I was too tired to bother with filtering and way too exhausted to listen to Melissa snark the whole way home. "My life has gone nuts. This is me dealing. And maybe I'm dealing with everything badly, but you don't get to criticize. You walked away. I don't get that luxury."

Melissa rolled her eyes and pushed me into the car, slamming the door behind me. "I can criticize all I want. You called me, remember? If you want nice Melissa, try calling at some time other than three in the morning smack dab in the middle of midterm week. We can't all charm our teachers into getting good grades."

I clenched my jaw. Was she serious?

Melissa narrowed her eyes. "Hey, you're welcome for coming to get you. I'm not supposed to be at your beck and call anymore, remember? You promised me space. Calling me sounding half-dead and giving me half answers isn't space. It's just annoying." She dropped into her seat with a huff and started the car. "Seriously? Burnt ozone? 'I'm dangerous.' That's all the explanation I get? Should I be worried? Are we in danger? Should I be driving faster? I mean come on, Persephone. I'm too tired to—"

"You're tired!" I exploded. "Oh gods, how inconsiderate of me to wake you up during midterm week. You must be so damned stressed!"

"Oh that's right, anything less than a goddess-sized problem is just completely irrelevant."

"Oh, would you get over it! I'm a goddess. You're not. It sucks. If I could trade places with you I would, if only to shut you up!"

Melissa closed her mouth with a click and pulled out of the parking lot.

I ignored her silence. It was *so* Melissa to shut down the minute someone else had a point. "I've *never* rubbed in my powers, I've *never* treated you like some sort of subspecies, and I've *never ever* acted like your problems didn't matter just because mine are bigger. And yeah, they are bigger. Are you seriously jealous of that? Do you know what I would give to be worrying about midterms right now instead of trying to figure out who's going to die next? My whole *life* you've acted like my friend, but I think you just liked having something over me that I didn't know, because the minute I learned my secret, you stopped acting like a friend and started acting like every other stupid girl at school."

Melissa opened her mouth, but I plowed ahead, talking over whatever she was about to say. "Got any more snarky complaints you want to throw my way? That's the normal you wanted? That's what you wanted so badly? Well congratulations, Melissa, if being normal equals being a bitch, you've arrived. I always thought you were above that, but whatever."

"You left the school! Those are the only people left to hang out with. And yeah, they're snarky, but at least they aren't—"

"What? Better than you? So it's only friendship if you get to feel superior? You told me to leave the school with *her!*"

"You weren't supposed to go! You weren't actually supposed to pick her over me. Gods! I tell you your new perfect friend makes me feel insecure, and I'd appreciate it if I didn't have to hang out with her anymore, and you cut off all contact? What is that?"

I gaped at her. Stupid humans and their stupid ability to lie. I'd sell my soul to be able to break my word just once, and she was using her ability for the same kind of double speak my mom used? "I'm not supposed to have to read between the lines with you. I'm not supposed to have to watch every word I say so I'm not rubbing something in. I'm not supposed to have to downplay the problems in my life so you don't feel stupid stressing over your problems. We're supposed to be friends. You're supposed to be there for me when things get crazy. You have no idea what I've been through-"

"Because you won't tell me! You never kept anything from me before you found out you were a goddess, and now all of a sudden you're hiding things from me and spending all your time with Aphrodite and

Hades. I get that I'm just a human, but I can still listen."

"I don't want to keep anything from you. Believe me, if I could, I'd tell you everything. I hate keeping secrets."

Melissa stiffened. "If you could? Why can't you?"

I opened my mouth then closed it again. I sighed and slid my necklace back and forth on its chain. "Nothing, never mind, I just—"

"What did you mean by 'can't'? Tell me."

We stopped at a red light, and she turned to face me. I opened my mouth again, but the words caught in my throat. I shook my head, feeling suddenly sick.

"You've been bound." Melissa's eyes widened. "I know that look. I've had that look. Your mom bound me so I couldn't tell you what you were when we were kids. Remember? Holy shit! Who did this to you? Hades respects you too much, and your mom wouldn't dare. She'd have to answer to him."

I couldn't say anything.

"I know," she said. "I know exactly what that's like. I'm sorry. I'm so sorry. We'll find a way around it. I promise."

"Where are we going?" I asked, looking out the window and noticing where we were for the first time. We were passing the strip mall on Alps Road. We should have been on the highway going the opposite direction, not in the center of Athens.

"The park. That's where the entrance to the Underworld is, right? I'm getting you to Hades, and I'm going to tell him you've been bound. Who knows what damage you did channeling the Reapers. Speaking of which, how did that work exactly?"

"I don't need to go to the Underworld." I couldn't agree to go back. I couldn't do anything that would help Hades figure out Thanatos' betrayal without breaking my promise. "Just take me home."

Melissa reached over and flipped down my visor. "Have you seen yourself?" She indicated the mirror. "You need help."

"No, I need sleep. Hades will just give me more power to offset the deficit. Whatever he gives me will come back to bite me when I recover my powers tomorrow. I already have more than I can handle."

"So tomorrow he can take it away."

He would see what happened tonight. I wasn't strong enough to shield my thoughts. He'd see the lightning storm, the Reapers—everything.

"Please, Melissa. I can't see him right now. Please just take me home. Or better yet, your house. I need to talk to your mom anyway."

Melissa sighed and turned the car around. "Why do you need to talk to my mom?"

"You two are going to Iowa State this weekend to take a tour of the campus."

Melissa gave me a wry smile. "I don't think she's going to go for that. She wants me to stick around here and be your priestess, remember?"

"It's not your mom's place to decide who my priestesses are. Orpheus said something to me, about how I need to choose between being your goddess or your friend. But he was wrong. I can't be either. Not right now, it's too dangerous. You need to go. Go there for the weekend, stay away from me the rest of the year, and then go enjoy four years of normal. After that"—I avoided Melissa's eyes "do whatever you want. There will always be a place for you here when all this craziness dies down. But you don't have to do anything you don't want to do."

Melissa shook her head. "I'm not leaving you. Besides, normal is overrated. If I don't have you to talk to about everything that's happened, it's like it never even happened, you know? I've missed you."

I smiled at her. "I missed you, too. But I *really* need you to go for now. Just a few days, please? I couldn't take it if something happened to you. It would take such a load off my mind if I knew you were safe."

"What's to stop Zeus from following us?"

"Nothing." I waved my hands in frustration. "But what's to stop him from taking you right here, either? It's not like I can protect you. We might as well not make it easy for him. Why would he ever think to look for you in Iowa? Besides . . . " I gulped before adding, "I think he likes it when I watch. If I'm not around to see you get hurt . . . " I thought of Melissa's words from earlier. "It's kind of like it didn't happen."

Melissa shrugged. My phone buzzed. I glanced down and saw Joel was calling and clicked ignore.

Melissa's eyes flickered over my phone. "Are you still seeing him?"

"I'm breaking things off with him tomorrow." I shrugged. "Well, maybe."

"Maybe?"

"I have every intention of breaking up with him, but once I see him, I'm not sure I'll follow through."

"Are you in love with him?"

"No, it's not that . . . " I trailed off, uncertain how to explain. "When I'm not with him, I know it's not working. I just don't like him like that. He's a great friend, and he's nice, but he's not Hades. I know

I'm putting him in danger and taking advantage of him and all that horrible stuff. So I tell myself, that's it. We're breaking up. And then, I see him. I look in his eyes, and all of that is gone." I smiled. "For a few minutes, I forget everything. All my responsibilities, all my problems. For a few minutes I can just be normal. And so I let him kiss me, and we go out, and we do . . . stuff—"

"Stuff?" Melissa's voice was incredulous.

"Not that." I shot her a look. "Just making out stuff."

"How much making out stuff? Like what base?"

"It doesn't matter." I crossed my arms and hunched down in my seat. "It makes me feel sick. Not right away, when I leave. Because he's not Hades, and that feels wrong."

"But is it more than you did with Hades?"

I shot her a murderous look, and she raised her hands in surrender. "Fine, but I want details later. So why aren't you with Hades? Are you still freaked out about him and my mom?"

I shook my head. "It's this thing." I searched for a way to explain.

"The thing you can't talk about?"

"Exactly." I clutched my necklace. "Once he finds out, he's going to hate me."

"Not possible." Melissa sounded so certain that I found myself believing her.

"You don't know what it is."

"It doesn't matter. He couldn't hate you. Have you *seen* the way he looks at you? It's like you're some long-lost part of him come whole. He couldn't hate you if he tried. No matter what you've done."

Hope fluttered in my chest, and I swallowed hard. "I really hope you're right."

IT WAS LATE WHEN I got home, but I felt better knowing Melissa and Minthe were leaving after school today. I waved at the Reapers I'd left stationed around my house and fumbled with my keys, cursing as my phone rang.

"Hello?" I asked, shoving the key into the lock.

"Kora? I've been trying to get a hold of you all night!" Joel exclaimed. "Look, about what happened with Aphrodite—"

"I don't care." I dropped my purse in the entryway and walked to the staircase.

"Just let me apologize—"

"Joel, I don't think you understand. I don't care. And I should." I took a breath and leaned against the banister. "Look, this isn't fair to you. I think you like me more than I like you, and I don't want to lead you on."

"You're breaking up with me?" Joel sounded incredulous. "Look, the thing with Aphrodite, it was nothing——"

"It's nothing to do with her." I paused. "Though I think you should stay away from her. She's dangerous, Joel."

Now why had I said that? My brow furrowed, but the thought that had made me say that slipped away from me like it was never there.

"See, you do care." Joel sounded hopeful. "Look, it's late. Maybe we should talk tomorrow, in person."

"Joel, it's not going to change anything." I didn't want to see him in person. I didn't trust myself not to change my mind.

"Well, if you've actually been leading me on, you kind of owe me, right?"

I frowned. He had a point.

"Fine. Tomorrow, usual time."

"I'll bring smoothies."

I hung up and rounded the corner into the kitchen. Mom sat at the kitchen table, thumbing through a back issue of *Better Homes and Gardens*. "Busy night," she commented without looking up. "Shouldn't you be in the Underworld?"

I grabbed a bottle of water out of the fridge and twisted the top off. "Do you ever sleep?"

"The need diminishes when you come into your powers."

"Hades sleeps."

Mom raised her eyebrows at me. "Does he now?"

I flushed. "That came out wrong. I didn't mean . . . I mean, not . . . you know, with me. I just know he sleeps. I . . . um, I healed Eurydice."

She gave me a wry look. "Sure, we can change the topic. For *now*. I heard about Eurydice. That's quite an achievement. What ended up working?"

I explained as best I could, and then, barely pausing for breath, I explained about Melissa's admission to Iowa State.

Mom nodded. "That was a sound decision. Your priestesses should not be unwilling. I only wish you would have told me what was going on. I could have explained to Minthe. Do you have any ideas for a replacement?"

I hesitated. "I was thinking about Orpheus. He already accidentally started that cult. Think of what he could do on purpose? And his new CD, *The Eleusinian Mysteries*, it's all about us. Plus, he's a demigod. He gets all this stuff. More than I do half the time."

"Are you going to curse him and his wife with immortality?"

I took a long sip of water. "I kind of already did. They don't know yet. It was an accident. When I healed Eurydice, I used Orpheus' soul. I'm not really sure how, but when I healed her, I just felt it. Their souls changed. They felt . . . different."

Mom nodded. "I'll check when I next see them, but I wouldn't be surprised. A healing that involved could have all manner of unintended side effects."

We lapsed into an awkward silence. I studied her face. She looked tired. Weary even. I looked down at the table. This fight . . . we'd never fought like this before. It was draining. I thought about what Orpheus had said and realized he was right. I needed to establish boundaries, but nothing good would come from hanging onto all my anger.

"Mom, can I trust you?"

She looked up at me in surprise. "Of course, honey."

"I want to believe that, but I really need you to be up-front with me. I can't deal with all the deception and double speak anymore. But I don't want us to fight anymore, either. I just want . . . I want my *mom* back. I feel like . . . ever since I found out what I am, and what you are, we stopped being . . . *us* and became these gods. I just want you to be my mom."

She pulled me close and gave me a hug. "I can do that."

I relaxed into her arms. "I know you don't like Hades—"

"Oh honey, it's not that. He's just so much older than you."

"I know."

"I don't think you do. There is so much history between all of us that you just weren't a part of. Lifetimes, and those lifetimes shape a person. Hades and I weren't always at odds. Once he was my closest friend."

I closed my eyes and asked the question I'd been dreading. "Did you two ever . . . ?"

She shook her head, breaking free of our embrace. "We might have had the timing ever been right. But he was hung up on Hera for so long. And then everything with Zeus happened, and after that, we all split up. We were all so angry, so betrayed. Zeus was . . . He made us hope."

"What happened between you and Poseidon?"

She stiffened. "Did Hades tell you about that?"

I shook my head. "Poseidon kept bringing you up, and it seemed to really piss Hades off."

She clutched her magazine so tightly that the pages crumpled. "We were together for a time. I lost interest. He didn't." Regret flickered behind her eyes. "He kept following me, trying to make me see reason. I told him I wasn't interested, and he . . . " She shrugged. "He doesn't take no for an answer very well. Never has." She stood abruptly. "Would you like some cocoa, dear?"

I nodded numbly, processing the words, spoken and unspoken. Concentrating on what she didn't say. I remembered how weird she'd gotten when I mentioned Poseidon the night I'd had that dream. How Hades had promised he wouldn't let anything happen to me. The way Hades' face had contorted with rage when Poseidon mentioned how much I looked like my mother. How he wouldn't so much as let Poseidon touch me, even to shake hands. "What do you mean Poseidon doesn't take no for an answer?"

"That's all ancient history." Mom waved a dismissive hand. But I already knew what happened. I could read the lingering horror in her face. "You know what's funny?" She poured the steaming cocoa into a cup and set it in front of me. Her magazine went into the recycling bin, and she reached into the pantry for marshmallows. "Hades helped put me back together afterward. He was so furious with Poseidon, but so kind to me. I think that's why I lost touch with him. He reminded me of when I was weak. But I know you're safe with him." She met my eyes, and I read the message there loud and clear.

"Mom, I love him."

She sighed. "I understand that you think so—"

"I know so."

"He saved your life, he's handsome, he understands you," she continued as if I hadn't spoken. "I can see why you would be infatuated."

I took a deep breath. "I understand and appreciate your concern. But I think you got so used to raising me like a human that you forgot I'm not one. This is *not* some crush or infatuation. I'm not some human girl you need to have 'the talk' with. I'm a goddess. I've seen things and done things and had things done to me that no normal person has ever had to deal with. And the only consistent thing through all of that was him. I need you to understand and respect that my feelings are real. Yes, he's older than me. Yes, he has history that I'm not a part of. But pretty much any god that's left is going to have that history and be as old as dirt.

Age doesn't matter to immortals any more than genetics. If it were Aphrodite instead of me, would you think anything of it?"

She blinked. "No. I guess I wouldn't. But Persephone, you've got a very long life ahead of you, and I don't want you to make any decisions now that will impact you—"

"I'm not stupid." I sighed and grabbed her hands from the table. "I need you to listen to me."

She squeezed my hands in response. "I'm listening."

"The way I feel about him now, I get that it may not last forever. I can't imagine my feelings ever changing, but I'm not going into this blindly." I sighed, trying to collect my thoughts. "At what point do I get to stop worrying about the way my choices will impact the rest of my life and start living it?" I let go of her hands and raked my hair back. "We're drifting apart Mom, and I don't want to look back and wonder what if, not with Hades."

"Honey, I've never seen Hades look at anyone the way he looks at you." Mom took a sip of her tea. "He won't mind waiting until you're ready."

"It's not even him I'm worried about; it's me." I spoke too fast, all my thoughts pouring out of me in a jumble. "He might be willing to wait centuries until he thinks I'm ready for a serious relationship, but what if *I'm* not? Mom, I'm different without him. And I don't mean that in a co-dependent 'I need him to live' type way, but to some degree the choices you make and the people you surround yourself with shape who you become, right? I don't like the person I'm becoming without him." I took a deep breath. "What if we do wait on pursuing this and the person I become isn't *me* anymore. What if I could have been someone else? Someone better."

Mom took a long sip of her tea. I knew the look on her face well enough not to ask any more questions. She was mulling over everything I'd said and trying to phrase her next sentence. Interrupting her thought process seldom improved things.

"I just worry," she said finally. "The people he loves always get hurt."

"Isn't that kind of true for every god?"

"It doesn't have to be true for you. I don't want you to get hurt."

"You don't want me to get hurt?" I laughed. "Where have you been? My entire life's shattered, and all that's left are shards that cut and scrape and slice when I try to put it back together. I am *so* past hurt." I blinked back tears. "I'm completely and utterly broken."

Mom gave me a sympathetic look. "And you think Hades can fix that?"

I shook my head. "No. But fighting you every time I need to lean on him isn't helping."

She let out a slow breath. "Touché." She stared down at her teacup. "You've grown so much." She bit her lip and blinked rapidly. "It's bitter-sweet, you know. Watching you become this strong, independent, powerful young woman." Mom took a deep breath. "There's this saying, 'Mother is God in the eyes of a child.' You used to have absolute faith in me. You looked at me like I had all the answers in the world." She smiled and stirred her tea. "You cried every time I dropped you off at pre-school, and when I picked you up, you'd hold me *so* tight." She cleared her throat. "It's better than worship. It's potent and pure and utterly addictive." She raised her eyes and looked at me. "I never wanted to give that up. I never wanted to let you go, but you grew." Her eyes shimmered with unshed tears. "And I messed *everything* up."

I slid the necklace back and forth on its chain. "Mom—"

"I should have told you, honey. I should have told you what you are. I should have told Hades about Zeus. I should have handled everything differently. I'm sorry."

I gave her a hug. "I don't know that I would be who I am if you had handled it differently. I'm sorry I was mad. I love you."

"I love you too." She stroked my hair and took a shaky breath. "But you shouldn't be here." She pulled away from me. "It's not safe."

I looked up at her, surprised. "I was actually going to talk to you about that. I should stay down there until this gets settled. Then you two can focus on finding Zeus. I wanted to go back to my regular life, but I don't have a regular life, and I just ended up getting in the way."

"You weren't in the way."

"I'm a distraction. You should be looking for those missing demigods."

Mom's eyebrows shot up. "He really tells you everything, doesn't he?"

I nodded. "As much as I hate having to hide, I'm doing more harm than good here."

Mom put her cup on the table and grabbed my hand. "I know it feels like you've lost something, and that's mostly my fault. I let you think you were human, so you're feeling this loss that's not real. What you have—" she paused, gaze locking with mine like she wanted to make sure she had my attention "—it's going to be so much better in time. Once all this craziness ends, you'll find a new normal. You won't have to hide in the Underworld your whole life either."

I nodded. "I hope so. Do I have to go back tonight? If I'm going to be staying there, I'd like to bring a few things this time, and I'm really tired."

"You'll go first thing in the morning?" she asked.

I nodded. "As soon as the sun comes up."

She considered for a moment then nodded. "Goodnight sweetheart, I love you."

"Love you too." I gave her another hug and went upstairs to my room feeling like a huge weight had been lifted from my shoulders. I unclipped my necklace and slipped into pajamas. I'd made things right with Melissa and Orpheus and my mom. Tomorrow I'd set things right with Joel, and assuming the power from the Reapers didn't burn through me, Hades would have to realize something was going on. I just had to put up with this headache until then. My heavy eyes closed, and I settled in for what I really hoped would be my first Reaper-free night when a heavy weight dropped on my back.

Someone yanked my head up by my hair then my pulled a sheet over my head like a hood. A deep voice chuckled, and my blood went cold. I knew that voice.

I flailed, trying to buck him off me, but he pulled the sheets tighter, shoving my face into the pillow. I couldn't breathe. He straddled me, knees pinning my covers to me like a cocoon. My hands groped at the sheet, trying to pull it off my head so I could breathe, but Thanatos yanked them back.

"What the hell did you do to my Reapers?"

Chapter XXVI

I SCREAMED INTO the pillow as my shoulders threatened to come out of joint. Thanatos pinned my arms behind my back. I'd teleport, but his grip on my hand insured I would only bring him with me. A shield was useless if he was already touching me. I forced myself to calm down, even though my lungs felt like they were about to burst. I couldn't die, and he couldn't have any serious intentions of hurting me or Cassandra would have seen this coming.

"They're my Reapers now." My voice was smug, if muffled. The sheets tightened, digging into my throat, and I forced myself to stay calm. "They swore fealty."

"That can't work on them. You can't charm the dead." He pressed against me, crushing me against the mattress.

I shifted my shoulders in an awkward attempt at a shrug. Pain shot through me, and I gritted my teeth. "I can charm you. It must have trickled down to them."

"So what? You're taking over soul collecting now?"

"No, you are. Your Reapers won't be gathering souls anymore."

Thanatos laughed. "That would be chaos! Souls would be left in their dead bodies for weeks. You wouldn't put the souls through that. You *care* too much."

I tried to shake my head, but couldn't manage in the tight space. I felt dizzy, breathing in my own air. Pain ricocheted though my body. Why was I in so much pain? "Either way, I win. If you can't keep up with the souls, Hades will know something's up."

"And if I can?"

I fully believed he could. My promise wouldn't have allowed me to do this much if I didn't. Just like I knew he wasn't going to slip and get Cassandra's attention. However angry he got, he'd keep his mind focused. "You'll be too busy to cause trouble. I never promised to make life easy for you."

He shifted, body pressing mine into the bed. "I'm supposed to bring you to Zeus."

I struggled to maintain consciousness. "You wouldn't dare. Cassandra will see."

"Cassandra's busy."

So why was I still here? I swallowed hard. "Doesn't matter. You won't risk Zeus finding out you've lost control of your army. If he has me, what possible use could he have for you?"

Thanatos' grip tightened, and I knew I'd hit a mark. He pulled me back by my hair and slammed my head into the metal bedpost. I yelped, and stars flooded my vision. "Exactly. I won't take you to Zeus, and if I leave you here, Hades is going to wonder why you felt the need to charm all the Reapers."

I smiled. "Checkmate."

"Not quite." Triumph surged through Thanatos' voice. "I just need a way to get rid of you. You made it so easy."

I struggled to understand him. Thanatos gave a dark laugh. "You don't realize what you've done, do you?"

Static filled the room. I frowned as a voice broke through the radio on my dresser. "And an unnamed source said they saw a blond, green-eyed, teenage girl leaving her room."

"Hang on," the co-anchor interrupted. "Like the jailbait Orpheus was seen leaving with from Terrapin tonight?"

"Hey, yeah. One of our fans just posted her picture on our Facebook page. Looks like it's already linked to a couple tabloids."

"Weigh in listeners. We have a miraculous healing and a mysterious girl. Could this be the Persephone that Orpheus keeps raving about?"

"Oh shit," I whispered.

The co-anchor laughed. "Yeah, sure. I figure she's just a mistress."

"Or both!" The anchor chuckled. "Post your opinion at—"

The sound cut off abruptly. My heart pounded in my chest. They had a picture! It was only a matter of time before they found where I lived. Or the shop, Demeter's Garden. Couldn't my mom have picked a less obvious name?

Last year Orpheus had told the world about me, and I'd nearly died. I didn't want to wait to see what would happen if people had an image to focus their energies. They wouldn't just be worshiping the *idea* of me. They'd be worshiping me.

"You're going to let me die." I realized. Typically gods only died from lack of worship, not too much. But I hadn't come into my powers yet. My body wasn't ready to handle powers. If Hades didn't channel the excess powers away, I could unravel. Die.

"That's the idea."

I threw my head back, hoping to catch Thanatos off guard, but he was ready. His hand twisted in my hair, and he slammed my head into the metal bedpost. I opened my mouth to scream, but the sound was whipped out of my mouth as the room swirled around me. Crap! He was teleporting.

Thanatos shoved my face in the sand that materialized beneath us. "Don't even try to make eye contact."

I coughed, gagging on the sand. I sputtered, spitting out what I could when I could get a breath of air. I lifted my head to gauge my surroundings and realized we were on a sandbar. Endless ocean surrounded me. I gulped and squirmed beneath him, trying to break free, but only managed to get myself further entrenched in the sand. It scraped at my skin, leaving it raw. I could hear water lapping around us.

"It's not that I want you to die. I actually liked you. If I thought you could be convinced to swear fealty—"

I spat out sand. "Never!"

"Yeah I figured as much. So I guess it's just a matter of waiting for you to die."

He wouldn't have long to wait. My head was throbbing in time to my heart. Erratic and fast. I needed to get to Hades.

I concentrated through the pain, pouring all of my energy into creating a thorny vine. It rose up, brushed against Thanatos' leg, and crumbled to dust. He laughed and snapped my wrist. I cried out.

"Have you forgotten that I'm the god of death?" He put pressure on my arm, and pain lanced through my body, sending me into convulsions. I screamed into the sand and pulled on the power of the Reapers to lash out. His grip loosened, and I bucked him off me, rolling away, coughing up sand and gold blood into the ocean.

Gold blood? That probably wasn't a good sign. I got to my feet, whirling to face Thanatos, but he was gone. His foot shot out from nowhere, kicking me squarely in the stomach.

I stumbled backward, coughing as Thanatos rained blows from behind his shield, invisible until he touched me.

I'm going to die. I was strangely calm with this realization. It was probably too late for me to get to Hades. But if I was going down, I was taking Thanatos with me. The next time he lashed out, I grabbed his hand, pulling him from behind his shield. My broken wrist screamed in protest, but I didn't let him vanish behind the shield. Just one look, just one look into his eyes, and I could charm him. Then this would be over.

"What is going on here?" A familiar voice bellowed.

I looked up in surprise. Thanatos didn't hesitate. He broke my grip and teleported before I could blink.

Poseidon met my eyes. "Are you okay?"

"I had him! You ruined everything!" I struggled to stay on my feet, cradling my injured hand.

Poseidon raised his blond eyebrows. "I didn't get a good look at the other guy, but from here it looked like he was winning."

He didn't look like a harmless surfer anymore. He still wasn't wearing a shirt. I couldn't believe I'd ever found him attractive. His muscular build brought bile to my throat as I imagined him overpowering my mother. I coughed, gold spittle landing on the sand.

Poseidon's swore. "You really are a child. That's why Hades married you, isn't it? You need him to channel your power. Come on, we don't have a lot of time." He stepped onto the beach, and I made a sharp noise.

"Stay back!"

Poseidon furrowed his brow. "I'm helping you."

"I don't want to owe you any favors."

Poseidon rolled his eyes. "You're not thinking clearly. Look, it wouldn't be a favor. What do you think would happen if Hades or your mother found your body washed up on my shore? I'm covering my own ass here. Come with me." He reached out his hand.

"Don't touch me!"

"Persephone—"

"Don't come one step closer! This might not be much land, but it's still earth, and you are *not* welcome here. This is my realm. Get out!"

I doubled over, clutching my stomach. It hurt. I hurt so badly. Poseidon stepped closer, and the ground rose up beneath him, shoving him back into the water. "Get *back!*"

"Look," he kept his voice patient and calm, as if he was talking to a wild animal, "I'm not going to hurt you. I've got a son about your age, actually, he—"

"Stay away from me," I warned when his foot crept toward the sand.

He ran his fingers through his bleach-blond hair, just like Hades did when he was frustrated. "It isn't your realm, you know. It's your mother's."

"You don't get to talk about my mother. I know what you did."

Poseidon drew back like I'd struck him. "That was a long time ago—"

"You're scum! You're worse than scum. And I am never ever going to put her in the position of owing you *anything*. Least of all my life. Now step *back!*"

He raised his hands in surrender. "Can you teleport to Hades?"

I gritted my teeth against the wave of agony that washed over me. I went through a mental list of all the entrances of the Underworld. Not the park, Thanatos would probably be waiting there. Or maybe he was waiting at the one in my backyard. Damn it! I didn't have time to be wrong.

Italy! Orpheus had mentioned one in Italy.

It doesn't matter, I realized. Why would Thanatos camp at one entrance when they all led to the same place?

"He'll just be waiting for me in Tartarus. I'll never make it."

Poseidon stepped onto the beach. My gaze flew to him. "If you come any closer, I'll let Hades think you did this to me."

He paled and stepped back into the water. "If I don't help you, you are going to die."

No kidding.

"Why not skip Tartarus?"

I shook my head. "I can't teleport between realms."

"So make an entrance."

Could I do that? I'd never tried before, but it was just as much my realm as it was Hades'. I pictured Hades' chambers and poured all my energy into that image. The ground beneath my feet shuddered and split open. The Underworld yawned beneath me in an open chasm. My feet hit Underworld soil, and I teleported straight to Hades' room.

Hades saw me and went sheet white. He dropped the book he'd been reading and bolted to me, catching me before I crumpled to the floor. He swore when he felt the power rushing through me. "Okay, okay, it's going to be—" The lie caught in his throat. His hands shook. I latched onto his wrist, staring at him wide-eyed with fear. It was too late. I'd taken too long. I was going to die.

"*No.*" His lips found mine, and he channeled the energy away from me. The images flashed through my brain as he searched for the explanation. I saw Eurydice and Orpheus, the news reporters, Joel, Thanatos—

I wasn't in control of my thoughts. I couldn't shield them. My mind screamed in protest, and my back arched in pain. I couldn't gain control of my thoughts fast enough to stop the flow of information. The promise ripped through me in a flash of white-hot agony.

Hades saw everything.

Thanatos in the clearing, charmed into taking Boreas' soul. Thanatos asking me not to tell anyone. The months of agony at hiding the truth from Hades. The Reapers tormenting me. Discovering I could charm the Reapers. Thanatos attacking me.

Hades' fingers dug into my shoulders, anger flaring through him. Tears coursed down my cheeks. He knew, he finally knew! He'd hate me forever for hiding this from him, but he knew!

The pain was gone. Even my wrist had been mended. Hades released me, going very still.

"I'm so sorry; I tried to tell you, I—"

"Don't apologize." His voice was low and scary calm.

I looked into his face and blanched. His eyes were cold and flat. His face, shrouded in shadow, seemed to be made of granite. I couldn't feel *anything* from him like I normally could after channeling.

"Come with me."

I swallowed hard and followed him up to the throne room.

"Moirae. I need a name."

Moirae jumped in surprise and turned to Hades. She stepped back when she saw Hades' face. "M-Mario Smith," she stammered.

"Where?"

She closed her eyes, and Hades nodded. "Thank you."

Confused, I followed him to the surface. We emerged on a bustling city street. I looked around for a familiar land marker to get my bearings.

"Wh-Where are we?" I asked. "What are we doing?"

Hades didn't answer. He stepped onto a crowded sidewalk, shoving his way through the crowd until he reached a man in a brown coat. I blinked, suddenly aware of the shield that kept the pedestrians from seeing or hearing us.

"Look over there." Hades pointed behind me.

I turned around, searching the crowded street. "What is it?"

I heard a crack and a thud and spun around to see the man in the brown coat fall motionless to the ground, neck twisted at a strange angle.

Chapter XXVII

"WHAT DID YOU DO?"

"Persephone—" Hades reached between me and the man.

"Get away from me!" I shoved Hades away and fumbled for the man's pulse even though I knew I'd find none. I focused my powers and tried to heal him. It wouldn't work. Even I couldn't bring people back from the dead.

"Persephone—"

"Someone should call 911." I reached for my phone, but of course I didn't have it on me. It was sitting on my nightstand, right where I'd left it an hour and a lifetime ago.

"Persephone, listen to me!"

I shook my head and struggled free from his grasp.

Hades swore. "Persephone, look!" He pointed me toward the intersection as an old Buick sailed through a red light and into a crosswalk, followed by a police car with flashing lights, but no siren. Pedestrians scattered out of the way. I stood, scanning the road. No one had been hurt.

"That was supposed to be him. He would have gotten hit and fought for his life for *hours* in excruciating agony. Got it? Now step away from his body."

I swallowed hard and moved away as Hades dropped another shield between the fallen man and us. "But . . . but . . . You killed him. Why?"

"Thanatos has to respond to divine deaths."

"Speak of the devil." Thanatos grabbed me from behind. "Don't move, Hades."

Pain ripped through me, but what else was new? I gritted my teeth and slammed my foot down on his with a satisfying crunch, then twisted and plowed my elbow into his gut. His grip loosened, and I sprang free. Hades pulled me behind him, grabbed Thanatos by the throat, and slammed him into a brick wall.

"Charm him." Hades blindly groped for my hand.

I grabbed it and felt power surge through me. I looked at Thanatos, and his pupils widened.

Hades met my eyes. "Don't kill him yet. The power will just go to Zeus, and he could gain access to the Underworld. Ask him to swear fealty to you."

"Why not you?"

"I'm not in Zeus' bloodline; it won't work."

Thanatos stared at me with mute adoration. "I swear," he managed in a strangled gasp.

Hades eased up on his grip fractionally. "Good. Now give her your powers. All of them." Thanatos hesitated, and Hades tightened his grip. "Persephone, tell him."

I looked at Thanatos, remembering the hell he'd put me through the last few months. The pain and misery, the fear. I took a deep breath, steeling myself to give the order. Unbidden, other images rushed through my head. Thanatos teasing Cassandra, joking with Charon, laughing with Hypnos, moving his hands around while he explained something to me. The whole group sitting around the table at dinner. It might have all been an act, but it was a convincing one. He'd been my friend. I gave Hades a helpless look. "Isn't fealty enough?"

"Thanatos, when you attacked her while she slept—" his grip seemed to tighten more with each word. "—when you beat her on the beach, tried to kill her and leave her for Poseidon—"

"Hades stop it, he's charmed. He can't fight back." I reached out to touch Hades' arm, but something in his eyes stopped me.

"Whose idea was that?" Hades let go of Thanatos so suddenly that he fell to the ground with a thud.

"Mine."

"Did Zeus even know about it?"

"Not to my knowledge."

Hades gave me a look. I closed my eyes and nodded my head. I understood. Fealty didn't mean absolute loyalty and devotion. It wasn't charm. When the charm wore off, Thanatos would still be tied to me through fealty, but he would hate me even worse. He'd never stop looking for a way to get rid of me so he could be free.

"But he'll die."

"Just like Boreas."

I stepped farther away, trembling like a leaf. "I didn't know that would happen when I charmed Boreas. I was just talking. I didn't know—I can't do this. Don't ask me to do this. Please!"

Hades closed his eyes. "Fine, tell him to give you most of his powers, but keep enough so he won't die."

I nodded at Thanatos. His power rushed through me, dark and strange. Hades' hand around mine was a lifeline, preventing the new powers from overwhelming me. It felt like something slick and wrong and incompatible had entered my blood stream. Like oil on water. Foreign yet inseparable.

When it finished, I smiled at Hades. "He's mortal now, I can feel it. No powers, no threat at all really." I breathed a sigh of relief, glad to have found a way around the unspeakable.

Hades channeled enough of Thanatos' powers away to allow me to let go of his hand. "Go back to my chambers in the Underworld. Don't talk to anyone. I'll be down in a few minutes."

"What? Why?"

The look he gave me sent shivers down my spine.

"But he's not a threat," I protested. "Hades, you don't have to do this."

"He knows everything about us. Go, Persephone."

"No." I swallowed hard. "This . . . this isn't you. You can't. People can't do—"

"We are not people."

His voice. It was so hard, so cold that I scarcely recognized it. "Please."

Hades turned back to Thanatos. "Fine, stay and watch if you'd rather."

Horrified, I left.

Chapter XXVIII

ONCE I MADE IT back to Hades' room, I burst into tears. I sank to the floor, pulled my knees to my chest, and covered my ears as though curling safely into a ball would stop what was happening on the surface.

The worst part was that part of me, a big part of me, agreed with Hades. If Thanatos was allowed to live, I'd always be afraid of him. I'd always wonder what else he would try. Hades was right. He was a threat.

But knowing that and being a part of it were two very different things. I remembered watching superhero movies with Melissa. At the end of the film when the villain was safely behind bars, I'd complain that the hero should have just killed them. Everyone knew the bad guys always escape from jail.

I'd made it sound so simple. So easy. So inconsequential. Just kill them. No big deal.

My trembling hands wiped the tears from my face. I felt cold. Frozen. I climbed to my feet and looked around Hades' room. I stared at the familiar items as though seeing them for the first time, trying to fit them back into my mental picture of Hades. His books on the shelf. The glass doors overlooking the library, filled to the brim with his eclectic collection. My hands found a worn psychology book, something about the seven stages of grief, and I smiled. He tried so hard to help the souls adjust to life in the Underworld.

I flipped it open and found a note from Cassandra. *Thought you'd like this one. Note: Please don't talk to me about this book. No one wants to hear your psychobabble. ;) xoxo, The Prophet.*

I smiled and sat the book down on the dresser. A silver picture frame caught my eye. It held one of the pictures from the photo booth on St. Mary's Island. I touched Hades' face.

The door opened. I set the picture down. "Hades?"

"Yeah." The single syllable was saturated with bitterness.

"His soul?"

"I destroyed it."

I blinked, too shocked to even process that.

"We don't have a lot of time. I need you to give me Thanatos' power. It's going to feel different from channeling—"

"Are you okay?"

He gave me a look that sliced through me like a knife. Anger was radiating off him in waves. "How could I have been so *stupid?*" He smashed his fist through the mirror. The mirror shattered, sending broken shards of Hades crashing to the floor. "It was bad enough having Zeus use you as a puppet."

What did he mean by that?

Hades saw my questioning look, and his jaw clenched. "But Thanatos!" His eyes landed on the silver picture frame. He picked it up, preparing to hurl it to the floor.

"Not that!" I grabbed his hand. It was a stupid thing to do, but this was Hades. It just wasn't in me to be afraid of him. No matter how loud and angry he got. No matter what he did.

He went as still as a stone. "Right." He removed my hand from his very carefully and turned the frame over to reveal the picture of us. "Right." He set it down and stared at the picture, seeming to grow angrier. I could feel his thoughts swirling around in a bitter void. "This whole time? This whole fucking time?"

I blinked back tears. "I know. I tried; you have to believe I tried. I'm so sorry—"

"Stop apologizing!" Hades slammed his fist into the dresser. "You weren't responsible for this, he just used you like a fucking pawn, and I allowed it to happen. I trusted him! Worse, I trusted him with you." The anger seemed to drain out of him, leaving him lifeless and hollow. He sagged against the bed. "I made him your guard. Gods, the Reapers. How could I have been so stupid? I let them hurt you."

I stared at him in disbelief. All this time I'd been convinced he would blame me. That he would hate me. It had never even crossed my mind that he would blame himself. I sat next to him on the bed. "You didn't *let* him do anything to me. You didn't know! I never thought—I knew, I knew if I could just tell you, that you would fix this."

Hades stared at me. "That's even worse. This whole time you were waiting for me to see what was right in front of me. I'm sorry. I'm so sorry."

I couldn't think of anything to say to that. For the thousandth time I wished for a lie. Humans don't appreciate the power of false platitudes. I couldn't tell him that it was okay. I couldn't say I didn't blame him. I wasn't mad at him, but when it had gotten bad, part of me did blame him for not getting it. For not hearing what I couldn't say.

I couldn't lie, but I could mislead. I remembered Hades glancing up to my room when my mom asked where I was. My actions could lie. I put my hand to my forehead with a wince.

Hades swore and cupped my face with his hands. "Right, Thanatos." He closed his eyes. "This is going to be different than just channeling. It's not so much lending as it is giving. I will give it back when you're old enough to handle it. You have a right to this—"

"I don't want it. It feels . . . wrong."

Hades nodded. "It's on the complete opposite end of the spectrum as your abilities. I imagine it feels strange." He ran his fingers through his hair. "What I'm about to do . . . I—"

I put my finger on his lips. "It doesn't matter. I trust you."

"You really shouldn't."

I kissed him. I poured all my thoughts and feelings into that kiss to show him what I couldn't vocalize, to show him what he was to me. I pushed Thanatos' power to him, along with half of my own. He drew in a sharp breath, and I locked gazes with him. "I trust you. Absolutely. And there is nothing you could ever do to convince me that trust is misplaced."

"Persephone—"

His eyes were so full of anguish that even if I hadn't been able to feel his pain it would have broken my heart.

"Hades, do you know what the worst part of the last few months has been for me?"

He shook his head.

"Thinking that once you finally found out, I was going to lose you. I was sure you would hate me for being stupid enough to make that promise. I can't lose you. I think it would kill some part of me, I just—"

Hades shushed me, brushing a tear from my cheek. "I couldn't hate you. Do you know why?"

It was my turn to shake my head.

"After everything he did to you, you still couldn't bring yourself to kill Thanatos."

"So you had to kill one of your best friends? If I wasn't so weak, I would have done it."

"That's not weak. That's strong. Stronger than you know. It's easy to give into vengeance. But you rise above it. I saw that in you from the very beginning. You're so much better than us. And if he'd managed to take that from you . . . " Hades trailed off. "I almost lost you, and that would have destroyed me." He looked at me and nodded his head. "I love you. These last few months of trying to give you space and wondering what was going to happen, they were terrible." He shook his head. "Thanatos used me too. He knew all my hang-ups. He used that. Had I just trusted you . . . me . . . us, as completely as you do . . . this never would have happened. I love you, and I knew one day we would be here. I shouldn't have waited. I should have just jumped." He ran a finger along my jawline. "I trust you. Absolutely." He kissed me.

My life wasn't in danger or anything. His power flowed through my veins.

But won't that—The thought hadn't even fully formed before he brushed it away.

I can filter it. Keep it safe for you. You might be seeing more of me than before.

I smiled at that. Equilibrium. Our connection solidified with a snap. My mind cleared, and I saw everything that had happened since meeting Aphrodite. I saw myself charming Hades, running to the park, promising never to hurt him, and getting charmed. I broke off and stared at Hades wide-eyed.

"It really was her." He shook his head. "I didn't think she had enough power to charm you anymore. I'm sorry—"

I waved a hand, cutting him off. "You've been trying to tell me ever since you figured it out. Do you think she's Zeus?"

Hades shrugged. "I think I would have known. But I haven't seen her since that day on the beach. Maybe that's not Aphrodite at all."

I thought back to the day I'd met Aphrodite. How grateful she'd been that I'd come for her. She thought of me as a sister. How screwed up would it be if she'd been replaced and I hadn't even noticed?

"We'll deal with her," Hades promised. "Later."

I realized that I was still holding on to Hades. I flushed and dropped my hands from his arms, but I didn't move away from him. I couldn't. It was like fighting gravity. I gazed into his eyes and saw him struggling against the connection we shared.

"Persephone . . . "

My lips brushed against his. He kissed me back then wrapped one arm around me, crushing me to him, and propped his other arm on the bed behind me, stabilizing us. He drew back in a sudden jerk.

"This is you?" He searched my face, looking for any sign I was acting under charm like the last time.

"Yes," I whispered. "Is this you?"

His mind flitted to the last time I'd charmed him, and he nodded. "But I don't think—"

"Do you trust me?" I asked.

"Absolutely."

"Then stop thinking."

My lips found his, and we were kissing again. I knew it sounded stupid and trite to say we belonged together. How many times had I rolled my eyes when I'd heard others say those words? But we *did* belong together. Ever since that first kiss in the clearing. We'd given each other a part of ourselves, and that could never be undone.

I sank beneath him. His hand flew to the back of my head, blocking it from hitting the wooden headboard. He tangled his fingers in my hair. His other hand ran down my body. He hesitated, and I knew I could speak now and end this. He wouldn't be mad and wouldn't think less of me. I was completely in control here. Whatever happened next was my choice to make. I met his eyes, and he read the decision in them.

Chapter XXIX

JUST BECAUSE Thanatos was dead didn't mean that our troubles were anywhere near over. We still had Zeus or Aphrodite to contend with, but before we could even do that, we had to make sure there weren't more traitors in our midst.

"So why can't you charm anyone or teleport on the surface?" I asked Hades as we waited for everyone to gather in the throne room.

"It doesn't work like that. We have half of each other's powers, so our abilities will be enhanced. Not traded off. Otherwise we'd only be half as good at what we could already do. Everyone would lose. You'd have to pull a Boreas for me to be able to charm anyone."

"But I could touch souls like the Reapers."

"That's fealty; that's different. Besides, souls are just as much your domain as flowers."

I blinked. I'd never thought of it that way. "But I can teleport down here."

"Because I rule this realm. Your mother has given you a claim to her realm. You don't rule it, so you don't get to say who teleports there. She's pretty nice about it. Beings born native to her realm are allowed to teleport within it. Anything else . . . " Hades shrugged. "You have no idea how much negotiation it required for her to allow Thanatos and his Reapers the same privileges."

I frowned. The Reapers. I couldn't feel them anymore. Had I given them to Hades?

He shook his head, following my thoughts. "They were released when we reached equilibrium. They swore fealty to you, not us."

I started to reply when the door opened and Cassandra, Moirae, Charon, and Hypnos walked in. Cassandra's eyes were red-rimmed, like she'd been crying, and I realized she must have seen what happened.

"What's going on?" Charon asked.

"Where's Thanatos?" Hypnos pushed his grey hair out of his face and scanned the room. "Is he coming?"

My heart wrenched when I remembered they were twins. Hades

shook his head slightly. *That doesn't mean as much to him as it does to you. He's just asking.*

Hades explained what had happened to Thanatos in a quick, dispassionate summary. Only I could feel the pain and anger hidden behind each word, but Cassandra wasn't fooled by his apparent disregard. She took her place beside Hades and squeezed his hand. There was silence while everyone digested Hades' words.

Charon's face flipped through a whole range of emotions. Grief, anger, concern. The last was aimed at me. "Gods, Persephone. Had I known . . . "

I shrugged uncomfortably. "My fault. I promised."

Hypnos shook his head. "You didn't know any better at the time. So, what's the plan, then? I assume the first thing we need to do is make sure Thanatos was acting alone?"

Hades nodded. "Did any of you know about this?"

"Of course not," Cassandra said.

"I'm not working with Zeus. I had no idea Thanatos was," Charon said.

"I had no knowledge of this conspiracy," Moirae answered.

"I don't suppose our word is going to be enough in this case?" Hypnos said softly.

"For you three—" Hades indicated Cassandra, Moirae, and Charon "—it's going to have to be. For you . . . "

Hypnos nodded, giving me a defiant look. "Try it."

Hypnos was still alive. He could still swear fealty. I could charm him if he'd sworn fealty to Zeus. I met his eyes and breathed a sigh of relief when they didn't widen.

"He's clean," I told Hades.

"I'm not working with Zeus." Hypnos held his chin high. "I was not working with Thanatos. I'd never betray you. And I'd never be party to something—" he looked at me "—that would hurt *her.*"

I looked down at the floor. "Thank you."

"So what's next?" Moirae asked. "Do you need me to round up the demigods and the Reapers?"

Hades nodded. "I've suspended the Reapers' access to the surface until next Samhain, when we can charm and question them again. Which means, we're going to be very, very, busy for the next few months."

"Why would you need to round up the demigods?" I asked.

"They can cross between realms."

I blinked. "Wait, they can do that even if they're dead?"

"Of course. Where do you think ghosts come from?"

"Can I charm them?"

Hades shook his head. "Not if they're dead. We'll round them up per zone and keep a guard on them. Keep it civil, guys, innocent until proven guilty. Cassandra, can you keep an eye on the demigods in this zone?"

She nodded.

"Okay, Hypnos, keep an eye on Tartarus, Charon, the Elysian Fields—"

"This has crippled us." I realized. "We're going to be acting as Reapers and guards and keeping things running down here? Just the six of us?"

"Four. You and I are going to find Zeus and end this."

I shook my head. "Put Zachary in charge of Reaping. You can trust him. If we can find two, maybe three other souls we can trust on the surface, I think they can handle it."

"Zachary?" Hades gave me a quizzical look.

"Asclepius' new persona," Cassandra explained.

"What makes you think you can trust him?" Charon gave me a surprised look.

"He helped me when the Reapers were attacking me. And he never had to be charmed. He swore fealty on his own. Who's Asclepius?"

"He swore fealty? To you?" Hades' eyebrows shot up. "Well . . . okay then. You'll still have to try to charm him, but if you say he's trustworthy . . . "

"Who is he?" I asked again.

"He's the first Reaper." Hades was talking fast, indicating we needed to move on from this conversation. "He was a god of healing, and he tried to stop death. That violated the rules of nature We put into place. Rather than changing the nature of the dead, it changed him."

The way he said "We" emphasized the capital letter, and I understood he was talking about my mother, Zeus, and the rest of the original six. When they created the world, they'd all agreed on its natural laws. Earth and all its inhabitants formed a complex system involving all their powers. To protect their creation, they'd even given up the ability to lie. Words had power; the wrong words could unintentionally change the nature of something. I'd never considered the ramifications of a god intentionally trying to change the rules.

I felt sick. Poor Zachary. He'd tried to stop death and become its first agent.

"I can Reap too," Charon said with a grin, bringing the conversation back to its focus. "Call it multitasking."

I had a million more questions about Zachary and how the rest of the Reapers were made, but I forced myself to concentrate on what was important right now. "Good. Helen can watch the demigods here. Orpheus can watch the demigods in the Elysian fields—"

"Orpheus?" Hades asked.

I nodded. "He owes me." I hesitated. A regular soul, demigod or not, couldn't handle Tartarus. That required power. "Hypnos?"

"I'll watch Tartarus."

"Thank you."

Hades smirked. "Anything else, Majesty?"

I scowled at him. "Actually, yes. Zeus is going to know Thanatos is dead, right?" When Hades nodded, I continued. "But he doesn't know how it happened. Let's use that to our advantage."

Chapter XXX

TAKING A SHUDDERING breath, I dialed Aphrodite's number. It had taken seconds to teleport back to my house and grab my phone. I grabbed my necklace too. I felt weird when I wasn't wearing it. I teleported out before Mom realized I was home. The fewer questions I had to answer right now, the better.

Mom was going to have a fit when she found out I'd added Aphrodite to our family plan, but I was glad I'd added at least one more way to keep tabs on her. Him. Whatever. I was still reeling with the betrayal.

She'd said we were like sisters.

"Persephone! I've been looking everywhere for you! Where have you been?" She spoke so fast I could barely separate the words.

"Aphrodite?" I kept my voice soft and infused it with worry. Hades sat beside me on a picnic table, keeping watch over the park from behind our shield.

"What's wrong?" She actually sounded worried.

"Thanatos is dead. He attacked me, and I charmed him, and oh gods, Aphrodite, I don't know what to—" I took a shuddering breath instead of finishing the sentence. I *did* know what to do.

"Are you okay?"

"I'm not hurt," I replied, keeping my voice thick with what could be interpreted as unshed tears. I kept my answer vague on purpose. I was great actually, but it would be weird for me to be too happy after killing someone.

"Have you told Hades?"

Not technically. Hades had been there, so I hadn't told him anything. "No. Aphrodite, that's his best friend." My voice wavered, and I took a quick gasping breath that could be taken for a sob.

"It's okay. We'll . . . we'll tell him together. I'm sure he'll just be happy you're safe."

I raised an eyebrow in surprise. She was good. "I don't know, Aphrodite."

"Was Thanatos working for Zeus?"

"Yeah, he said he was supposed to take me to him."

She took a deep breath. "You could still be in trouble. Look, I can meet you at the park, by the Underworld entrance. Stay shielded till I get there, okay?"

"Thanks, Aphrodite."

She hung up.

I exchanged a glance with Hades. Now all we had to do was wait. If we could get Aphrodite to stand on the entrance to the Underworld, Hades could make a powerful barrier and trap Zeus in Tartarus with the rest of the Titans.

The sound of a car pulling into the parking lot jolted me from my reverie. Aphrodite was a reckless driver, but this was too fast even for her. The rain bounced off the shield like pellets. We'd assumed we'd have the park to ourselves. Who else would come here today?

My breath caught as I recognized Joel's green Chevy Thunderbird. I'd promised to meet him. . . . I glanced at my phone . . . now. I swore and shoved my phone into my pocket.

"What's wrong?" Hades asked.

"Joel's here." I met Hades' eyes. "I don't want him to get caught up in the middle of this."

"Seriously?"

"He's here to talk me out of breaking up with him."

Hades raised an eyebrow. "Far be it for me to get in the way of *that*. Go ahead. Get him out of here. Just be quick about it."

Joel got out of his car, shielded his eyes from the pelting rain, and looked around. He balanced a sad-looking bouquet of daisies and two smoothies.

I pressed my lips together against the wave of guilt that washed through me. What had I been thinking going out with him? I'd hurt him by leading him on, and I'd hurt Hades. And, for some reason, Melissa seemed to really resent that I'd dated Joel.

"She likes him," Hades murmured, following my line of thought. He gave me an apologetic glance. "I'm in your head every night. I make observations. And I'm not hurt. Jealous, yeah, but that's dumb. I told you to see other people. You listened."

My eyes widened. Melissa liked Joel! How could I have been so blind! I thought back on our conversations in a new light. It was so obvious.

"Did I mention that you needed to be quick?" Hades reminded me as Joel headed off toward the walking trail.

I blinked and stepped out from behind the shield right into a puddle. The rain was cold and quickly soaked the hem of my skirt.

"Joel?" I swore and hurried up the trail. "Joel!"

I ran up the hill at breakneck speed, keeping my eyes out for Joel. I saw a flash of a blue shirt through the trees. He was headed for the pavilion. Duh, probably trying to get out of the rain.

"Joel?" I teleported around the curve of the trail. We were deep into the woods now. I dashed the final few yards and grabbed his shirt. He turned, surprised, pulling the headphones from him ears.

"Oh hey! You're early." A grin broke out across his face. "How long have you been behind me?" He offered me the wilted bouquet of flowers with an apologetic grin. "Daisies are kind of hard to find. Look, I'm really sorry about that thing with Aphrodite . . . "

I shook my head. "We need to get out of here." I met his eyes. "This is going to freak you out, but you won't remember, so don't worry about it."

"Kora?" he asked uncertainly when I grabbed his hand.

I tried to teleport, but it didn't work. I was yanked back, my hand on his acting like a tether, pulling me back to the earth.

My gaze traveled up his arm as I tried to decipher what this meant. An old conversation with Hades popped into my mind.

"You can't teleport with me. This isn't my realm."

I met Joel's eyes. I could teleport with humans. They were native to this realm. Demigods too. I'd teleported Orpheus to the hospital.

"Right," Joel said, meeting my eyes. "You're going to forget you just tried that, and you're going to walk with me, deeper into the woods."

I felt power sweep over me. Familiar power. Charm.

I shook it off like water. "What? No! Let me go!" I tried to pull free, but his grip tightened.

"What is this?" Joel laughed. "There's quite a bit more power in you today."

"What are you?"

His face rippled, and the glamour protecting him faded. His blue eyes lightened into an impossible sky blue, his hair shone like the sun. He looked taller, stronger, and overwhelmingly perfect.

He gave me an easy grin and answered in a voice as smooth as silk. "Aw, come on, you know the answer to that."

"Zeus," I swallowed hard, yanking my hand away from him. It felt it like it had been seared with heat. "What did you do to Joel?"

He laughed, flashing a mouthful of gleaming white teeth at me. "You're pretty thick sometimes, you know that? There was no Joel."

"But Aphrodite—"

"That was a handy distraction. She wasn't too happy about it, but it's not like she could say no. We are family."

I closed my eyes. How had I missed that? All that talk about us being sisters. Her complete and immediate trust of me. Gods didn't have family loyalty. Zeus and Hades had never referred to each other as brothers. My mom and I were an oddity. But Aphrodite had trusted me from the beginning. Why hadn't I realized how strange that was?

Zeus didn't need her to swear fealty. He'd programmed her to have unconditional loyalty to family when he created her. She'd always done everything I asked, even while complaining about it.

"But I charmed you." My voice was weak, I felt sick.

"No. I charmed you. But you almost got me once." His sky-blue eyes sparked with amusement. "I was impressed. I'd been watching you for a while, but the first time you tried to charm me, that last day of school before winter break, I knew you were strong enough to be useful."

I blinked. I had charmed Joel just days before Pirithous came to the flower shop. I'd been walking to Professor Homer's class.

That's what set this all in motion? I felt sick to my stomach. My head was spinning. Zeus was Joel; he'd charmed me. I'd been wrong about Aphrodite. I'd set this in motion on that one stupid day. My mind couldn't decide what to focus on; it was all so horrifying.

"Why—what do you want with me?"

"At first I just needed a vessel. Someone to collect worshipers without attracting too much attention. I was supposed to rescue you from Boreas."

"Asking fealty in return?" My throat felt dry as I remembered my speculation on how he'd planned to rescue Aphrodite.

He shrugged. The gesture was so reminiscent of Joel that my breath caught in my throat. "That was plan B. Plan A involved the only god with a clairvoyant by his side."

Hades. He'd known Hades might intervene if Cassandra asked him to. And the only way to rescue me from Boreas would be to bring me to his realm. The only way to do that—my head was spinning. I felt like my whole world had been tilted sideways. Zeus had been behind everything. He was behind us.

"Oh yes, I've been planning you for a long time." He grinned at me, and I shuddered. "I've watched you. Waited for you. I *made* you." His grip tightened on my arm. "And then I set everything in motion and culled you from your darling little herd. And you were so cute, trying to piece it all together. I would have saved you from Boreas." He shrugged. "Eventually. I owed him a favor. But then Hades intervened, and you became so much more valuable." He shook his head. "Queen of the Underworld. With you, I wouldn't even need Thanatos. What happened to him, by the way?"

"Hades destroyed his soul."

Zeus blanched. "He did what?"

I smiled. "Consider it a preview of what's to come if you don't let me go *right now——*"

"No chance. Now you're my only hope to rule the Underworld. See, that's where I messed up before. I was shortsighted. Humans lose their belief sooner or later. We were doomed to die. But the humans in the Underworld . . . their worship lasts forever."

"You want to take over the Underworld?"

"I was going to let Thanatos rule it for me. The worship I got from him would have sufficed, but you have a legitimate claim to the throne. If you swear . . . I won't even need a mediator. It could all be mine." He smirked. "You really are the perfect package. Three of the realms in one silly little girl."

"I *kissed* you!" I realized, horrified.

Zeus gave me a sideways glance. "We did more than kiss."

My stomach heaved, and I was suddenly glad I hadn't eaten break-fast.

"Oh, don't be such a *human,*" he admonished.

"You're sick," I managed, stumbling away from him.

A familiar, warm voice filled my head. *Hate to interrupt, but Aphrodite is here. If you teleport to where I am behind the shield* . . . Hades trailed off, realizing something wasn't right. *What's happened?* His voice ricocheted through my head.

Hades! I took a sharp breath when I realized he hadn't been listening in to what he'd thought was a breakup speech with Joel. I summed things up as best I could and felt his shock.

Get out of there!

Our plan.

No! Just teleport. Leave! Hades' voice was frantic.

I can get him to the entrance. Hades, this is our best chance. This could all be over. All I had to do was run.

" . . . there was still the matter of gaining more power." I blinked when I realized Zeus was still talking. He must really love the sound of his own voice. "Once I saw what Orpheus had done, I saw so much potential . . . "

"Eurydice." I realized. "When I healed her, someone told the press . . . And they had the picture . . . "

"I didn't want to take you until you had enough followers to be worth it. Now you do. Look, we could drag this out all day, I could torture some of your pet humans, or we can get this over with now. Swear."

"Never," I hissed.

Zeus grinned at me, stroking my cheek. I slapped his hand away, and he laughed. "You really think you stand a chance against me? You're no better than Icarus challenging the sun."

"People forget that Icarus also flew," I quoted.

Zeus' face twisted in a smirk. "Didn't do him much good."

"Bet it pissed you off though." I smiled at him and he moved closer to me. "Humans don't give up very easily, regardless of the odds. And I think you've forgotten something very important."

"What's that?" Zeus asked, brushing my hair off my neck.

"I was raised human." I drew my leg up and kneed him in the groin.

Zeus yelped and sprang backward. I tore free from his grasp and ran as fast as I could. I veered off the path into the woods toward the park. I needed to get to the entrance of the Underworld.

Just teleport! Hades' mental shout was so loud my head hurt.

Suddenly the air changed around me. My hair felt like it was standing on end. A bolt of pain coursed through my veins, and I fell to the ground screaming. I threw up a shield before the next blast hit and managed to get back on my feet. Footsteps pounded behind me. The lake shimmered through the trees. *I'm so close!* I thought.

Another bolt hit my shield, crumbling it. I spun to face Zeus. Fight or flight. And flight was out.

No! Don't try to fight him. You'll only get hurt. I could sense Hades running up the path. *I'll be right there.*

Electricity coursed through my veins, and I hit the ground screaming. Through blurred vision, I saw Zeus walking to me at an unhurried pace. He gave a flick of his wrist, and the pain lashed through me again.

Persephone! Hades' voice sounded so frantic, so desperate. I struggled to answer to say anything to ease the fear in his voice. Then everything went dark.

Sneak Peek

The Iron Queen

(Excerpt)

Chapter I

Persephone

GETTING STRUCK by lightning hurts. A lot. Most people die. I don't have that luxury. But there is something that hurts worse. Healing from a lightning strike at godspeed.

When I came to, my veins felt like they were filled with molten lava. *Gods,* I thought as an inhuman moan tore from my throat. *What happened?* It wasn't until the bed shifted that I realized I wasn't alone.

Hades. I let myself relax. If my—yeah, thinking of him as my husband was still too weird. *What should I call him?* Husband sounded weird, but calling the god of the Underworld my boyfriend was just as strange. *Doesn't matter. If he's here, everything is going to be okay.*

Unconsciousness threatened to pull me back under, so I forced myself to take steady breaths. It was too soon to open my eyes. I knew how to stay conscious through horrific pain. Thanatos had taught me that.

What's happened to me? I wondered. Less than a year ago, my biggest problem had been that I didn't fit in at school. I hadn't known I was a goddess. Then Hades pulled me into the Underworld to save me from Boreas, the god of winter who tried to abduct me.

It wasn't all bad. A smile came to my lips. I'd gotten Hades out of the whole debacle. And for a minute, everything seemed like it was going to be okay. But then I found out that Boreas hadn't been working alone. He'd been working with Zeus, who was apparently not dead like everyone thought. Everyone but my mom.

My mom ruled the living realm, Hades the Underworld, which meant I had irrevocable access to both. Unfortunately that made me very valuable to someone who wanted to take them over. Someone like Zeus.

I breathed in too deeply, and a bolt of pain lanced through me. I let out a low moan and shifted positions to try to get comfortable. There was no comfortable. The lightning had seared every single nerve ending in my body. Healing from this didn't feel good at all.

His hand brushed the hair out of my face.

"Hades?" I croaked. I struggled to open my eyes.

He shushed me, stroking my arm. I leaned into his touch. The memories rushed back. Hades finding out about Thanatos. Killing him, destroying his soul. Memorial Park, waiting for Aphrodite. Joel had been there. What happened to Joel?

The voice shushed me again, and the hand on my shoulder didn't feel comforting anymore. It felt . . . wrong. My eyes flew upon, and I bolted upright.

With a horrible certainty I turned to see who sat next to me on the bed.

Chapter II

Hades

EARLIER THAT DAY:

It wasn't easy watching my wife chase after a human boy. I tore my gaze away from her as she scurried up the hill leading to the wooden path that ran above Memorial Park and watched the parking lot for Aphrodite, or Zeus, or whoever he, she, it may be.

Rain fell, pinging against my shield with pleasant plinking sounds while I sat comfortably dry atop a metal picnic table. My fingers worried a spot of rust, and I tried not to think too hard about whatever else had touched the shining surface.

This realm was disgusting. Insects swarmed the park, and birds flew through the air, dropping waste indiscriminately on the world below. I couldn't wait to return to the Underworld. The surface had its charms, but I had no desire to stay for very long.

Joel!

Persephone's voice rang through my head, and I tossed up a mental wall. It wasn't just good manners preventing me from listening in. I'd seen this boy in her thoughts every night. Seen the way he looked at her, seen the way he touched her. I clenched my jaw and studied the parking lot like it might change shape any moment.

She'd probably think less of me if I ripped him apart.

Not that her opinion was all that was stopping me. It wasn't my habit to go around killing mortal children. And not just because I'd have to deal with them in the Underworld. I liked humans. Just not when they groped my wife.

My heart thudded at an uncomfortable speed in my chest, filling my body with adrenaline. I couldn't seem to catch my breath. My hands gripped the edge of the picnic table, and I leaned forward, muscles tensed. That was strange. I had no reason to be this anxious. He was just a kid. And Persephone was Persephone. She had no idea what effect she had. I couldn't really fault him for being interested, and I had encouraged her to see other people.

I took a deep breath to force myself to calm down, but it didn't seem to work. What was the matter with me? I'd channeled Persephone's power away every night. That had given me a very unwanted front-row seat to their developing relationship. I'd seen every kiss, everything, and not felt *this* before. It hadn't been pleasant, but—

Cold dread filled the pit of my stomach, and I frowned. This didn't even feel like rage. My heart was still beating a mile a minute, like it might burst free from my chest at the slightest provocation. My entire body felt alien, strange, terrified.

That was it. Fear. But why was I—?

It wasn't mine.

My thoughts flew to Persephone, and her abject terror washed over me. The human boy had a tight grip on her arm. He was saying something. I rose from the picnic table, ready to relieve him of that limb, when his voice filtered through her thoughts.

. . . Hades.

How would he *know* my *name?*

A red sports car squealed into the parking lot, and I swore. *Hate to interrupt,* I directed the thought to Persephone.

The boy locked gazes with Persephone and seemed to look through her to me. I knew those eyes. Images and thought fragments flashed from Persephone's mind to catch me up. But I already knew everything I needed to.

Persephone, run! I tore through the parking lot to reach the path.

Hades, it's Joel! He's Zeus!

The whole story passed through my mind accompanied by waves of fear and guilt. Persephone gripping Joel's arm to teleport but nothing happening. Her realization that Joel wasn't from this realm. His glamour melting away. Why wasn't she running?

Get out of there, now!

I couldn't keep the panic out of my thoughts. If Zeus hurt her . . .

Our plan, she protested.

She wouldn't. She'd be a fool to risk going through with our plan now. We'd intended to trap Zeus by having him stand on an entrance of the Underworld and bringing some of my realm up and around him. A little slice of Tartarus. It had worked to imprison some of the Titans before, and it could work with him. But not like this. Not with her alone with him. She was hopelessly overpowered.

But this was Persephone. The girl that had fled the safety of the Underworld to confront Boreas with nothing but righteous indignation on her side. It was foolish of me to expect her to do anything else.

I swore and scrambled up the hill. *Just teleport. Leave!*

I can get him to the entrance. Hades, this is our best chance.

Her determination pounded through me. She was so desperate for this to be over. She wasn't going to run. If I couldn't reach her in time . . .

I rounded the corner, and a bright light seared my vision. She screamed, and intense pain flashed through her. I stumbled, blinded by white-hot agony. Another flash. My head felt like it exploded. My vision cleared for a split second, and I saw the ground rush toward me. Then everything went black.

Chapter III

Aphrodite

A SCREAM ECHOED through Memorial Park, and I knew I was too late. The air hummed with energy, setting my hair on end as I jumped out of the cherry-red convertible I'd "borrowed" from some random guy.

I sloshed onto the wet pavement, twisting my ankle in my haste, and made a mental note not to wear heels next time Persephone called for help.

I hurried up the wooded running path and almost tripped over a crumpled shape. Hades. How had Zeus managed to knock Hades out?

"Aphrodite." A voice as smooth as silk sent shivers up my spine.

I looked up, and Zeus emerged from a grove of trees. He held Persephone in his arms like some knight out of a painting. She lay limp, arms dangling, golden hair cascading in waves toward the ground. He strode toward me, strong and radiant, like the sun had reached through him to get just a little closer to earth. It would have been breathtaking, like something out of a storybook, if it wasn't for the sinister expression on his face.

Damn it, I'd hoped it would never come to this. She was my sister and my friend, and I'd stabbed her in the back by pretending "Joel" was anyone but Zeus. I'd helped to keep her oblivious, but only because I had to. I never wanted Zeus to win. But now he had Persephone, and with her, access to the Underworld and the living realm. We were all doomed.

"You said you wouldn't hurt her." I'd meant to sound defiant, angry, but it came out petulant and scared.

"I said I didn't have to. There's a difference."

I closed my eyes. Of course there was. "You're leaving me here, aren't you?"

Zeus grinned. "I'm sure you'll make yourself useful."

I was surprised it still hurt. I'd known from the beginning that I was no more than a pawn to Zeus. He'd created me from the remains of Uranus to give me unprecedented levels of charm and then abandoned me in the world without the knowledge to control it.

Charisma, or charm, is kind of like mind control if you know how to use it. I can smile at pretty much any human and make them do what I want, but uncontrolled it's dangerous. Used without direction, it steers humans toward their baser instincts. They'd be obsessed with me, jealous, enamored, whatever, to the extreme. Anything could have happened to me, but either way, it served Zeus' purpose. He had back-up plans for his back-up plans.

Now he was leaving me with two very pissed-off deities that would move heaven and earth to find Persephone. No telling what they'd do to me.

I wondered if she knew how lucky she was. I'd sell my soul to have just one of the followers she seemed to collect anywhere she went.

"Tell Hades and Demeter I'll take their realms in exchange for the girl." Zeus shifted and grabbed the necklace Persephone always wore and gave it a yank. The silver chain broke and he tossed it toward me. "Give him that, will you?" He vanished before I could answer.

I plucked the necklace out of the puddle it had fallen into. A small plant was anchored in a wire basket. I shook the water off it and dried the pomegranate charm on my shirt. Oh yeah, Hades was definitely going to kill me when he came to.

I'd run, but it wasn't like I had a choice. Zeus had created me with an extra-special tweak. I was loyal to family. Loyal to the point of obedience if they outranked me enough. That was why I was almost glad I was still "useful" to him. I had a feeling the minute he didn't need me anymore, he'd ask me to swear fealty and give him all my power. Suicide by devotion. And I'd have no choice but to oblige.

I sat beside Hades and pulled my knees to my chest. I felt hollow inside. Hopeless. The rain dripped down my face, mimicking the tears that I didn't dare cry.

Hades groaned and shifted positions. I shook his shoulder.

"Hades?"

His eyes snapped open. He bolted up and glanced around the park, gaze falling on a nearby patch of scorched earth. Myriad emotions flickered over his face, too fast for me to identify. Then his gaze hardened in rage and he looked at me. "Where is she?"

My voice was shaking as I held out the necklace. "Zeus will take the Underworld in exchange for—"

I found myself on the ground, Hades' hands wrapped around my throat. Agony spread from his fingertips. The ground beneath me crackled and shriveled. The leaves turned dark with decay.

I screamed, or tried to, but all that came out was a strangled yelp.

"Let's try that again. Where. Is. She?" His voice was dark and dangerous, and there was murder in his eyes.

Melissa

A Bonus Short Story

A Goddess's BFF Tells All

I WAS THE WORST friend ever. My best friend in the whole world was stuck hiding out in the Underworld from a psychotic serial rapist, and here I was hanging out at school like everything was normal. Except for the part where I was being asked out.

By the guy she liked.

And I was probably going to say yes.

Yeah, I deserved to burn for this.

"Melissa?" Concern flickered behind Joel's easy grin. "Did you want to catch a movie tonight?"

"You're . . . asking me?" I clarified for the third time, wincing even as I heard myself ask the question. It's not that I'm stupid. Like, I actually do have an understanding of the English language. But no one had actually asked me out before.

I'm not ugly or anything, just human. A tall, twiggy human with boring brown hair, brown eyes, splotchy skin, and curves as flat as a pancake squished in a Panini press. My best friend, on the other hand, was a goddess. Literally. A petite, curvy little blonde goddess with amazing green eyes and the uncanny ability to make all the light on the room sparkle around her like a beacon shouting, "look at me, look at me, aren't I perfect?" With her beside me, I might as well be wallpaper.

"Who else would I be asking?" Joel sounded amused, but it was a strained amusement. Could he really be worried that I would reject him? Joel might not be a god, but divine wasn't a bad way to describe him.

"Kora," I replied like the answer was a no brainer.

Persephone preferred her middle name on account of hers being so . . . unique. I didn't blame her. Not that my name was much better.

Melissa may sound normal, but in Demeter-land it's not an actual name. It's a title that used to identify her priestesses back when they were well enough known and numerous enough to have a title. My mom must have been feeling nostalgic when she'd been ordered to have me so Demeter's daughter would have her own personal playmate and priestess. To say my entire life revolved around Persephone would be an understatement. But she hadn't known until a few weeks ago that she was a goddess at all, so it wasn't like she had anything to do with me being named after a job position, instead of, you know, a person. But I'm not bitter or anything.

"Kora isn't here," Joel replied. "Besides," his bright blue eyes looked me up and down. "I'm sure she's nice and all, but she's kind of quiet, you know?"

"Not really." Persephone comes off as shy to most people, but one-on-one she never stopped talking. She's got an opinion about everything. And it generally came from the moral high ground, which I guess made sense. Gods don't do so well with shades of grey. It's not easy for a mere mortal like myself to live up to her ideals of right and wrong. But I manage.

Joel cleared his throat and I realized I still hadn't answered his question. I put a hand on my hip and studied him for a moment. "What movie?"

"Lady's choice." His blonde hair fell into his eyes in a fashion meant to appear careless, but I knew better. He probably spent forever in front of a mirror, preening. How shallow.

My smile tightened and I ordered myself to stop doing that. Not every encounter I had with people required a sarcastic narrative. I didn't have to take the psychology elective to know that my penchant for insults was probably a pathetic attempt to compensate for playing second fiddle all my life to a goddess. But I'm not bitter or anything.

"Pick me up at seven." I turned on my heel and walked away before he could respond. Yeah, jerk move, but my heart was pounding in my chest and any second now I'd turn beet red and all the snarky thoughts in my head would spew out of my mouth like verbal vomit.

Joel cleared his throat. "From . . . where?"

Right. I rushed back to give him my address.

"See you at seven," he promised, flashing me an easy grin.

My lips moved and words fell out but I couldn't for the life of me guess what I'd said. Probably something stupid. That whole conversation with Joel felt like one of those cheesy movie scenes where all the details fade into the background except his face. When his gaze locked to mine, everything and everyone else vanished.

Including time apparently. A quick glance at my phone confirmed that I was late for class. The wooden bridge solidified beneath my feet as I rushed across the steady beams too fast to appreciate the vast away of colorful trees and bushes thriving around campus like something out of an over enthusiastic landscapers wet dream. I ducked into a white, window-walled building and made it to my classroom a few minutes after everyone else had settled. Smiling apologetically at my Latin teacher, I slid into my desk.

With my thoughts bouncing back and forth between the excitement of Joel asking me out, my worry for Persephone, and the guilt that came with both, I didn't hear a word in Latin class, or any other class for the rest of the day. Oh, who was I kidding, it wasn't like I paid attention on normal days either. What was the point of working my but off in school when my whole life was already laid out for me? It didn't matter what I learned or how I applied myself or what I wanted. My future was set.

It wouldn't be a bad life. I'd have my best friend, lots of money, and not to mention immortality. All I had to do was believe in someone standing right in front of me. It was a good deal. If I'd been asked about it, I probably wouldn't hesitate before saying yes. But no one had bothered and that bugged me more than I cared to admit.

But none of that mattered right now because Joel asked me out.

On a date.

Me!

It's wrong right? Being this happy while your best friend hides out in the Underworld?

My stomach was in full revolt against my emotional whiplash by the time I got home. Thinking of Joel set butterflies flapping against my insides. But thinking of Persephone drenched those wings in poison.

"I'm home!" I called, pushing open the door. The faint sound of the television from deeper within the house was my only reply. Shrugging, I grabbed a cookie off the bar that separated my living room and kitchen. I waited for her to say something disapproving about my choice of snack (hey, she made them, if she really didn't want me stuffing my face with unhealthy snacks, why would she bother? Mixed messages, anyone?), but her eyes were glued to the television set.

Despite her silence, my guilty conscience got the better of me, and I grabbed a cantaloupe and pineapple cut to look like a flower out of the vase she placed strategically in front of the cookies to inspire feelings of guilt, inadequacy, and pressure all without saying a word.

When I grow up, I want to be just as manipulative as my mother. I smiled at my own sarcasm and bit into the flower fruit. My mom made a killing selling whole fruit baskets designed to look like flower arrangements out of the fruit grown by Demeter's priestesses all over the world.

The sound of Orpheus' name coming from the television caught my attention and I turned to see what was going on. The rock star sat in a chair next to a hospital bed speaking in a somber voice. Weird. He was usually pretty upbeat.

But for once, his golden features just didn't do it for me, so I headed to my room instead of obsessing over his every word. I had a date to get ready for. But after finishing my fruit, two cookies (take that, Mom!), and draining a glass of milk, I still hadn't managed to pick out the perfect outfit for tonight.

As I rummaged through my closet for the seventh time, my hand paused on a dress Persephone borrowed at the Orpheus concert. I drew back like I'd been stung as the memories from that night came flooding back.

I'd imagined every reaction Persephone could possibly have to finding out she was a goddess, every question, every conversation, and every fun thing we do with her powers. But I'd never thought she'd be mad at me. The look she'd had on her face when she'd realized everything I'd kept from her had felt like a punch in the gut. And then she'd nearly been abducted by Boreas, and was trapped down in the Underworld and everything went wrong. It wasn't supposed to be like this.

I'd spent the first few weeks after she'd gone under in a daze of worry and fear. But then, once the fact that she was safe sunk in, I felt something else. Relief. For once, I was free to do what I wanted.

Wasn't that terrible? Persephone was my best friend. It wasn't her fault every minute of my life had revolved around hers since my conception. I shouldn't feel relieved or happy or anything good right now, should I? I shouldn't be going on dates and picking out clothes and having fun.

Yet here I was, so might as well make the most of it.

After careful deliberation, I chose a short, green sundress that almost made it look like I had curves and modeled it in front of the mirror. Casual enough but still dressy. Perfect.

Next I rummaged through my bathroom drawers searching through an array of what my mom referred to as dollar a drop shower gels. My allowance, my choice, and guys liked smells, right? Every magazine harped on how important scent was to guys because they were like, super connected to their scent glands or something. Time to put that to the test.

I avoided the floral scents on principal, finally settling on a purple concoction called Love Spell because I had shampoo and conditioner that matched, then took a long shower. Choosing the right makeup and jewelry took almost twice as long as usual, but soon I was as satisfied with my appearance as I'd ever be.

The doorbell rang, startling me from my reverie and I glanced at my phone. Six-thirty? He was early.

"Melissa!" Mom called.

When I walked into the living room, I found Joel shifting uncomfortably under my mother's steely gaze. He saw me, and his eyes swept up and down in a once over Mom couldn't miss.

"You didn't tell me you were going on a date." Mom's smile did nothing to warm the chill in her tone.

I shot her a smile of my own. "You didn't ask." Or say so much as a single word to me since I walked in the door for that matter.

That realization gave me pause. The cookies might be an act, but my mom did care enough to at least feign interest in my day. I'd never be her top priority, not like Demeter was, but I did rank on the list.

I turned and looked at mom, coming out of my own thoughts enough to see her clearly for the first time. Mom looked worried. Tired. There were circles under her dark eyes, and her brown hair hung loose, not in one of her usual half-bun like things she kept trying to bring back (it wasn't happening). She hadn't even put on make-up today.

"Is she—" I couldn't finish the question, not without making Joel curious about the whole situation and we didn't need that right now.

"Everything is fine." This time Mom's smile reached her eyes. "I'll tell you all about it when you get home."

Something had happened. I watched Mom carefully for a minute, determined she was telling the truth about everything being fine, and then nodded. She could lie, only gods lacked that particular ability, but she wouldn't dare lie about anything involving Demeter or her daughter.

"Okay. See you tonight." I walked out the door, motioning Joel to follow. I paused at his car, a juniper Chevy Thunderbird and waited for him to unlock the door.

"Be home by ten!" she shouted after me.

"What are we seeing?" He opened the door for me, wisely refraining from commenting on the exchange with my mother.

"A chick-flick of course. I'll pick when we get there." When I sat down and pulled on my seatbelt, I caught his eye to show him I was joking. "What do you want to see?"

He listed off a few movies, and one caught my ear. Some superhero's origin story.

"It starts in ten minutes," Joel pointed out. "Did you want to grab dinner first and catch the nine o'clock instead?"

That would make it difficult to be home by ten. "Nah, the first fifteen minutes are previews, we won't miss much."

He grinned and stepped on the gas. The drive to the theater was harrowing but on the bright side we didn't miss a second of the movie. My pulse pounded with adrenaline from the wild ride as I watched the hero's journey unfold on screen.

The movie was all right, nothing spectacular. Not from the little bit I saw anyway. Somewhere after the first preview Joel stretched and put an arm around me. It got hard to pay attention after that.

My breathing went shallow, and my pulse pounded in my throat. I looked up at Joel, the lights from the movie gleamed in his blue eyes and my mouth went dry. Was he going to kiss me?

You know what? No. I was not going to be the weak-kneed nervous girl waiting for him to make the first move. I'd spent my whole life waiting on the whims of other people. Not this time.

I shifted out from under Joel's hand, and tossed my hair back.

"Sorry," he whispered. His face went red. "I—"

I cut him off with a kiss. He got over his surprise quick enough, his arms wrapped around me, and he kissed me back.

A lot.

When the movie ended, something I only noticed when the house lights rose, we stumbled out of the theater. My hair was disheveled and I had the beginnings of a hickey on my neck but that didn't stop me from yanking him back into a kiss before his car door closed.

We paused long enough to drive somewhere else, not far. Just behind the theater I think, I wasn't exactly paying attention, and then we did more. A lot more. Like . . . yeah.

I never figured I'd be easy. But this was Joel. Persephone was going to come back from the Underworld at winter's end, and then guys like him were going to forget I existed again. I needed to live this up now even if that meant I was a terrible friend or an insult to women everywhere or a rotten human being. Whatever. It was amazing.

I didn't say anything on the ride home. Not in a bad way. There was just no need to speak or think. I didn't know how I felt about what just happened.

My blood pumped too fast making me jittery, but I couldn't tell if I felt sick or excited. A part of me was disappointed in myself, but the rest of me had enjoyed it. Did that make me a slut?

Joel kept up an easy conversation the entire way home so the silence wasn't awkward. I appreciated that. When he pulled up to my house at nine-fifty-eight, he turned to me and asked, "Next Saturday?"

I smiled at him. "Buy me dinner next time, huh?"

His eyes widened in surprise and he burst out laughing. "We skipped that, huh?" Then he seemed to think over his words. "I'm okay with just dinner too, you know? I'm not expecting–"

"I know." Joel really was a nice guy. I leaned over and kissed him then slid out of the car. "Night."

Mom sat on the porch and I waved at her but didn't go in the house right away. Instead I walked. I was buzzing with so much extra energy that I felt like if I stood too still I might explode.

As I ventured further into the woods behind my house, I rubbed my arms to ward off the chill. It was cold all of the sudden. Really cold.

A cracking sound caught my attention and I glanced down to see a thick carpet of frost creeping across the ground toward me. Boreas. The ice spread everywhere, crawling over the ground and up the trees as it closed in around me.

"Mom!" I shrieked, dashing in the direction of the house.

My feet flew out from under me and I hit the ground hard enough to knock the breath out of my lungs. In a stunned moment of clarity I realized that even if I made it to the house, I wouldn't be safer. My mom couldn't go up against a god.

It had to be Boreas, the same freak who'd gone after Persephone. He was the whole reason she was in the Underworld. But what would he want with me? I wasn't anything special.

But I mattered to her. She would come for me through hell or high water. But I refused to be used against Persephone like some kind of divine bargaining chip. I made a quick decision, and turned away from the house. There was a ravine about a half a mile to the west. If I fell down that, there was no coming back.

I tore through the woods, keeping just ahead of the ice as I dodged branches and rocks. He wouldn't be able to pretend I was alive and in captivity somewhere. Demeter would know if I dropped dead since I was bound to her, had been since birth.

A white mist materialized around me and a man appeared in front of me. I tried to stop, but lost traction on the ice that spread beneath me and plowed into him. His ice-cold arms wrapped around me and I screamed for help, but my voice was lost on the wind.

I fought, kicking and screaming. My nails raked across his face. He grimaced and loosened his frigid grip. For all of two seconds, I broke free, then his fist plowed into my face so hard I saw stars.

Then I didn't see anything at all.

If I'd been someone else, this would be when the ground would have split open beneath me. If I were special, this would be the part when someone would whisk me away to safety in the Underworld. But I wasn't Persephone. I was just her human friend so there was no one to save me.

But I'm not bitter or anything.

Acknowledgments

Thank you to Kathryn for the read throughs and to Debra Dixon for the amazing cover art. To my husband, thank you SO much for listening. And of course I owe my writers' group for reading this story in 5,000 word chunks every other week three times. You guys rock.

It takes so many people to make a book. Thank you. Thank all of you.

About the Author

Kaitlin Bevis spent her childhood curled up with a book and a pen. If the ending didn't agree with her, she rewrote it. Because she's always wanted to be a writer, she spent high school and college learning everything she could to achieve that goal. After graduating college with a BFA and Masters in English, Kaitlin went on to write The Daughters of Zeus series.

www.kaitlinbevis.com

CPSIA information can be obtained
at www.ICGtesting.com
Printed in the USA
LVHW112210070119
603102LV00002B/378/P

9 781611 946345